THE FOURTH PASSENGER

Mini Nair

ROMAN *Books*
www.roman-books.co.uk

ISBN 978-93-80905-25-9

Typeset in Adobe Garamond Pro

First published in 2011
Paperback Edition 2012

1 3 5 7 9 8 6 4 2

British Library Cataloguing in Publication Data.
A catalogue record for this book is available from the British Library.

ROMAN *Books*
26 York Street, London W1U 6PZ, United Kingdom
2nd Floor, 38/3, Andul Road, Howrah 711109, WB, India
www.roman-books.co.uk | www.roman-books.co.in

Printed and bound in India by
Roman Printers Private Limited
www.romanprinters.com

For Aaliyah and Aaria

1

Anusuya Alhat

She yanked her *sari* and tucked it firmly in the folds of the cotton petticoat cinched around her waist. The loose end of the *sari* fell over her shoulder. Deftly she wrapped it around herself and tucked it into her waistband. She clutched her purse close to her chest, smoothed her hair with the other hand, and swung her long black braid to the front. Her expressive kohl-lined eyes darted nervously to both sides and gauged the situation. One wrong step and she would lose her life. There were many others waiting to execute the same operation, so she would have to move fast, elbow her way to the front so that she emerged first. The time was 7:10 in the morning. The maneuver would start at 7:12. She looked apprehensively at the giant clock at the railway station. Swiftness was the name of the game. She had to jump in when the speed was right. If she were too slow or too quick, she would land up with a broken arm or leg or, worse still, dead. Or could it be *better still,* dead?

She had a small frame, with slim arms and legs, and a natural ebullience that came to her rescue in such situations. The arrow-like needles of the archaic clock now indicated 7:12. A pin-drop silence ensued. There was a brush of perspiration on her upper lip and she bit her lips nervously. She adopted a stance with her right side inclined at an acute angle and her right hand slightly outstretched, as if to grab something passing by. The other contenders stood in the same manner. Then she heard the sound — like a bugle announcing the beginning of battle. The train was approaching.

The 7:12 local train pulled into Mumbai's Andheri station. During peak business hours, the compartments were packed with people. Young boys perched on top of the train, daring the overhead electric wires, just to reach their destinations on time. Limbs and hands hung out of the wide entrance. One more passenger and the train would burst from its seams. It was a daily battle for Anusuya and thousands of other Mumbaikars. But she knew the trick. When the train hurtled into the station, she ran along the platform and quickly jumped into the moving compartment, holding onto a steel bar at the entrance. Soon she was surrounded by the incessant chatter of women compressed against each other, leaving barely any room to breathe.

Every morning, Anusuya napped till the train reached Bandra, four stations from where she boarded. She tried to, at least. An informal system of reserving seats in the local trains meant that a number of women would inquire about her destination, only so they could take her place as soon as she vacated it. They called it *booking*. She could not nap till someone came and booked her seat. It was common knowledge that people would wake even the dead to book a seat.

Finally, a young girl motioned to Anusuya with her hands and mouthed that she would sit in her place. But there was more to be taken care of — the fourth seat. The fourth seat was gratis. It was Mumbai's compassion and represented the spirit of the city. The train seats were designed for three passengers to sit comfortably. But, at times — most of the time — the three crammed and adjusted to make place for a grateful fourth passenger, precariously balancing herself on the edge. Today, a reed-thin girl who kept reading her prayer book was the recipient.

All taken care of, Anusuya Alhat closed her eyes while the train chugged on.

Anusuya worked as a housekeeper for an aging film actress in Bandra. Bandra was called the Queen of the Suburbs and many

Bollywood film stars lived there. She earned nine to ten thousand *rupees* a month. It was a decent sum, but the efforts she made to get this decent sum were strenuous. Sweeping, swabbing, cooking, at times nursing the actress's imaginary ailments and listening to her nagging chatter — all of it took a toll on Anusuya. She worked without a care for her health, because a day's absence meant no money. But there were days when extreme tiredness took over, the whole world seemed to spin, and she wanted to quit the race.

The force that egged Anusuya on was her daughter, Sarangi, who was in class nine of a convent school so that she could learn to speak English fluently. The noise and brawl around the *chawl* in which mother and daughter lived were unbearable. The *chawl* was a three-story grey building with twenty apartments on every floor. The doors to the apartments were seldom closed, and privacy was enjoyed only by the newly married. Everything was public there. The quarrels, the patch-ups, celebrations, bereavements. But at least Anusuya felt assured by the proximity of the neighbors, leaving her daughter when she went to work, what with horrible things being done to girls elsewhere. During the festival season, when the young boys blared the loudspeakers, Sarangi could barely read her lessons; however, Anusuya had better sense than to complain. It would simply lead to a quarrel. It was incredible how Sarangi studied through the din.

Anusuya did not have the luxury of waking up late in the morning like the women on the afternoon television soap operas. Anusuya watched a heroine lying on satin sheets, stretching a manicured hand, and groping to find the alarm clock. An old aluminum alarm clock with a shrill throat woke Anusuya faithfully at four every morning. She rose and walked across the 150-square-foot apartment to the corner that was called the kitchen.

Anusuya paid an exorbitant rent for such a tiny hole. The kitchen walls were lined with stainless steel pots and pans. In the corner, a replica of a temple with a few gods asserted its place.

Her husband, despite being an alcoholic and wastrel, enjoyed his status as the master of the house. Consequently, he occupied the only iron bed in the apartment while Sarangi and she slept on the floor.

She moved on as if the day were prey and she a predator.

Anusuya brewed some tea for herself in a dented aluminum saucepan. Many a morning, she had looked at that saucepan and felt like it — battered, dented, but still functional. One cup of tea down and she'd begin to move like someone had pressed the fast-forward button of a video player. Collecting water, waking Sarangi up, serving her breakfast, cooking lunch, packing lunch for herself and Sarangi, washing the clothes, folding the clothes — and the climax of it all was rushing off to work. Two burners on a gas stove and a middle-aged woman accomplished all of it in a span of two hours. She prayed that her daughter would pay complete attention to her studies and would not have to go through the same grind. There were times, though, when Anusuya did not dare to dream for her daughter. Perhaps they were all preordained to suffer…

Before Anusuya left for work, she gave her husband a perfunctory shove in an attempt to wake him. He would not rear his head till noon.

Times had not always been like this. Her husband, Sakharam, was once employed at a bank, and Anusuya didn't have to work for a living. But Sakharam was suspended from work for consuming alcohol during the bank's business hours. He was not an alcoholic when he married Anusuya. But at times, his friends coerced him to have a glass or two of country liquor in shady bars that shielded the identity of their clients with a curtain, often dirty, strung half-heartedly across the door. Sakharam steadily deteriorated, and the times that he was sober and coherent were rare. The bank started sending memos of suspension after he disappeared for days at a stretch and surfaced only after a week or so. Soon enough, he was fired.

Instead of reforming after the setback, very readily, without a care for the family, he gave up to the surrealism of alcohol. At times, his so-called friends would drop him at home drunk, literally on all fours. That was the beginning of the doom. Everything changed. Anusuya had to think of ways to eke out a living. She had not completed her studies and was not skilled.

"If only I had finished school...," she thought ruefully.

She was the eldest of three daughters of a poor farmer in Satara, a place nearly three hundred kilometers away from Mumbai. Her father had believed that the sooner the girls were married off, the better. Her father's land was always parched, and she spent most of her time taking care of her siblings. At seventeen, she was married off to Sakharam Alhat. A good marriage and moving to a city like Mumbai were indeed strokes of good luck! And now she had been reduced to this state of despair.

Anusuya became desperate as expenses mounted. Debtors came to the door every day. She could not step out of the apartment for fear of being accosted by someone to whom her husband owed money. The stink of poverty was nauseating.

And then her friend and next-door neighbor, Nootan Vakharia, provided the answer.

2

Nootan Vakharia

The recurring dream that haunted Nootan frightened her enough to prevent her from going to bed. The dream was almost always the same. Her three-year-old daughter and she were running. From whom and what, she did not know. The landscape of the nightmare was arid, with no sign of green vegetation, and Nootan felt almost suffocated. Her daughter's head bobbed to one side and saliva dribbled from her mouth. When the little girl stopped from exhaustion, Nootan dragged her along, her feet making designs in the sand. To escape the dream, Nootan rarely slept. She spent nights either sewing or gazing out at the city, bright even in the darkness. She knew that she was being punished. Punished by someone superior, first by giving her a daughter who was not normal and then by depriving her of sleep.

Apart from this, her life was no different from Anusuya's. True, Nootan only had to fend for herself and her daughter, unlike Anusuya, who had a husband like a stone around her neck. Also, Nootan did not have to undergo the torment that Anusuya went through to get to her job every morning. Nootan worked in someone's house, but she did not have to make use of public transportation. She just walked a few blocks to her employer's home. All in all, Nootan's day was very similar to Anusuya's, and her struggle was just the same.

They hadn't always been the same, though. A string of beads, or *toran,* hung across the main entrance of Nootan's home, and on the wall was a picture — black and white — of an affluent family. Women wearing puffed blouses, silk *saris*, and ornaments. Men wearing *sherwani* suits and pearls. And in the arms of a woman, smugly sat little Nootan, unaware of her future. The picture was a reminder of what might have been…

In her home town, Nootan had taken up a job as an accountant with a small-time grocer. She had a natural aptitude for figures, was adept at counting, and managed her money very well. Nootan had moved to Mumbai immediately after her marriage to Dilip Vakharia, who worked as an electrician. More importantly, though, he was a member of the Hindu United Party, or HUP, a right-wing party that vowed to protect the rights of Hindus. Nootan's father found the latter qualification befitting for the match. Hindus and Muslims were the two main religions in India and for centuries had lived together. The Muslims had also formed a party, to counter the HUP. Skirmishes between the two were very common. With not many suitors for the short, plump Nootan, the decision was made by her father, who did not consult her. He just invited her for her own wedding like all the other guests.

Dilip was an active member of the HUP, and soon after their marriage, he took Nootan along for the meetings. For the first time, Nootan witnessed the turbulent nature beneath Dilip's calm exterior. He was intolerant of every other community but Hindus and expected Nootan to be the same. He did whatever the HUP party leaders instructed the cadre. She just attended the party sessions quietly, not expressing her opinions.

"They destroyed our Somnath. Our temple! They are criminals, and their boys come and steal our young girls…." And so on and so forth. Nootan heard it all without reacting.

She almost came to believe in what the leaders said.

"It is true that most of *them* are criminals, and it is also true that *they* destroyed our temples," she thought.

At home, Dilip nagged her to get involved in the women's wing of the HUP and reminded her that this was what he expected of her. She never had any inclination to comply. When Dilip sensed this, he perversely pushed Nootan further.

But no matter what she heard at the HUP meetings, or how the party manipulated her opinions, she could never truly hate *them* — those who were not Hindu — because of her affection for Ahmed Syed, Farzana's *Abbajan.* He was *Abba,* or Father, to Nootan, and his family were Muslims.

Dilip did not know Ahmed Syed and his daughter Farzana. They were a part of Nootan's past that would have shamed her husband. She could not even invite *Abba* to her wedding, though she had met with him two days prior to the event and sought his blessings. There had been tears in his eyes as he shook his head. Nootan had given *Abba* the address of the place where she would be living with Dilip. She had asked *Abba* to send it to Farzana, who was also married and living in Mumbai by then. Nootan had not been permitted by her brothers to attend Farzana's wedding ceremony. Like Dilip, her brothers were members of the HUP.

Within two months of marriage, Nootan was pregnant. In the spring of the following year, she gave birth to Pooja. By that time, Dilip was getting increasingly frustrated with his job, and the HUP too was not living up to his expectations. The action they had promised was not happening, and that made him restless. Dilip was a man whose blood was always at the boiling point; he lived in a perpetual wait to attack. He was always the first one to participate in or initiate stone-throwing incidents, common in Mumbai, or to create disturbances in the *mohallas,* or local neighborhoods. He was further enraged when a doctor certified that Pooja was mentally impaired. That he could produce such a child infuriated him.

Dilip was responsible for his elderly parents, and finances were always a problem. When bad times hit, he began to borrow money at high interest rates, believing in his dogged way that he would pay it all back. One day, he had an altercation with a man to whom he owed money. Dilip, being obstinate, could not control himself. He was so enraged that he began raining blows, resulting in the man's death at his hands. There were no means to hire a lawyer, so Dilip languished in jail. He hoped that the HUP would help him, and he asked Nootan to meet with a few people. The experience was humiliating to her. When she told him about it, he accused her of provoking their refusal to assist him.

That was the last straw. Nootan took charge of her daughter's life and put the marriage far at the back of her mind. She had to work to keep herself and Pooja alive. She found the strength to do all of this when she remembered what *Abba* had always told her: "Act; don't blame." She thought of *Abba* on the veranda, walking up and down and loudly reading the news from all the newspapers in his booming voice for everyone around to hear.

She spread the word that she was looking for work. Any type of work. The watchman of a nearby colony of apartments told Nootan about a lady who was looking for a housekeeper and a governess. Nootan readily took up the job and grossed seven thousand *rupees* every month. She stopped visiting her husband in jail. The HUP sent mailers every week that she used as lining for the dustbin. If anybody asked of her husband's whereabouts, she replied that he had deserted her. She trained her daughter, Pooja, to give the same reply.

"Being a jailbird's offspring will not get my daughter anywhere. As it is, the poor girl is afflicted," she thought.

Her daughter went to a special school that was expensive for Nootan. But there was no other way. She understood the importance of education and made sure Pooja attended an English-immersion school. She also made sure that her daughter ate Britannia bread with Amul butter and had a cup of milk every morning. All of this was a matter of great pride to her.

Unfortunately, Nootan was an unimaginative woman and did not even consider the better options she had. She was a good seamstress, and her childhood friend Farzana had taught her the most fashionable embroidery. Farzana had purchased old magazines to study the designs, and the two of them, as young girls, would sit and sew in silence.

"Where will I get money to buy a sewing machine? Who will give me dresses to embroider?" She thought of a thousand obstacles when she was confronted with the problem of earning her livelihood after Dilip was incarcerated. So her talents were wasted on making little gifts for Anusuya's daughter, Sarangi, and the other neighbors.

Nootan always helped people in times of crisis, and there was a steady flow of relatives, distant and close, from her village to her home in Mumbai. In her own life, however, there was no one to help. She simply let herself be maneuvered by life and stayed afloat. Nootan never blamed the gods or her destiny. She was a woman who waited for a miracle. In the daytime, she went about her work diligently; in the evenings, she watched soap operas and cried openly. That was the only time Nootan cried. She had an immense sense of pride about her, and even though she realized that she was merely a housekeeper, she went about the work with dignity.

Anusuya Alhat was her next door neighbor and friend. Nootan was a very good cook and often prepared delicacies for Anusuya and her daughter, Sarangi. In the past, her old friend Farzana had always insisted Nootan cook for her. And Nootan had. Very gladly. She would have done anything for Farzana.

Abbajan had given Farzana Nootan's phone number, but she never called.

"Does she know? Did *Abba* tell her?" Nootan sometimes thought ashamedly.

Very soon, Farzana was just a memory, and in a way, Nootan was glad that Farzana didn't try to contact her. She simply did not have the courage to face Farzana, and guilt was the fence between her and Javed.

Nootan got along well with her neighbor Anusuya, and they were good friends. She mentioned Farzana, her childhood companion, to Anusuya and often lamented their separation. When Nootan first went out to work, Anusuya remained at home, because at that time, Sakharam was still bringing in money. Anusuya often helped Nootan by looking after her little daughter, Pooja.

Sometimes Nootan purchased henna and colored her daughter's hands and spoke to her about her Aunty Farzana. Pooja looked at her and smiled like an innocent baby.

Nootan never colored her own hands with henna.

Not after that day the peacock, the tiger, and the man became one.

The color had smeared.

Did Farzana know?

3

Farzana Javed Sheikh

Farzana Javed Sheikh wiped the sweat off her brow. The heat was killing her and her cheeks were red with the strain of stirring the cauldron of *khichda*. She looked down to see that the lamb and wheat had mixed well with the *ghee,* or clarified butter, and the spices. The aroma smelled right, and in a few minutes she would take the brass *handi* off the stove. *Eid,* the holiest day, when the prophet had readily agreed to sacrifice his son in accordance with God's wish, was around the corner, and her neighbor Parinbi had ordered two kilos of *khichda* for her relatives. Farzana would make five hundred *rupees* off this deal. Of course, Parinbi would haggle and urge Farzana to reduce the price. But Farzana resolved that this time she would not. All the earlier times that she had cooked for feasts, she'd been coerced into charging less by the pleas and tears that flowed copiously from the cheeks of her customers. She pulled her *purdah* closer and continued stirring. She would tell Parinbi of the good ingredients she had used and the labor that she put in. Farzana thought of her *Abbajan* and was relieved that he couldn't see her unfortunate situation. Of course, Javed, too, was unaware of her side business. If he'd known, it would have infuriated him to no end. Independence was the one trait he deplored in Farzana.

"Javed is not the man for you. This is the flush of youth," her *Abbajan* had said much too often.

But Farzana was stubborn and insisted that if she got married, it would be to Javed. Finally, *Abbajan* relented. Her best friend,

Nootan, did not attend the wedding, and Farzana had not forgiven her for it. Anti-Muslim sentiments were running high, but their friendship scored above all, didn't it? Farzana knew that if Nootan looked inside the trunk of the huge oak tree, even today, she would find the henna Farzana had ground and kept for her in an iron vessel.

Farzana and Nootan had studied in the same school. Her *Abbajan* insisted on education and sent Farzana and her elder sister to school. Somehow, a friendship was struck between the quiet, pudgy Nootan and the effervescent Farzana. Nootan visited Farzana's home often and took to calling her *Abbajan* affectionately *Abba.* Farzana also visited Nootan's home and performed the *garba,* the traditional dance during *Navratri,* the nine-day festival of the Goddess Amba.

The girls sailed through school and were admitted to the government college together. Then things changed. The atmosphere around them was filled with suspicion. History was used as a weapon to retaliate. That a good thousand years ago Muslims destroyed Hindu temples was suddenly remembered as a justification for selfish discrimination. The destruction of the Somnath temple by the Muslims was cited as a prime example of Muslim intolerance. The Muslims also conveniently found something from history to rationalize striking back. Communal tension prevailed. Nootan's brothers had become members of the HUP, openly advocating against the Muslims, and they were involved in a campaign asking the Muslims to leave India and go to Pakistan. Their argument was that Pakistan was created for the Muslims.

Farzana stopped going to Nootan's home. Nootan's brothers often looked at her uncharitably and Farzana was afraid of them. Their anti-Muslim views were known by all. She knew that Nootan could not stand up to them, so she had no chance of being accepted as her friend. Nootan did not stop visiting

Farzana, though, and when her brothers asked her to do so, she began visiting Farzana on the sly. The girls sewed, cooked, and applied intricate henna designs on each other's hands. Farzana picked the leaves from the henna shrub in her back yard, ground them with a stone mortar and pestle, and kept the dye overnight for the color to develop.

"This is my home. I want to be buried here, near my father and his father," Farzana's *Abbajan* would say with a smile.

Abbajan was religious but also secular. He educated his daughters and instilled in them a fierce sense of patriotism and pride. But Farzana's love for Javed ruined her father's plans. *Abbajan,* as usual, gave in to his daughter's request. He smelled a change in the wind. Perhaps, he thought, it would be better that Farzana move to Mumbai with Javed. After all, Mumbai was known to be more multiethnic. The times were not very good. Farzana had seen her male relatives forming groups to attack Hindus. Everywhere, people were whispering and conspiring.

Farzana remembered very clearly her first thoughts on the groundswell of religious intolerance.

"I think we must ban all history books and historians," Farzana pronounced one day as she and Nootan sat side-by-side sewing. They were on the veranda outside Farzana's home, looking over a green field of millet. Farzana tightened the wooden embroidery ring on the muslin cloth and looked at the design very carefully. She was embroidering flowers in different colors, and later on she planned to attach the trim to the neck of her *kurta*. Farzana had helped Nootan stencil the flowers on the piece of muslin. She peered to see Nootan struggle with the embroidery of the leaves of her flower. A slight wind blew, and Farzana absently brushed away the errant hair that had escaped her tight braid. Nootan looked up to see the dark westward clouds dancing with glee in the blue sky. Very soon, it would rain.

"Why?" Nootan asked.

"Nobody would remember who did what to whom. Everything would be forgotten and both of us could be friends forever."

"If historians were banned forever, then what would happen to that handsome professor Mr. Patnaik?"

They both laughed.

During *Eid* that year, everything transformed. Javed, a friend of one of Farzana's cousins, arrived from Mumbai to celebrate *Eid* with his family. Javed wore his hair like Amitabh Bacchan, the popular Hindi film actor who, in most of his movies, played the role of the angry young man. The youth of India identified with him.

Everyone was tired from the strain of fasting, and each evening the *azaan,* their call to prayer, was the most welcome sound. But Farzana was not overwrought at all. The fast seemed to have purified her. Javed's presence exhilarated her and brought a cherry red color to her cheeks. She was besotted by Javed and listened with rapt attention to all that he bragged about Mumbai and his life. She liked staring at him, and her stares were not lost on Javed, who reciprocated. Very soon they were in love.

Javed kept coming to Farzana's house on one pretext or another. For Farzana, it was a heady time. They rarely spoke. But Javed's glance made Farzana blush, and she felt an urge to lose herself in his arms.

After many days, Javed found a chance to speak with Farzana. She was hanging clothes to dry on the clothesline when Javed came from behind stealthily, confessed his love to her, and proposed marriage. Farzana blushed and ran into the house without saying anything.

Of course, she had to tell Nootan all about it. Right after Javed proposed, Farzana ran to Nootan's house and called out to her. Her eyes twinkled with joy as she told her friend about Javed's proposal. Nootan felt happy for her friend.

"Tomorrow, usual place, same time. I want you to meet him!" Farzana said as she spun around and ran back towards home.

The usual place was under a huge banyan tree. The trunk was so large that both the girls could lean against it and spend afternoons. Nootan skipped a heartbeat when she saw Javed the next day. Holding onto the root of the tree, he looked like a film star. She was tongue-tied. She could not explain what she felt when she gazed at him. There was a tingle down her spine. Javed saw a slightly plump girl who had run all the way to meet Farzana and her fiancé. Her bosom moved up and down with the strain.

"So, do you like him?" Farzana asked after Javed departed, leaving the girls alone. Nootan's opinion mattered. Farzana wanted Nootan to like Javed and approve of her marriage to him.

Nootan said nothing, her heart wanting to jump out of its cage.

A day before *Eid*, Farzana brought some henna and drew a design of a forest — complete with a peacock, a tiger and, strangely, a man — on Nootan's hands. It was the last *Eid* they were to spend together. Farzana's impending marriage and the worsening situation around them would make it the last.

"Come home tomorrow to get the *Idi*," Farzana reminded Nootan. *Idi* was a gift given by the elder members of the community to the younger ones on *Eid*. Nootan collected her *Idi* every year from *Abbajan*.

Nootan walked back home holding her hands up, hoping that the wind would dry the henna. In the distance, she saw a familiar-looking man who walked towards her like a tiger and displayed his plumage like a peacock. She wished to run in the opposite direction, but her legs refused to pay heed. Her heart yearned for an encounter with this stranger. The henna on her hands smudged. The peacock, tiger, and man became one.

The next day, when Nootan went to her friend's home to collect her *Idi*, her *Abba* looked at her as if he knew.

When Farzana introduced Javed to her father and stated her desire to marry him, her *Abbajan* objected. The reason he gave was that Javed was a trader of timber, and ideally he would have liked Farzana to marry a man with a white-collar job. But Farzana stuck to her guns.

People speculated that Farzana's father was upset because Javed was a Sunni Muslim, while *Abbajan* was a Shia, a descendant of Hazrat Ali, the Islamic Prophet Muhammad's son-in-law. Nobody knew the real reason. However, seeing Farzana's stubbornness, her father relented and agreed to the marriage, fervently praying that he was wrong.

Farzana became Farzana Javed Sheikh and left her home town for Mumbai. Her last memory was of two girls sitting on the veranda and coloring each other's hands.

*

Farzana adjusted to Mumbai quickly. She was enamored by the city. Even though she lived on its outskirts, the city's scents wafted to her. She tried to come to terms with her marital life, because Javed was not as liberal as her father. He was a conservative person who thought that his wife should remain in the confines of the home. She wrote long letters to *Abbajan* and always asked about Nootan. *Abbajan* replied but never mentioned anything about Farzana's childhood friend. One day, however, he sent her a letter with Nootan's telephone number, explaining that she was married and living in Mumbai. Farzana folded the letter and kept it between the clothes in her dresser. For the first few months after her marriage to Javed, she had avowed that she would write to Nootan; however, the pressures of being a good bride took their toll and time passed. She somehow never contacted Nootan at all. It was as if that chapter of her life was best retained as a memory. Friends from one's youth often were lost when life took new paths. And so Nootan, too, was lost to her.

Farzana, by then, had slipped into a private hell of her own. Javed was not the man she had thought he was. Nothing had turned out the way she had planned or imagined. Javed worked with his cousin, the owner of a timber shop on Reay Road. The employment was frustrating for Javed. He had to play second fiddle to his cousin, who was five years younger. Whenever his cousin asked him to do something, Javed considered it an affront and refused to work. Fights between the cousin and Javed increased. Javed cursed Farzana for the trouble with his twisted logic. "If it weren't for you, I would have kicked this job and sat at home."

He was also a womanizer. Philandering aside, soon Javed even began to beat Farzana at the slightest provocation. After just a few months of marriage to the man of her dreams, she was almost a prisoner, because he would never let her out of the house. Things were tougher because she lived in Mumbra and, being new to Mumbai, didn't know any other part of the city well. Javed stopped her from reading newspapers and was hell-bent on pushing her back in time, preventing any kind of momentum.

She was patient with him, and some amount of ego prevented her from returning to *Abbajan's* house. Javed had lost a lot of property in the riots, and his female relatives consoled Farzana by saying that it was a woman's lot to suffer and that before the financial losses he was quite fine. Farzana cried bitterly, hoping that time would bring with it professional success and Javed's behavior would improve.

After three years of marriage, Farzana still had not conceived a child. Javed refused to go for a medical check-up and accused Farzana of being barren. He visited other women and pointedly held her barrenness as the reason. The connection escaped Farzana. Later that year, Javed did not let Farzana go home when *Abbajan* died. Her *Abbajan,* true to his wishes, was buried near his father and grandfather.

Farzana visited a fertility specialist alone. According to the doctor, there was nothing wrong with her, but he warned that she would need to take a lot of care if she wished to have a child. Her fragile frame and weak reproductive system would make it difficult to carry a baby to term.

When Farzana showed the doctor's reports to Javed, there was a fresh spate of violence. He accused her of implying that he was infertile. Farzana blocked her ears when he began bragging about his conquests with other women. By then, she had mastered the art of not reacting to what Javed said. Very slowly, he began hinting that he would take another bride, so he could have children to avenge his loss in the riots. Farzana smiled at the ludicrous thought. He presumed her smile was a taunt at his manhood. So, the wooden stick substituted, and he thrashed her. Each scream from her lips brought with it greater determination to escape.

Nootan was the only friend she had. The phone number was still in the letter written in *Abbajan's* firm hand. It had been more than five years, and Farzana had reached the limit. Many a time, she had reached for the phone, dialed one digit, and then hung up. She did not know why. Yet, when she was upset and needed solace, Nootan was the only person she remembered. She failed to understand why Nootan had disappeared from her life.

One night, Javed beat her so badly that she feared a few bones might be broken. Farzana took out *Abbajan's* letter and cried out loud. Finally, after all the years of being in the same city, she called Nootan.

4

A Meeting

"Hello," she said softly through her bruised lips.

Nootan recognized the voice immediately. For a moment, she was transported to the time when that same voice would call out loudly, "Nootan… Henna!"

There was a stunned silence. Nootan did not speak for fear of crying.

"How are you, Farzana?" at last she managed.

There were a thousand things that she wanted to ask but could not. Making conversation after so many years was very difficult, and Nootan couldn't remember where they had left off. But voices from the past seldom changed. Farzana's voice brought back other voices. *Abba's* baritone, the sound of children chattering. And smells. Green henna, the aroma of Farzana frying her special egg *bhurji.* An innocent childhood…. The pain of the betrayal haunted her, and the price Nootan had paid was her inability to sleep. But Farzana didn't know that. Or did she?

"I am not fine. I am broken," Farzana said.

"Who did that?"

"Javed. *Abbajan* was right. He's a no-good."

"Abbajan?"

"Died."

Another grave spell of silence.

"Are you married? Is your husband handsome? Do you have any children?"

"I am married. I have one daughter, Pooja. My husband... He... er... Can we meet? How did you get my number?"

"*Abbajan.* I live at Mumbra, and if Javed knows that I've gone out, he will murder me."

"Is there any safe place?"

"My doctor at Thane. It's the only place I'm allowed to go alone without my husband spying on me."

"Give me the doctor's address, and I'll meet you tomorrow at eleven."

"Bring Pooja along?"

"Some other time. Now you hang up and stay brave. Remember what *Abbajan* used to say: 'Act.'"

Farzana hung up the phone and cried. She cried for everything that she had lost. Only Nootan remained.

Nootan was very upset when she heard about Farzana's state. She had expected Farzana to be happily married with a brood of children. That Javed had turned out to be a fiend surprised her. Nootan looked at her empty palms and wept.

The next day, Nootan reached the doctor's dispensary. It was a gynecologist's waiting room, and pictures of fat babies adorned the wall. There was an air of expectancy all around. Nootan looked, but she could not see Farzana anywhere. In her memory, Farzana was frozen in time. The image she carried of her friend was of the time she confessed to Nootan her feelings for Javed.

That day, she looked frail and wore a pink salwar kameez. *Her pink chiffon* dupatta *covered her head. She was fair and had very sharp features. The nose was aquiline, the lips sharply defined with a brown lipstick, and the almond-shaped eyes lined with kohl. She kept pulling her falling* dupatta *over her head. Loose strands of her hair escaped and dared to sit with impudence on her forehead. She looked ethereal. There was an air of dignity around her. She rose with infinite grace, and her movements were full of character. Her hair was tied in a plait and rested on her back. She had removed her black* purdah *and thrown it across the branch of a tree. She crossed her legs and sat with ease.*

An hour passed and there was no sign of Farzana. Nootan thought maybe Javed had found out and locked her in.

Suddenly… "Nootan?" She heard a voice and felt a soft hand on her shoulder.

She looked up to see Farzana.

Her friend looked frail. She wore a blue *salwar kameez.* Her head was covered, and she looked tired. She crossed her legs and sat with ease, but Nootan noticed Farzana's lips were swollen and she had a black eye. Underneath the natural beauty, she reeked of domestic violence. Everyone in the dispensary turned to look at Farzana.

"Why did you forget me? I thought because I was a Muslim, you chose not to keep in touch with me," Farzana said.

Nootan kept quiet and looked at her friend. Farzana held her hand and squeezed it with affection.

"Husband?" Farzana asked.

"In jail."

Farzana looked questioningly.

"Killed a man he owed money to."

"Did he love you?"

"He was incapable of loving anyone."

"What about your daughter?"

"She is… special," Nootan said softly.

"It is because you can love… "

"No… no," Nootan said. "Can we go out somewhere?"

"Not today. Javed may have sent somebody to follow me. Maybe another time."

"Are you going to tell him that you met with me?"

"No!" He'll prevent me from leaving the house. He hates it if I have friends.

"Does he ask about me?"

Farzana shrugged her shoulders. She was so wrapped up in her problems that she didn't see the stricken look on Nootan's face, anticipating a reply to her question.

"Now, you are not alone. I'm there. Here's my address. You can come anytime," Nootan said.

Farzana did not reply. She looked at Nootan searching, then unraveling, and wondering why Nootan's gaze faltered.

"Promise that you won't desert me," Farzana said in an almost childlike panic.

"I won't," Nootan promised, and this time she meant it.

5

Anusuya Meets Farzana

While Nootan was reasonably optimistic, there were traces of disparagement in Anusuya. Anusuya was witness to Nootan's everyday struggle. She only knew vaguely what had happened to Nootan's husband. Not that she was interested. Anusuya also knew that Nootan worked as a housekeeper and it was not entirely a palatable fact for Anusuya.

"Work as a housekeeper! Now, that's not very good," Anusuya thought many a time.

"What else?" Nootan thought.

So the two of them kept quiet.

Their appearances were as different as their outlooks on life: one with a long, lanky body and the other with a round one. Their bond, though, had become stronger after Anusuya found employment. It had happened like this.

One evening, Nootan went to visit Anusuya; it had been over a week since they had last seen each other. Anusuya's eyes were red and her face was puffed.

"What's the matter?" Nootan asked with genuine concern.

Anusuya didn't reply; instead, fresh tears formed in her eyes. As if the concern shown by Nootan removed a plug that had stopped a leak, Anusuya burst out. Her thin body shook with sobs.

"My life is over. Get me some poison. I'll give it to my child and take some myself," Anusuya sobbed. "Death is the only way to end this misery."

Nootan remained silent. She had seen Sakharam come home

drunk every night. It was evident he wasn't working anymore. Nootan, seeing Anusuya's almost hand-to-mouth living conditions, had started to pay Sarangi some cash for tutoring Pooja. She knew that even the *Hindustan Times,* the English-language newspaper delivered every Sunday for Sarangi, had been stopped. Nootan knew that Anusuya was short of money. But her pride did not allow her to disclose the fact to Nootan or anyone else. Until that moment, when her defenses were down.

"That man squanders all our money, and now I have no money to pay Sarangi's school fees."

Nootan was sensitive towards the pride that Anusuya felt at Sarangi's academic achievements. Sarangi always stood among the first three in her class. After Anusuya stopped crying, she wiped her eyes dry and looked at Nootan for some answers.

"Why don't you earn some money?" Nootan asked.

There was a bewildered expression on Anusuya's face. She expected Nootan to ask her to goad Sakharam into working. But this was a surprise.

"But what can I do?" Anusuya asked, puzzled.

"Well! I can introduce you to some women in the buildings where I work. You can earn at least five thousand *rupees,*" Nootan said testily.

At first, Anusuya's face contorted with shock and horror. "How can I work in someone else's house?" she thought.

Nootan knew what was running through Anusuya's head. "You have no choice. You can't get a job elsewhere," Nootan said with finality.

Anusuya shook her head, a little miffed. Nootan sighed and walked out the door.

That night, Anusuya did not sleep. She heard her husband walk in drunk and crash with a resounding thud on the bed. Normally, it would have upset her, but that night she was preoccupied with Nootan's offer.

"If I don't do this, Sarangi will have to stop her studies, and all of us will probably starve," she thought.

Sarangi had offered to postpone her studies when she realized the family's economic state.

"No. Never," Anusuya had said with resolution. "As long as I'm alive, you'll study. I'll find a way out."

Sleep evaded Anusuya. In the early hours of the morning, she finally made up her mind. At eight, she walked next door to Nootan's apartment.

"Nootan, I'm ready. Take me with you."

The two women went to a block of apartments that was a fifteen-minute walk from their *chawl.* Nootan introduced Anusuya to a couple of women. Very soon, Anusuya found work as a housemaid in two of the apartments. She learned the trade quickly. There was no time to be wasted on any loose talk or banter, no carrying tales from one household to the other. Anusuya's hands flew at work. However, her physical health deteriorated. There were calluses on her hands and feet. Dark circles formed under her eyes, and her face became gaunt. Soon, Sakharam began to stay out of the house for days on end. At times, he demanded money from Anusuya, but she refused to give more than necessary. *Necessary* was an amount to get him drunk enough to stop bothering her or Sarangi.

Anusuya made sure that Sarangi knew of her struggle.

"This way, our daughters won't take their lot for granted," Anusuya told Nootan.

Nootan nodded, adding, "See how that young boy in 2B is squandering his father's hard-earned money?"

It wasn't long before Anusuya managed to save a bit. Often, Nootan visited her in the evening. They'd have a cuppa together or watch a half-hour sitcom. Nootan cried unashamedly when she watched weepy soaps. Anusuya wondered about the oddly touching aberration in the otherwise extremely practical Nootan. Nootan wept her heart out whenever she saw Amitabh Bacchan jilted or killed in a movie. Anusuya, on the other hand, was amused to see overtly made-up women forgive their erring husbands and smile with their pancaked faces.

"Hypocrites," Anusuya said disgustedly.

Someone noticed Anusuya at work and recommended her to an aged, eccentric actress living in Bandra. Nobody warned Anusuya about her eccentricities — that the actress was afraid of light and always sat in a dark room, or that she was an alcoholic. The actress's antics were well covered by the press, the most notorious gossip being that she opened the door in the nude, especially when the milkman and the newspaper boy knocked. The young boys were shaken out of their wits to see her in this manner. Anusuya, completely unaware of the woman's quirks, was in for a shock.

In the house, the curtains were always drawn, and Anusuya took time to get used to working in the rather badly lit surroundings. However, the actress paid Anusuya well, which compensated for the inconveniences. On the whole, the quality of her life improved, and she began paying off the debts her husband had incurred.

Soon, Anusuya, with Nootan's help, opened a bank account, and both of them toyed with the idea of buying life insurance policies. Anusuya wished that she could save enough money to buy things like new textbooks for Sarangi. Her daughter always read from old books and often grumbled that the answers were marked by the previous owners. At times, money seemed to be the answer to all of her family's problems, but when she inspected the lives led by the wealthy people she worked for, she became pretty sure money couldn't solve every dilemma. Sarangi was doing well in her class, and she maintained that she wished to study medicine.

"As long as I don't have to buy a college admission, like that Nita Parekh in 1A, then it's fine," she cautioned her daughter.

"You won't have to pay anything. My teacher says if I continue with this momentum, I'll enter medical school on merit," Sarangi said. "And once I become a doctor, you won't have to work so hard. You can sit at home and live like a queen and have somebody do *your* housework."

Anusuya just laughed, but somewhere hope began to float.

*

One day, when Anusuya was working at the actress's home, the telephone rang.

"All right! I'll call her. Who's on the line?" Anusuya heard the actress's sister say on the phone.

"Anusuya, there's a call for you — a Nootan on the line," the sister called out.

Anusuya shook her head and wondered what had happened to Nootan. She never called her unless something urgent had cropped up. Anusuya feared the worst as she reached for the phone.

"Hello," Anusuya said gingerly.

"Can you come a little earlier?" Nootan asked eagerly.

"Why? What happened?" Anusuya said almost tearfully.

"Silly! Nothing has happened. I want you to meet someone," Nootan said.

"Can't that someone wait?" Anusuya asked a tad hastily, as she did not want to spend time on the phone.

"No, the person cannot wait," Nootan replied. "She has to rush off."

"Is she Hema Malini?" Anusuya asked with sarcasm.

"Better! Rekha!" Nootan replied with a smile in her voice.

Hema Malini was Anusuya's favorite Hindi film actress, while Nootan preferred Rekha. They watched all the television movies featuring the two actresses. Anusuya sighed and mumbled an OK as she hung up. She left work early and went to Nootan's home.

She barged in to see Nootan stirring a pot of curry.

"Aha! Come in," Nootan invited. "I want you to meet my friend Farzana," Nootan said, turning from the pot of curry and pointing a finger to a girl-woman who sat in a corner.

Anusuya nodded her head, looking at Farzana, who nodded back.

"Farzana came to visit me. You know her, right? I've spoken to you about her. She stays at Mumbra. I stayed home to spend the day with her."

Anusuya smiled at Nootan's old friend.

Farzana had lied to Javed, saying she was going to visit a holy shrine with an aunt who lived in Bandra. She then phoned Nootan and said she wanted to meet her and Pooja. The reunion was bittersweet. Farzana cried when she was introduced to Pooja. Tears were also shared over lunch as the two friends spoke about *Abbajan* and old times. Later, Farzana took a cone of henna she had carried with her and began drawing little flowers and leaves on Pooja's hands. Pooja immediately smudged the dye, and the blob in the little girl's hand invoked peals of laughter from Farzana.

"Did you tell Javed that you saw me?"

"No, he would thrash me. He has changed completely."

"I want you to meet another friend of mine," Nootan said, relieved that the past would no longer drive Farzana and her apart.

"Nootan has mentioned you," Anusuya said.

"Farzana's in a bit of a fix," Nootan said, lowering her voice.

"What kind? I hope not with the police," Anusuya said hesitantly, looking at the black *purdah*.

"Don't be silly," Nootan admonished, not really surprised at her neighbor's attitude. There were many who harbored such feelings.

Anusuya turned to Farzana, ashamed of her pettiness. In an attempt to steer the conversation to a less embarrassing subject, she asked her about her journey.

"I took a train to Dadar and then another to Andheri," Farzana said in her clear voice. Her bangles tinkled when she gestured with thin arms covered by the sleeves of her *kameez.* Her fingers were long and shapely. The red henna on her fingertips was fading, and the blob of red on her palms looked fatigued. There was an underlying sorrow around her eyes.

"Did you have money? I forgot to ask you," Nootan said a little ashamedly.

Farzana nodded her head. She told her about the little money she earned cooking for feasts on *Eid.*

"Her husband's causing her a lot of grief," Nootan said, trying hard to keep a straight face.

"Tell me something new," Anusuya replied with a glint in her eye.

All of them burst out laughing.

"Hitting? Threatening to take another woman?" Nootan asked in a bored voice.

"Why don't you leave him?" Anusuya asked.

"And go where? I have nobody here. I don't have enough money to move to another place. I'm totally dependent on him," Farzana said with some rage.

There was a barren silence. Three women and one shared problem.

"Do you have your parents?" Anusuya asked.

"Not any more. *Abbajan* died. And I'm not sure whether I'm welcome in my home town. The HUP are gunning for our blood," Farzana said.

"No, the situation's not that bad. You're overreacting," Nootan said.

"Do you know Noor? That lame poultry owner?"

Nootan nodded her head.

"They burned his entire family alive, because his son was in love with a Hindu girl," Farzana said.

Nootan was quite certain that her brother must have had a hand in the arson, but she didn't say anything. She was aware of the HUP's methods. They would do anything in the name of reviving culture.

"Why don't you get a job?" Anusuya asked Farzana.

"It's not that easy. Javed would kill me if he found out."

"How will he know if you slip out?" Anusuya persisted.

"His aunt lives near us. She's a spy for him. Today, I lied to him and said I was visiting a shrine," Farzana explained. "That's why I'm here."

"What can we do to help you?" Anusuya asked.

"Nothing. I don't want anything. I just feel good knowing that I have two friends here in this city," Farzana said warmly.

Farzana put on her *purdah* and hugged Nootan. She stood for a moment, hesitatingly, in front of Anusuya and then quickly embraced her. She held her for just a second and then ran off like a startled crow in flight.

"Poor girl! I hope she can get through this," Anusuya said, looking at the black figure that had become a speck in the distance.

"Farzana hasn't laid down her arms. She's *Abbajan's* daughter. She'll give Javed a tough time. I know she seems frail, but there are very few women like her," Nootan said proudly.

"I know one — a relative, Shakuntala Ponkshe. She's a feisty woman. Her get-up-and-go attitude shames me," Anusuya said quietly.

The sun was nearly setting, and Sarangi would soon return from the college. Anusuya looked at the clock and sighed. It was time for her to leave.

Darkness was creeping over the city with a purpose, but the city refused to let it take over. Among all the bright lights in the streets, the pubs, the discotheques, and the high-rises, a 60-watt bulb's light shone on an old, much-read science textbook.

6

Shakuntala Ponkshe

Just three kilometers away from the *chawl* where Anusuya Alhat and Nootan Vakharia lived, there was a building called Govind that almost touched the sky. It seemed as if the wandering clouds, when tired, came and rested on its terrace. Far below those clouds, on its ground floor, Shakuntala Ponkshe sold soaps, detergents, and brooms to the secretary of the building.

When Shakuntala had left home to live in Mumbai with her new husband, her father had informed her of an Anusuya Alhat, whose mother had belonged to their village. At first, she visited Anusuya regularly. But later, the novelty of the relationship wore off. Shakuntala found the Alhats a whining couple. Moreover, that drunkard husband of Anusuya's was a pain — always moaning and grumbling.

Many years earlier, on a dusty Sunday morning, Shakuntala reached Mumbai in a state transport bus from Sawantwadi, her sleepy coastal village. The dirty red bus stopped with a screech at Dadar, and Shakuntala's first view of Mumbai was of streets lined with shops. She looked around, taking in her new surroundings. She had with her a large green jackfruit, a jute bag filled with coconuts, a suitcase of nine-yard saris, and a new husband.

Girish Ponkshe was a teacher in a state-funded school. He was a man devoid of ambition, wanting only to live until he died. Fond of good food, every Sunday he purchased mutton for lunch, and this was the only luxury he expected from life. In hindsight,

Shakuntala realized he might have married her only to have someone to cook for him.

All the buses from the villages stopped at Dadar. From Dadar, Shakuntala reached her new home in Andheri, a neighborhood fifteen kilometers away from Dadar, in a taxi. It was a complete contrast to her native village. In Sawantwadi, there was greenery as far as the eye could see. Summers were sultry, and the air was filled with the smell of mangoes and straw. Betel nut trees swayed in the wind while women pounded rice. There was none of that in Andheri, but she had agreed to the marriage to relieve her father of his responsibility. She was also secretly very ambitious and almost glad to leave her restrictive little village. She hoped to grow rich in Mumbai.

Although she was an industrious housewife and kept house very well, Shakuntala could not sit idle at home. She was a natural motivator and a born leader. Even back in her village, where life was slow, she had taken the initiative to sell at the bazaar all the local delights made by the village wives, with whom she shared the profits.

Shakuntala took some time to get acquainted with her new surroundings. She was a short, well-built woman with beady eyes. Her entire body, like her personality, was short and strapping. At first, cleaning and cooking calmed her turbulent spirits. She cleaned her home with a fury and got at every speck of dust with venom. Her husband never understood why she was so restless. For all her enthusiasm when at work, she never showed any emotion in bed, and he often wondered whether she was satisfied. She always rebuffed any discussion of it.

Girish Ponkshe had not even an iota of energy, and his inertia irritated Shakuntala. Girish had married a girl from the village so that she would stay at home and keep house. He hadn't bargained for an ambitious, restless wife.

Shakuntala soon learned of a woman who taught how to make soaps and detergents. She promptly enrolled herself for the course, causing Girish some ire. She started making soap and detergents at home and selling them to the maintenance staff in surrounding buildings and to other housewives who wanted cheap cleansers. She soon began making scented soaps, colored soaps, and animal-shaped soaps. She earned quite a bit to supplement Girish's income, and he could have had mutton all the days of the week.

Simultaneously, the already wide gap between Girish and Shakuntala was growing. One day, her husband did not return from work. She went to Girish's school and was humiliated to learn that he had eloped with a vegan Hindi teacher.

When Shakuntala reached home, she cried aloud like an animal. The lye had eroded her nails, and her palms and fingers were pink. She threw all her *saris* out and began dressing in masculine shirts and trousers. She thought that one could survive better in the world as a man.

It was retribution. She was an angry woman — angry at her fate, angry at her husband who had deserted her and run off with another woman. She informed her father, who was shell-shocked. He asked her to return to her village, but she refused. She was aware that if she had to move ahead, it would be in the city. Her village was not the place where she could fulfill her ambitions.

Shakuntala continued with her work and began supplying detergents to most of the buildings in her neighborhood. No men flirted with her. Her appearance frightened them off. But she was in store for another diktat that would change her life again.

"We do not want the detergents you make. We have begun doing business with a multinational company," the secretary of one of the buildings she supplied said one day.

"How am I going to live?" Shakuntala asked incredulously.

The secretary didn't answer. He simply walked away.

But Shakuntala did not lose hope. She returned home and paced up and down. She stared at the bare walls from which she'd pulled down all the pictures of her husband and their life together. There remained only a bed in one corner and a cupboard in another. The kitchen was the only area she invested in. It had an old Bajaj toaster oven, molds for making sweets, and every conceivable sort of wok, griddle, and pan. Her eyes fell on a basket of potatoes. She looked at them through her beady eyes, and a thought struck her.

She chopped the potatoes into fine roundels, dipped them in chick pea flour batter that was seasoned with cumin, chili powder, and turmeric. She fried the potatoes to a golden yellow. She arranged the fritters on a large tray she had received as a wedding gift, designed to carry cups of tea for visiting relatives. Then she walked to Andheri station. She stood there defiantly holding the tray in her hand. She had no place to rest her plate, and her arms ached. When anyone came to buy the fritters, she balanced the tray on her knees and packed the fritters in newspaper. In half an hour, she had sold everything.

Food became her new trade. She saved money and increased her stock, purchased a little wooden table to place her fritters on, rented a tiny stall just sufficient for herself and the utensils, and very soon she was making nearly one hundred and fifty *rupees* a day. But her imagination didn't stop there.

Shakuntala was truly a woman of vigor. She organized a local *kabaddi* team and competed in all the tournaments. Shakuntala had played the traditional Indian game in her village. It involved two teams trying to touch the opposing team, all the while saying *Kabaddi, Kabaddi* without breaking the rhythm.

She also became an active organizer of the local *Ganeshotsav,* the festival celebrating the installation of the elephant god Ganesha at homes and public places. She liked taking charge. And she gradually became secure in the knowledge that she would not be turned out into the street.

After the day her husband left her, she never missed having a man in her life. She stayed away from them. The one experience had been shattering. She kept the scandal to herself and did not even inform Anusuya Alhat that her husband had run away.

"In a city like Mumbai, there's simply no time to visit people," she though. "If I keep spending time socializing with people, I'll starve."

7
Dignity

Nootan Vakharia sorely missed having a man in her life, but she was too proud to admit it. Her husband had been jailed when she was in her early thirties. A neighbor who was happily married had since made it amply clear that, if she wished, he could make adjustments.

"To be honest, I was tempted, but then I shied away," Nootan told Anusuya one day in confidence.

Anusuya nodded her head. She had also experienced that dull ache.

"Do you know what I saw yesterday?" Anusuya asked, lowering her voice and looking around to see if there were any children hovering nearby.

"What?" Nootan asked, expecting something juicy.

"I was folding the clothes at that fat actress's home..."

Nootan giggled, knowing that the actress Anusuya worked for resented being called fat or old. She did everything to look thin and young, in vain. Nootan looked eagerly at Anusuya's face, indicating that she continue with the tale.

"It was around three o'clock. Four women came to visit. They were hugging each other and pecking each other's cheeks. A little later, a man came to the house. He must have been around thirty years old."

"And then?"

"She pulled him into a room and gave him a wad of notes. The other women were with her. The door was slightly ajar. There was no one else there except me. I was going about my work when

I heard some music playing in the room, so I peeped in. The man had taken his clothes off and was strutting around to the music!"

"He had no clothes on?" Nootan asked, more amused than surprised.

"Naked as the day! The ladies were laughing. Their faces were red."

"Were they touching him?" Nootan asked.

"I don't know. I think they were trying to, and he moved away." Anusuya laughed.

"How did it make you feel?" Nootan asked in a matter-of-fact tone.

"Please! I have not seen anything uglier. In the daylight, a man dancing naked with five women leering?" Anusuya thought of how the sunlight exposed the blackheads on their noses and the hair on their upper lips. "I felt nauseous," she said.

Nootan was taken back to a time when she and her best friend, Farzana, were young. Below the banyan tree. They dreamed of husbands loving them forever. But it was just that — a dream. Farzana had confessed that, after their marriage, Javed had forced her to have sex with him even when she was unwell. He forced himself on her in all the ways possible.

Nootan felt a little envious as she remembered the tiger in her past. And how she had ridden that tiger.

Anusuya was too fatigued to bother about missing a man. Her complete attention was on Sarangi.

*

Most of Nootan and Farzana's conversations revolved around their home town. Nootan's brothers and the other HUP members were actively talking about killing their religious rivals. The divide between the Hindus and Muslims was very visible. Nootan still had friends who wrote and kept her informed.

Before long, an incident occurred that was to change the course of Nootan's life.

In the house where Nootan worked, there lived a young girl of thirteen. One day, while sorting a pile of unwashed clothes, Nootan found panties soaked with menstrual blood. She was repulsed. She put the soiled item aside and while leaving, informed the lady of the house as her daughter stood by.

"But you're our servant. You're supposed to be washing everything," the young girl said.

Her mother supported her. Nootan stood fast.

"Don't come here tomorrow. We don't want disobedient servants," the lady of the house said.

Nootan walked out, knowing very well that the lady would spread rumors about her hostility, which could affect her reputation as a housekeeper in the neighborhood. Nootan thought of her grandmother, who had regaled her with tales of granaries filled with rice and wheat and food cooked in butter every day. Nootan did not blink for fear of tears spilling down her face.

"Some ancestor really screwed up," she thought angrily.

She related the incident Farzana, who was incensed. She told Nootan to go and yell at the girl and the mother and hurl the choicest epithets at them. Nootan suppressed a smile. Farzana hadn't changed a bit. Nootan informed her of her decision to quit the job. And to Farzana's questioning silence, she replied with bravado that she would find something better than such measly work.

"Even the poor have dignity," Anusuya said when she heard of the incident. The word *dignity* hung in the air.

Nootan was unemployed, but at least the weather was pleasant. The beginning of August was always kind to Mumbai. The sun set into the Arabian Sea and the sky was the color of Zinfandel for some. For others, it was simply a night to get out. There was a void in the sky where the sun should have been, like a tear in a blanket.

8
Sarangi

Sarangi was not too happy with her mother's job, but she realized and appreciated the sacrifice Anusuya had made for her future. Although the teenager in her refrained from telling her friends about her mother's employment as a housekeeper, she did feel a quiet pride in her mother's strength. Sarangi possessed a similar strength. She observed everything astutely, like a painter studying a subject, and her mother's suffering was not lost on her.

Sarangi was shy and, therefore, quiet. This added another dimension to her character, and she appeared to be very strong. She had to be resilient. At that age, coping with an alcoholic father and watching her mother struggle to survive must have fortified her.

Sarangi remembered her grandmother saying, "Anusuya, you are cursed. You have a beautiful daughter."

Having a daughter meant arranging for a dowry for her marriage, and having a beautiful daughter meant being extra alert to the threat of a man from a different caste and religion whisking her away.

"I am not cursed. I have a beautiful daughter who is someday going to make me proud," Anusuya replied.

Sarangi was indeed beautiful. She was tall and slim like her mother, with a pear-shaped face. Her eyes were fish-like and her skin was slightly dark but clear. Her fingers and feet were long and gracefully tapered, and she had long black hair that she usually braided. Anusuya oiled her hair every day and maintained that the oil calmed her and provided nourishment.

On Sundays, Sarangi washed the oil off and left her hair loose. She walked around, bouncing her hair up and down, and wondered why it didn't spring like models' hair in the shampoo commercials. Sarangi was an attractive girl but was still not aware of her beauty.

Sarangi's best friend was Elvira Pinto. Elvira was a schoolmate who lived in her ancestral home in Bandra. It was a nice, small house with a sticker of Jesus on the front door, welcoming everyone. The entrance to the street had a grotto with a statue of Mary and the infant Jesus. The street to Elvira's home was lined with shops that sold sausages, *sorpotel,* and *vindaloo masala* — all delicacies from Goa, the coastal area from which Elvira hailed. Sarangi liked visiting Elvira's home. It always smelled of cake and fish and mutton and Yardley's lavender and, above all, Elvira's older brother, Joachim, when he'd just returned from a soccer game with his friends.

Sarangi was in love with Joachim as only a teenager can love a boy to whom she has never spoken. Joachim was sixteen, dark, and curly-haired. Soccer was his passion, and Pele was his idol.

Elvira's mother, Asunción, was a widow who had lost her husband to cirrhosis of the liver. She worked as a receptionist at a grain merchant's office. She always wore dark lipstick and cropped hair, unlike Anusuya who wore her hair long and did not use any makeup except kohl.

Sarangi had seen an old photograph of Anusuya, and she could not recognize her mother. In the picture, Anusuya looked resplendent in a green sari and was wearing gold. In fact, she looked much better than Asunción. Those days, sadly, were gone, and Sarangi wished she could bring them back.

In the evenings, to break the monotony, Sarangi went to Elvira's house just in time to see Joachim rush out to play soccer. Sarangi always blushed when she saw Joachim. She was smitten by him, though he did not even acknowledge her existence.

Whenever she visited, Elvira gave Sarangi some baked treat that Sarangi nibbled at slowly, not wanting the experience to end. Every Christmas, Sarangi stayed for lunch at Elvira's. Sarangi didn't tell her mother that she was eating practically every day at Elvira's home. Her mother would have brought the roof down. Anusuya was extremely persnickety about issues such as abusing someone's hospitality. Also, Sarangi neglected to tell her mother about Joachim.

Once, Elvira had given Sarangi a red lipstick and a bottle of dried-out nail polish. Sarangi wore the lip color when she was at Elvira's home and wiped it off with her hands when it was time for her to return home. She hid the cosmetics in an old box, away from Anusuya's glance.

Slowly, Sarangi became aware of the differences between her life and Elvira's.

Elvira was allowed to speak with any boy, while Sarangi was never encouraged to do so. For the school Christmas parties, Elvira wore dresses with frills and pirouetted in front of the boys while Sarangi, on the rare occasions she was permitted to go, just gaped. Sarangi couldn't dance and became tongue-tied when Elvira introduced her to her innumerable friends. Sarangi wasn't the only one unaware of her quiet beauty. It was lost on boys her age too, and this worked well for Elvira, who got all the attention.

Elvira was vain about her appearance, while Sarangi did not have the luxury. She listened with awe when Elvira spoke about beauty techniques. Her knowledge, of course, came from beauty magazines that her mother brought home. In pursuit of the air-brushed ideals she saw on the glossy pages of those magazines, Elvira plucked her eyebrows and waxed her legs regularly. Her mother and she would go to Crawford Market to buy chicken and lentils. There, they purchased cold wax, which they heated at home and applied to strips of cloth, which they used to clean their legs of unwanted hair. The whole neighborhood knew that mother and daughter had hairless legs, arms, and armpits, because long strips of cotton cloth hung from their clothesline.

One day, Elvira coaxed Sarangi into waxing her legs. Sarangi was petrified.

"What if Ma gets to know?"

"Idiot! You always wear long *salwar kameezes*. Who's going to see your legs?"

Sarangi agreed, and when Elvira yanked the strips of cloth, Sarangi yelled with all her might.

"If you can't tolerate this, how will you ever have a boyfriend? It will pain when you do it the first time too," Elvira said conspiratorially.

"Have you done it?" Sarangi asked, shocked.

Elvira shook her head.

"Then how do you know?"

"Annette told me."

"Annette? Why, she's the most pious girl I've ever known!"

"She and Sheldon did it."

There was a look of shock on Sarangi's face. Just like when the hot wax strip was yanked off her leg.

Sarangi often pondered the disparity between their lives and concluded that it was because Elvira and her folks prayed to a God who had been crucified and who listened to prayers in English, while Sarangi prayed to stricter Gods who watched over her every moment and waited to crucify *her*. Sarangi decided that Elvira's god was much better. The only way out was to start praying to the English-speaking God.

One evening, as Anusuya and Sarangi did the household chores, Sarangi dexterously turned the topic to Elvira.

"Elvira and her mother are always so happy," she said wistfully.

"So are we," Anusuya countered.

"Of course! But we can become happier," Sarangi said, not giving up.

"How?" Anusuya asked, giving the bedsheet a final tug.

"We can pray to their God," Sarangi said gingerly.

There was an ominous silence.

"No God is going to help us. You get a good score on your exams, and we all will be very happy," Anusuya said, signaling the end of the conversation.

Sarangi was disappointed. She chose her own way out. She secretly began praying to the crucified God.

Soon, Elvira suggested that Sarangi change her name to a more Christian one. They went through a whole list of names, and finally Elvira chose Beverly. Beverly was a beautiful cousin of Elvira's who lived in Dubai.

Sarangi began having Christian dreams too. She dreamed of wearing a white gown and getting married in a church to, of course, Joachim. She scribbled on the last few pages of her notebooks "BEVERLY LOVES JOACHIM" or drew a wedding announcement with the words "BEVERLY WEDS JOACHIM." Elvira also gave her a rosary that she hid with the lipstick and nail polish.

Unlike Asunción, who largely left her daughter alone, Anusuya emphasized the importance of staying away from idle pursuits and stressed that men would come and go but life would not give any second chances. Sarangi's girlish fantasies were vague images of happiness and everlasting joy with Joachim. Sex and its power were yet unknown to her. Nor did she have any ideas to plot and plan the entrapment of Joachim. She was still untouched by the notion of manipulation.

One evening, when Anusuya and Sarangi were at the market, they ran into Elvira.

"Hello, Aunty. Hi, Beverly," Elvira wished them cheerfully.

Anusuya smiled at Elvira.

Sarangi cringed and smiled wryly, not encouraging any further conversation. But Anusuya held her ground.

"Elvira, you never visit us. Sarangi keeps going over to your house," Anusuya said in a tone that was hardly inviting.

Elvira understood Sarangi's body language and, not wanting to antagonize her friend, mumbled that she would visit some day and then ran off.

"What was Elvira calling you? Definitely not by your name," Anusuya probed.

"Oh! That! Elvira calls me by another name, affectionately," Sarangi explained.

"Hmmm..." Anusuya said menacingly, not entirely convinced.

Sarangi walked quietly by her mother. "I'll never let my mother be ashamed of me. She'll like Joachim, and we'll live happily ever after," thought Sarangi, otherwise known as Beverly.

Sarangi vowed to herself that she and Elvira would not share Nootan's and Farzana's fates. She would make sure that Joachim and she didn't end up like her mother and father or Nootan and the unfaithful Dilip. Sarangi knew that her mother depended on her to redeem them from their drudgery. At times, the white gown, the three-tiered cake, and the confetti seemed like a distant dream.

Sarangi was always conscious of the responsibility of saving her mother from further slavery, and the only way to ensure it was for her to study and earn money. She worked hard so her grades would not slip. She appeared for every scholarship exam and tried to reduce the burden of fees on her mother. Elvira had no such worry. Asunción would have been happy if her daughter became a receptionist, but Sarangi knew that Elvira wished to become an air hostess. Elvira's cousin Jean flew with Cathay Pacific, and whenever Jean visited Elvira's home, Elvira would stare at her, speechless.

Elvira declared her ambition to Joachim, who thought of nothing but soccer. Joachim was in a good mood that day, and looked at his short, dark sister gingerly.

"You'll have to hammer your teeth in," Joachim said unkindly.

Elvira took the advice very seriously and had steel braces put on her teeth. Sarangi found living with steel wire in one's mouth very strange but perhaps worthwhile, because Elvira did have difficulty keeping her mouth closed. Most of Elvira's pictures showed the white overbite of her protruding teeth.

Sarangi and Elvira were antonyms when it came to their ambitions. Elvira could never comprehend why her best friend thought that she would make it in life only by studying. Elvira's notion was that looking beautiful made all the difference. Yet, Sarangi was Elvira's sounding board, and she confided her current ambition to get a boy friendly with her.

"What will your mother say?" Sarangi asked.

"In *ours*, it's allowed," Elvira replied through the steel in her mouth.

Whenever Sarangi visited, Elvira played the Beatles for her. To the music of "Love Me Do" she would do the twist, to Sarangi's envy.

Another cause of envy was the celebration of their birthdays. Elvira's birthday was a day of frolic. Her grandmother and mother baked a cake — pink and creamy. They called over their friends in the evening, and Elvira blew out the candles on the cake and smiled to a 99-*rupee* Hot Shot camera. Asunción made punch, or *shandy. Shandy* was a special drink that Asunción concocted for guests. It was nothing but beer, lemon, and water.

Joachim took a swig of the *shandy* like a film actor, and Sarangi could not take her eyes off him.

In complete contrast, Sarangi's birthday was a boring affair. Anusuya woke her up at an unearthly hour, compelled her to take an oil bath, and walked with her to the nearby temple, where Anusuya made an offering of eleven *rupees*. Anusuya made *ladoos* and coaxed Sarangi to take some for her friends. But Anusuya's *ladoos* could not stand up to Asunción's pink cake. All of it reinforced Sarangi's belief that her gods didn't want her to have any fun, and it would be beneficial if she became Beverly.

9

An Idea

If Anusuya relied on Sarangi to rescue her from her life, Nootan relied only on herself to escape the misery. The row at her former employer's home had disillusioned her. Most of her time was now spent looking for a job. A cook was going on maternity leave in a fortnight's time, and Nootan agreed to fill in.

Farzana called Nootan on the telephone every other day. They had resumed where they had left off, but Nootan was still holding something back.

One Sunday, Anusuya and Nootan stepped out to run some errands. On their way back, Anusuya spied Shakuntala frying potato roundels at a stall. At first, Anusuya could not recognize Shakuntala, who looked like a man from afar. As she walked closer, she saw that the woman wearing a man's shirt and trousers was Shakuntala Ponkshe. Anusuya exclaimed in delight and reminded Nootan of the feisty relative she'd once told her about. They walked up to her.

"Why, Shakuntala, do you recognize me?" Anusuya asked.

Shakuntala stared at them, and then her eyes lit up.

"Yes, of course. Anusuya Alhat!"

"Meet my friend, Nootan Vakharia."

"Would you like to come home for a cup of tea with us?" Anusuya invited.

"Now?" Shakuntala asked, looking at her wristwatch. It was past the time customers would buy something to eat. Moreover, Shakuntala had exhausted her raw ingredients.

"Yes. Why not?"

"How is your father doing?" Anusuya asked Shakuntala.

Shakuntala had closed herself off to everything except her father. "He's OK," she said, remembering that she hadn't sent him a letter for weeks.

Shakuntala packed the remaining fried potatoes in two brown bags and handed one each to Anusuya and Nootan. She put away the utensils of her trade and walked with the two women to Anusuya's home. Anusuya brewed ginger tea for all.

Nootan offered to leave the two relatives alone, thinking that Anusuya and Shakuntala might have matters from the past to discuss. After all, they had known each other for a longer time. But Anusuya insisted that she stay.

"How's your husband?" Anusuya asked.

"Ran away," Shakuntala replied in a matter-of-fact voice.

Nootan and Anusuya were shocked at Shakuntala's tone. No emotion, just a statement.

"Where is your husband?" Shakuntala asked

"The less said about him the better," Anusuya started.

Shakuntala, seeing another typical sob story coming her way, cut Anusuya short by asking her about her job. "And where are you working now?"

"We both are working as housekeepers in a few houses and making nearly ten thousand *rupees* a month," Nootan said, a trifle proud and consciously avoiding the word *maid*.

Shakuntala merely managed a smile. "I don't like working for anyone. Humiliation, reprimands, admonishments — I've gone through all that. I broke my back making detergents and selling them to the secretary at Govind. At the end of it, he shooed me off without even a decent farewell," Shakuntala ranted.

Nootan absently nodded, thinking of her own mêlée with her employers. "She has a valid point," Nootan thought, as her pride melted away.

Seeing no defense coming from Nootan and Anusuya, Shakuntala warmed up to the topic. "I prefer running my own show, keeping my own hours, earning my own money, and — most importantly — earning it doing what I like the most."

The three women were quiet for a while. Anusuya and Nootan wished to be more like Shakuntala, but they knew neither what to do nor how to do it. Shakuntala seemed to be in control, unlike the two housemaids, who were virtual slaves.

Shakuntala finished her tea and picked up her belongings, ready to go back home. "We must stay in touch," she said.

"You stopped coming over," Anusuya accused.

"It doesn't matter who goes to whose house; we just need to stick together," Shakuntala said.

"Yes!" Anusuya and Nootan said almost in unison.

Before leaving, Shakuntala invited them to watch a *kabaddi* match on Sunday. Then she departed, leaving a visibly impressed pair.

"Even if she earns five hundred *rupees* a day, that makes it fifteen thousand *rupees* a month!" Nootan said, doing some back-of-the-envelope calculation.

"The scoring point is that she's her own boss," Anusuya said.

"Ah! I wish we could be like that," Nootan said dreamily.

"But I don't understand why she dresses up like a man," Anusuya thought.

Shakuntala actually felt sorry for the two women. They looked like hens to her. There was no blood in them. She could see them slaving away all their lives for others. Yet, Shakuntala liked Nootan's quiet demeanor, and there was a bright look on her face.

"I could get them to do something. But those hens have no heat between their legs," Shakuntala thought.

Anyway, Shakuntala would have no time, since *Janmashtami*, the celebration of the birthday of the Hindu god Krishna, was approaching and her hands would be full. This time, the prize money for the *dahi handi* was ten thousand *rupees,* and Shakuntala was forming an all-woman team to get the money. It required practice and determination.

Another day had slipped into the sea for Anusuya and Nootan, while in other parts of the city, glass slippers for a ball and drugs to escape reality emerged, presaging the beginning of day for some.

10

"I think she can make us do it"

Sarangi came down with a bad bout of influenza. The doctor pronounced that it would take her at least three or four days to recuperate. The 'flu was doing the rounds of the city, and the newspapers reported that film actors were stricken by it too. Anusuya was worried and had no heart to set out for work, leaving a fever-stricken Sarangi behind. So she stayed home for two days, while Nootan informed her employers that she had taken leave since Sarangi was unwell.

"I'm sure they'll understand. After all, they have children too," Anusuya said.

Two days later, Anusuya returned to work and was in for a rude shock. The aging actress announced that she no longer wanted her housekeeping services. Absenteeism was something she would not tolerate, even if it were due to a daughter's illness. Anusuya's spirit broke, and she had no energy left to fight. She had never expected to be sacked from her job. Now, she had to go through the headache of finding a new one. She reached home early and waited for Nootan to return from her job-hunting spree.

"Everyone knows she was notorious for not turning up at shoots, the bitch," Nootan said viciously, when she learned of what had happened to Anusuya.

"Now, what will the two of you do? Have you saved any money?" Farzana asked when Nootan mentioned Anusuya's predicament to her on the phone.

"Yeah, a little bit. We'll look for other jobs," Nootan said a bit cheerily, more in an attempt to convince herself that things were not so bad.

In her own personal hell, Farzana was almost under house arrest. She was not sure whether Javed knew she'd lied and visited Nootan. It wouldn't have been difficult for him to find out, since he had many friends who did nothing except while away their time. They'd readily act as spies in exchange for a little money. Farzana didn't want to precipitate matters by going out, so she stayed at home, cooked, sewed, and read the *Quran*. Whenever she got an opportunity, she called Nootan to reminisce about times gone by.

Both Nootan and Anusuya were morose. The future was uncertain, and they had no plans.

Sakharam was making Anusuya's life more tedious. He kept pestering her for money, disregarding the fact that she had no job. At times, she felt sorry that he'd chosen alcohol as a vehicle of escape from reality. He was a weakling who preferred to sit in the only easy chair in their apartment during the day, on the occasions he happened to be at home, and feign being the lord. When the sun set, he would go out. Anusuya didn't expect anything from him now. As far she was concerned, he was nonexistent. Sarangi didn't even bother to talk to her father and was so disgusted by his attitude that she generally ignored him.

Anusuya, who had been subjugated for so many years, never once thought of running away. She stayed in her morass and fought back, for she knew the key to her freedom was her daughter. Sarangi would eventually rescue her. It was with this belief that she lived every day.

"Let's meet with Shakuntala. She might suggest something," Anusuya said.

"Yeah! If nothing else, she'll cheer us up with her tales of *kabaddi*," said Nootan, who always managed to find some optimism.

They walked to meet with Shakuntala. The sky was the color of oranges, and a few clouds moved about. A major change was to occur after their meeting with Shakuntala that day, yet both women walked in complete ignorance, only aware of the fact that they were low in spirit and needed a good bout of merriment.

Shakuntala spotted them from afar and waved to them to indicate that they should wait till she finished her work.

"This time, my place," Shakuntala said, packing up her stuff.

The three of them went to Shakuntala's apartment, which was modest but maintained very well. Over tea, Anusuya described how she had lost her job. Shakuntala kept quiet, her silence a little strange.

"Why are you not saying anything?" Nootan asked.

"They aren't concerned about our problems. They think having more money makes them superior to us," Shakuntala said matter-of-factly. "But why should we accept what they dole out to us? Why can't we stand on our own?" Shakuntala hissed like a rankled snake.

Nobody spoke.

"I was thinking," said Shakuntala. "Why don't the three of us get together and start something on our own?"

Nootan's face had an expression of incredulousness, and Anusuya did not even bother to show her emotions.

"Stop being ridiculous," Anusuya said.

"What's ridiculous? That we can do something on our own? That we can run an enterprise? What's wrong with you people? Or are you happy being exploited by everyone around you?" Shakuntala nearly screamed.

Anusuya and Nootan kept quiet.

"You have no idea what you can do. You have no fire in your bellies, bitches!" Shakuntala said unkindly.

"Hey! No foul language!" Anusuya said.

"Thank God! At least you reacted!" Shakuntala said in mock relief.

Outside, on the roads of Mumbai, there was a cacophony of cars honking. The noise of the traffic suddenly seemed louder. Motorbikes jostled with bicycles. Auto rickshaws sped to catch up with cars. The cars sped to catch up with god knows what.

In Shakuntala's apartment, the conversation continued.

"But what can we do?" Anusuya asked in a low voice that was almost inaudible.

"Thousands of things," Shakuntala said.

"Like what?" Nootan asked.

"Run a cleaning service, a housekeeping agency, a food stall, or whatever," Shakuntala said, her ideas dying out.

"But don't we need money?" Anusuya asked

"There are banks."

There was silence. The scheme sounded preposterous to Anusuya. According to her perspective, the rich conducted business and the poor slaved. That was the rule.

"But the first thing we have to decide is what we're good at," Shakuntala said.

"Running a cleaning agency or housekeeping would be difficult," Nootan said, looking around at the others, not wanting to be autocratic.

"Everything is difficult," Shakuntala said.

"Hmmm…!" Nootan said, running out of arguments.

"I, for one, know that nothing sells in Mumbai like food. This city is always hungry. Need or greed, either way," said Shakuntala.

"And all of us like to cook," Nootan said, hitting the nail on the head.

"Then, let's discuss setting up a food stall and decide our plan of action," Shakuntala said, wanting to close in before they changed their minds.

"I'm not very comfortable with this... What if we lose all our money?" Anusuya whined.

"Why are you thinking so morbidly? Maybe you'll *make* money!" Nootan said.

Anusuya nodded her head slowly, not wanting to rush into anything unknown.

"Let's meet again and discuss the pros and cons after you've had a chance to think about it," Shakuntala said sensibly before the women dispersed.

On the way back to their apartments, Anusuya was silent, but Nootan seemed excited. Anusuya was always afraid of venturing into anything new. The fear of loss always dissuaded her.

"I have Sarangi to think of. I can't risk my daughter's future for some harebrained scheme. And you have your daughter to think of, Nootan."

"We're not expected to make a decision right now. Let's meet again," Nootan said as they parted ways.

Once at home, Anusuya related to Sarangi the events of the meeting at Shakuntala's place.

"Ma, it sounds simply perfect. You must do it. I feel bad when you have to slog at someone else's house."

Anusuya caressed her daughter's hair, and both of them looked out of their apartment window. All they could see was darkness.

The next week, thanks to Shakuntala's bullish obstinacy, they all met at Nootan's place.

"What do you think?" Shakuntala said, without preamble.

"Sarangi seemed to think that it was a good idea," Anusuya said.

"I asked what *you* think. Sarangi is far too young to know what's right and wrong," Shakuntala snapped.

"Let's assume that we're going ahead with a food stall. Next what?" Nootan asked pragmatically.

"We have to find a location, get permits, and buy the materials to start with," Shakuntala replied.

"Where do we get the money?" Anusuya asked, indicating that she was not willing to shell out any of her hard-earned savings.

"I have the utensils. All we need is the resolve," Shakuntala said.

All of them seemed to be deep in thought, each with her own worries. It was not in Nootan's and Anusuya's natures to be speculative, and foresight was not a trait they possessed. Shakuntala was impatient with the two of them. They were taking far too long to reach a conclusion. She had more things to worry about.

The main issue gnawing Shakuntala Ponkshe at the moment was *Janmashtami*. She was spending far too much time on two women who did not have enough gumption. She should have been with the team, trying to win the prize money. Ever since the day they had first discussed a possible business venture, the outcome had remained inconclusive. Shakuntala was irritated at the ficklemindedness of Nootan and Anusuya. The two simply refused to commit to anything. A week had elapsed with no communication from either side before this second meeting.

Shakuntala did not attempt to force the issue. "I was trying to make donkeys run like horses," she thought.

For the next ten days, Nootan and Anusuya judiciously avoided Shakuntala for fear she'd coerce them into a scheme that would naturally fail. They began scouting for work. Nootan did not take up the job of temporary cook, because she foresaw that she would have to look for employment all over again once the permanent employee returned. Instead, she found employment with a tailor, helping him sew and embroider clothes. Anusuya secured a temporary placement as a nurse for an ailing old woman.

Nootan had arranged for an elderly widow who had been thrown out by her daughter-in-law to take care of Pooja while she was at work. The old lady and Nootan had become acquainted while Nootan was working as a housekeeper. They were employed in adjacent homes. Pooja took to the old lady, who was also happy taking care of Pooja. At some level, it managed to assuage her pain at not being with her own grandchildren.

The crisis, for the moment, was over. However, the insecurity remained.

*

One day, Shakuntala visited Anusuya who also called Nootan over. Shakuntala was too irritated to broach the topic of starting an enterprise, and she could see that the two women were more or less settled in their new jobs. The real reason Shakuntala was there was to invite them for the *Janmashtami* celebrations.

"This year, we're going to win the prize," she emphasized.

All over Mumbai, in its narrow streets, on *Janmashtami,* an earthen pot filled with curd, the *dahi handi,* hung from a rope stretching between two buildings at a height of no less than twenty-five feet. Young men formed human pyramids and broke the pot amidst much shouting, revelry, and the battle cry "*Govinda ala re!* Govinda has come!" The event was formerly entirely a male bastion. This time, however, Shakuntala defied norms by forming a women's team. She collected a motley group of unmarried girls and housewives and formed a team. Every evening, they met and practiced. It was a challenge for the women, who wished to break the coveted pot and take revenge on the men who made them break their backs every day.

On *Janmashtami* day, Nootan and Anusuya went to Shakuntala's neighborhood. Shakuntala appeared to be busy talking to a group of women who acted like they were heading out to battle. She called Nootan and Anusuya over and instructed some boys to let them stand in the front so that they could see.

"This year's *Govinda Ala Re* is ours!" she said smugly.

Anusuya realized with a start that it was an all-woman team, and they were making a bid for the pot with the curd.

"How, in the name of god, is she going to manage?" Nootan asked, surprised at the audacious venture.

Anusuya was too stunned to say anything.

They saw Shakuntala issuing last-minute instructions to her team. Two male pyramids were formed but they fell into heaps. There were shouts of *Govinda ala re!* everywhere. Then, Shakuntala's team took their stances. Crowds came to see the all-woman pyramid, and the whole area was teeming with people. A women's team making a bid for the pot was indeed daring.

Shakuntala looked up to see the pot dangling high in the air, as if tempting her. The sunlight caught her eye and she almost felt dizzy. The team began forming the pyramid, one woman over the other's shoulders, with Shakuntala walking all around them, egging them on like a coach does when his team plays. At last, the pyramid was formed. Everyone watched with bated breath, and then, in the second tier, a woman slumped. The whole formation fell down. There were taunts all around.

"Go home and cook."

"Your wrists are meant for bangles!"

Shakuntala did not give up. She urged the team members to try again, all the time shouting and coaxing. Energy surrounded her as she gave cries of encouragement. They made a second attempt. There was determination on each woman's face. Anusuya and Nootan looked up expectantly at the pot and at the slim girl on top of the human pyramid. She was perspiring, whether from the effort she was making or from fear, nobody knew. Then, like a woman possessed, she grabbed the pot. The rope swung and everyone watched in suspense. She couldn't break it. The sun's rays were falling on her face and she made the mistake of looking down. That did it. She tumbled to the ground with the entire pyramid.

"Don't look down! Every tier has to be strong. We can do it!" Shakuntala screamed.

This was their last chance. The women were tired but not defeated. They formed the pyramid again, each tier of women adding more strength. They muttered some kind of war cry. The slim girl valiantly reached for the pot. Her t-shirt was wet, and it stuck to her slim body. The balconies of the surrounding buildings were lined with people who had come to witness the extraordinary spectacle of a woman breaking the earthen pot. The girl at the top tugged at the rope, screamed loudly, and smashed the *handi* to smithereens with her fist. Her timing was perfect. If she had waited any longer, the others below would have been too exhausted to hold the pyramid steady. As the pot broke, the white curd fell all over her. She yelled, "*Govinda ala re!*" and they all tumbled down, screaming with joy.

The slim girl who smashed the pot was called by the local sponsor of the contest to collect the team's prize. But she called out for Shakuntala*tai.* Shakuntala collected the award, her face beaming. Anusuya and Nootan had never seen such a performance.

Nootan was very impressed with Shakuntala, who had encouraged, pushed, identified the weakest link in the pyramid, and changed that link. Anusuya and Nootan made their way through the teeming crowds, all the while thinking of the tall and strong structure formed by the women.

"I think we can do it," Nootan said quietly.

"I think she can make us do it," Anusuya replied.

11

A Menu

Nootan and Anusuya were in a state of confusion after they returned from the *Janmashtami* celebrations. Their confusion oscillated between belief and total disbelief. Somehow, they felt that they could make things happen, but at times, waves of pessimism took over them. They had witnessed Shakuntala take charge and lead her team to victory. They debated for a long time whether they should go along with Shakuntala or continue as they had always done. Nootan seemed to be in favor of teaming with Shakuntala.

A fortnight and many discussions later, they visited Shakuntala, who purred like a cat when she saw them.

"Did you see how we smashed that pot?"

"What about us?" Nootan asked abruptly.

"You people are better off working for someone. Let's not waste each other's time," Shakuntala said, a trifle bored.

"I think we can do it. The pyramid formation at *Janmashtami* was fascinating," Nootan persisted.

"Ha! It's very difficult. It required fortitude. You saw the number of times we fell. But every time they tried again without whining," Shakuntala said, looking pointedly at Anusuya.

"You have a point. But we can try," Anusuya said earnestly.

Shakuntala smiled. And the discussions began.

Shakuntala truly believed that an eating place would thrive best in Mumbai. She had noticed that even a two-bit stall selling sandwiches at the right location reaped profits. Ram Kisen, who could not even pronounce *sandwich* and whose signboard read

Sandwitch, was now the owner of a motorbike. Shakuntala was aware that the smorgasbord of life did not offer her much from which to choose, but she was resourceful enough to make the best of what life offered.

"Have we decided that it will be a food stall?" Shakuntala asked, resuming their last discussion.

"Yes, we have," Nootan said.

"Let's start small," Shakuntala said sensibly.

They agreed to sell a few delicacies from Shakuntala's existing business location, so they could get a feel for the trade.

"Why don't you spend some time with me at the stall after you finish work? You'll see the dynamics of the crowd and understand the business better," Shakuntala suggested.

"Hmmm! That sounds good," Nootan agreed.

"On an average, I make about five hundred *rupees* a day. Ten *rupees* per plate and two *rupees* extra for *pao,*" Shakuntala said. She had arranged for a baker to provide the *pao,* a type of Indian bread.

The best part of the plan for Anusuya, however, was that Shakuntala did not insist they quit their jobs.

"Imagine us doing something on our own!" Nootan said excitedly to Farzana on the telephone.

Farzana's silence was rueful. Nootan understood her friend's helplessness.

"Would Javed let..." Nootan let the sentence trail.

"Don't even think about it," Farzana said. Then she offered what she could. "My prayers are with you."

For three months, the trio cooked small portions of popular snacks and stood in the evenings at Shakuntala's stall. The food sold out in no time as hungry commuters swarmed the place and asked for more. In Mumbai, people ate not only to sate hunger but to kill time while waiting for a train; to spend a few additional moments with their dates; or, if they were college students, simply for the sake of eating. In three months' time, the three women realized the potential of their new business and felt that it was worth moving to a bigger place.

Now, they had to act. Just as *Abba* said: act. Nootan wished that his daughter Farzana could join them.

They spent week after week meeting and discussing, at first, what could go wrong. When all the horrific possibilities — including being run over by a bus — had been exhausted, they moved on to discuss all the good things, as well as the operational difficulties like location and capital.

"Can't we check the availability of an existing space for us to operate from? It makes more sense than starting from scratch, right?" Nootan asked.

"Hmmm… I think we have to be at Nariman Point. There are lots of offices over there, and I've seen the rush during lunch hours. Come 12:30, everybody makes a beeline for food," Shakuntala said.

"Nariman Point! That seems so far way," was all Anusuya could say.

"Nothing is far away in Mumbai. Thousands of women get into trains filled to the brim and travel from as far as Vasai and Ambernath to Nariman Point," Nootan said.

Anusuya remained silent.

"Let's visit Nariman Point this Saturday. Nootan and I can go and do a survey," Shakuntala said.

"And what would the rent there be like?" Anusuya asked.

"Let's cross that bridge when we get there," Nootan said consolingly.

The women were not looking for a restaurant. They wanted to open a little place where customers could stand and eat. Relatives and friends made various suggestions. Some recommended Bandra, with its swanky glass-covered office buildings, or Worli or Lower Parel. Shakuntala, however, had decided that their food stand was going to be at Nariman Point. Nootan and Anusuya took her at her word when she told them the place abounded with large crowds. Most of the tallest buildings in Mumbai were there too.

Named after a Parsi Municipal Corporation corporator, Nariman Point was built on land reclaimed from the Arabian Sea. Ironically, the three women were reclaiming their lives. Nariman Point was to become their battleground where, in the coming years, they would win, lose, and most of all… grow.

The new business partners visited Nariman Point a couple of times, but they couldn't find anyone who would rent space to them. They considered changing their location and starting something at Bandra. Anusuya felt it was a bad omen. She was of the opinion that if something was destined to happen, then everything fell into place immediately. Any postponement was divine discouragement. The delays bothered her so much that at times she wanted to back out.

One evening, a distant cousin of Anusuya's visited her. In the midst of their conversation, the cousin mentioned a friend who was winding up his trade at Nariman Point and returning to his home town because of some family problems. Anusuya subjected her cousin to a Spanish Inquisition and wormed out the details. When her cousin questioned her curious interest, she lied and said she'd never traveled that far and was simply curious.

"Sounds like she's inquiring about London," the cousin thought.

Anusuya wrote down the address of the place on a piece of paper, thinking, "Maybe I shouldn't show it to them. Let them find out on their own. They probably won't find out about it, and the whole scheme will go kaput."

Anusuya was frightened of being independent. It suited her to go to work every day like a robot and get paid at the end of the month. It didn't matter whether she was belittled or berated, as long as she was certain where her next paycheck was coming from.

There was no one to talk to and reassure her. Sakharam was by then completely in the clutches of alcohol, and when he was sober, he was always demanding money from his wife and nagging her. Anusuya preferred him in his drunken state. He was at least quiet then.

"I won't tell them about this," Anusuya resolved.

As the time to decide on a location for their new business drew near, Anusuya was the one most frightened. One night, as Sarangi studied late, Anusuya paced the little room, restless with the knowledge that she had an address her friends were looking for, and she hadn't given it to them.

"Fine! I'll give them the address and ask them to let me out," Anusuya thought.

Sarangi understood her mother's discomfiture and went to her side.

"I don't know what to do," the mother confided in her daughter.

Sarangi heard her out.

"Ma, I think you must join them. At least you can work with dignity," Sarangi said softly.

"What if it doesn't work out?"

"You can always go back to your old work. Anyway, I'm with you," Sarangi said.

The next morning, Anusuya rushed off to Nootan's and gave the address to her friend, who was delighted and a bit surprised that, among the three business partners, Anusuya, the unlikeliest candidate, had solved the problem of finding a location. The information was conveyed to Shakuntala, who acted immediately by fixing an appointment with the owner of the stall. Nootan and Shakuntala met with him that Saturday. The owner seemed in a hurry to vacate, and Shakuntala managed to negotiate a nominal rent. She heartily agreed to give him a share in their profits and skillfully made the owner waive the security deposit. The deal was struck.

The stall was a horizontal, flat-roofed structure with a counter at which to serve patrons and ample space behind to prepare meals and maybe even accommodate a hotplate.

"Nootan, you must quit your job. Ask Anusuya to do so also," Shakuntala said, knowing that the venture required everyone's full attention.

That evening, all three were bubbling with excitement. Shakuntala generously volunteered to donate her toaster oven and sandwich-maker to the endeavor. She also agreed to bring her wok, griddle, and ladles. The previous owner of the stall had left behind some cookware.

"What should we serve?" Anusuya asked.

"Before that, when do we start? We need a deadline," Shakuntala said.

"Next month," Nootan suggested.

"OK. By the first week of next month, we should be operational," Shakuntala said.

Nootan nodded, not very sure that it would be possible to set up shop in such a short span of time.

"Now, what do we serve?" Anusuya persisted.

"It'll be like a takeaway restaurant. No sitting around and wasting time," Shakuntala said. "Sandwiches, onion and potato fritters — or *bhajjiyas,* rice with onion — or *kaanda poha,* and sago with peanuts — or *sabudaana khichdi,"* Shakuntala prattled, as if she'd thought about the menu long ago.

"And not to forget tea, coffee, and buttermilk," Shakuntala continued.

"Sounds fine. But what about people who want a proper lunch?" Anusuya asked.

"Yeah! We need to think about hearty eaters. *Biryani* or egg *bhurji* or something like that..." Shakuntala said abstractly.

"*Bhurji... biryani...* Farzana!" Nootan practically yelled.

"Who is this Farzana, and what has she got to do with bhurji?" Shakuntala asked.

"Farzana is a friend of Nootan's. She cooks the most delicious *biryani* and *bhurji,*" Anusuya said.

Farzana excelled at making *biryani,* the rice dish spiced with cardamom and cinnamon, and *bhurji,* scrambled eggs with onions, tomatoes and green chilies. The *masala* she used was special, and even after so many years, Nootan remembered the taste of both. Nootan would eat the bhurji with *roti* and sometimes even with bread. She would plead with Farzana to make the bhurji as often as possible.

"Call her up and find out whether she's interested in joining us," Shakuntala said at once.

Shakuntala had no problem adding business partners. She knew that the greater their numbers, the greater their chance of success. And if Farzana was a friend of Nootan's, then she really did not mind including her. The *biryani* and *bhurji* would clinch the menu; they could offer their customers a complete meal.

Nootan was uncertain Javed would let Farzana join them. Calling her might only make Farzana more aware of her helplessness. Nootan mumbled that she'd call her friend later.

"Do it now," Shakuntala argued, not wanting to waste time.

Nootan couldn't let Shakuntala think she was putting off talking to Farzana.

"It's her husband. He won't let her," Nootan said.

"That's not a problem. Men have to be kept in their place. Free your friend," Shakuntala said earnestly.

Nootan found solace in work. Maybe Farzana would find redemption through it. Nootan decided to show her the place at Nariman Point first and then talk to her about it. Seeing the location might make a difference.

"Ask her to bring us some *bhurji.* Let me taste it!" Shakuntala said, running her tongue over her lips.

"When do we have to start work?" Anusuya asked, remembering the days when she had to be on the job very early in the morning.

"OK, about our hours of operation. Since most of the offices open by nine in the morning, we have to be there by nine, stay through lunch, and leave by four," Shakuntala said.

"That sounds perfect," Anusuya agreed. She was still not entirely confident of taking the plunge, but Nootan and Shakuntala's enthusiasm propelled her. If Nootan planned to include Farzana, then it had to be a foolproof scheme.

Nothing ever remained the same. The people Farzana and Nootan left behind in their home town had changed radically. Everything was touched by religion — Hinduism or Islam. A propaganda phase had started. Muslims were targeted systematically. Venom spread. The violence that was the next phase would follow five years later.

Nootan's brothers actively participated in the spadework that would lead to genocide. Hindus were asked to boycott services offered by Muslims. Young men wearing saffron bands and clutching tridents rode around town on motorcycles, spewing terror. Politicians encouraged people's raging emotions. After all, only the elections mattered!

Young Hindu women were asked to stay clear of Muslim men who, it was claimed by some, would marry, convert, and breed with them for the sole purpose of propagating their religion. In retaliation, the Muslims regrouped.

Nootan's brothers and their ilk were unhappy with her for mixing with the *others* but were placated when she married Dilip Vakharia, who seemed to have a bright future in the party. They tried contacting small-time politicians to secure his release from jail, but they failed.

Now, after intelligent deliberations, the women had taken a step alone. They dreamed of a better life in the city and probably knew that they alone could make it happen. The sun set, a little confident that it would return tomorrow to another day of surprise and intrigue.

12

The Reconnaissance

"Do you think her husband will let her join us?" Anusuya asked. She wanted to avoid a conflict with Farzana's husband, whoever he was. She'd heard that such men were trouble-mongers and wished to avoid them.

"I'll talk to her. Who knows? He may agree," Nootan said.

For a change, Nootan called Farzana on the telephone. Normally, Nootan's fear of Javed answering the phone prevented her from dialing, but today she was excited and couldn't hold back.

Such was not the case for Farzana, who answered on the first ring.

"Can you leave your house tomorrow? My home?" Nootan asked excitedly.

"Why?" Farzana inquired in a hushed tone.

"Something that I need to talk to you about."

"Urgent?"

"Sort of."

"What time?"

"Around eleven. You can have lunch with me."

"You don't have to go to work?"

"No… I quit!"

"Are you OK? Leaving your job?"

"Yes, I'm OK. Can you make it tomorrow? And get some *bhurji* for me!"

"Who is it?" Nootan heard Javed's stern voice in the background.

"No one," Nootan hear Farzana say, followed by a click and a dial tone.

"You barren bitch! Who was that you were talking to? A new man? Your *Abba* cheated me," Javed screamed. "He was a pimp!"

"Call me names, if you wish, but spare others from your viciousness," Farzana said softly.

"Aha! That hurt you. But you don't mind maligning your husband!" Javed said and moved forward, slapping her on the cheek.

Farzana had learned to deal with the pain of being hit by Javed. The terrible humiliation he inflicted didn't bring a teardrop to her eye. But if she hurt herself while performing a household chore, then she'd wail in pain.

"I haven't maligned you," she said quietly.

"Then why does everyone accuse me of torturing you?"

Farzana shrugged her shoulders, infuriating Javed even more.

"After my new bride comes, I'll throw you out, you barren bitch!"

Farzana shut herself off to the rest of her husband's tirade. She thought of Nootan's news and remained nonplussed. She wondered what her friend wanted to talk to her about. It must be serious. She'd sounded excited. And egg *bhurji* for her? Was she pregnant? She'd mentioned that they were doing well with the food business. What could it be?

After Nootan's phone call, Javed increased his vigilance. Farzana had no idea how she would leave home to keep her appointment with Nootan. If she slipped out in the afternoon, then Javed's aunt would report her departure to him. Farzana didn't want Javed to prevent her from ever going out and make things worse for her. She didn't put it past him to ask the neighbors to keep a watch on her.

And then she knew how she would do it.

After dinner, Farzana went to the bathroom and pretended to vomit, making sounds loud enough for Javed to hear. The whole night, she groaned in pain and clutched her stomach. The next morning, Javed threw a hundred *rupee* note at her and asked her to visit a doctor.

"Of course, if you're pregnant, then I will go to Ajmer tomorrow," Javed said devoutly. Ajmer was home to the Sufi saint Moinuddin Chisti, and Javed was a devotee.

Farzana nodded weakly, but there was a little worry nagging her. Javed would definitely send someone after her to watch her movements. She might have to pretend to go to the doctor and then give the person the slip, cooking up a story that the doctor asked her to go for some further check-up.

She left home but not without carrying the *bhurji.* She could see no one following her but, to be on the safe side, she visited the doctor and complained of some imaginary pain. She reached Nootan's home at around twelve o'clock, the heat having dehydrated her almost completely.

Nootan seemed to be brimming with excitement and refused to tell Farzana what the reason was. Nootan talked nineteen to the dozen while she pleated her best sari. She clutched her purse and dragged a bewildered Farzana out of the house.

Farzana had expected to see Nootan in some kind of trouble, with no job and no steady income, and her friend's behavior stunned her.

"Where are we going?" Farzana demanded.

Before Nootan could reply, Anusuya joined them, and a few minutes later Shakuntala arrived. Nootan introduced Farzana to Shakuntala, who gave her a warm smile. Farzana smiled back, not really knowing whether Shakuntala was a man or a woman. Shakuntala was wearing a shirt and trousers that left no trace of femininity. Her hair was cropped close to her head, her wristwatch was a large gold one, and the boots were definitely manufactured for men. Yet, on closer inspection, Farzana could see a woman in her eyes and in the softness of her smile. Shakuntala immediately liked Farzana and mentally likened her to a troubled doe, watching and listening for any trouble with her ears twitched, and suddenly the doe would run.

A few minutes later, Farzana had a look of utter confusion on her face. She couldn't understand what was going on, nor could she comprehend the babel that the other three women had created.

"At least tell me where we're headed," Farzana asked.

"Nariman Point," Shakuntala said.

Farzana almost fainted. As far as she was concerned, Nariman Point was as distant as Mecca.

"Javed will kill me if he gets to know that I'm traveling so far."

"How will Javed know?" Nootan asked naughtily.

"Why in Allah's name are we going to this place?" Farzana asked.

In reply, she was dragged to Andheri station. Shakuntala purchased return tickets for all of them. They boarded a local train to Churchgate for the thirty-minute journey. They sat quiet on the wooden seat, all four women as different as the four seasons. Each was lost in her own hell, and even the discordant songs of the waif in the train did not disturb them. Electric poles, buildings, dried turds, and slums marked the journey.

"I hope this works out," Anusuya prayed.

"Nothing can go wrong," Shakuntala assured herself.

"I'm sure I know what I'm doing," Nootan affirmed to herself.

"What's going on?" Farzana wondered.

*

They alighted at Churchgate station and walked ten minutes to reach Nariman Point. Shakuntala was their navigator, and she gathered them like a mother hen. All the Western suburb trains originated and terminated at Churchgate. At no point of time was the station without people. They walked out of Churchgate, saw the colorful display at the Asiatic store, the art deco Eros

Theatre, the lush green Oval Maidan, and the Rajabai Tower. They turned to the right and passed Mantralya, the seat of power where state meetings were held. En route, Nootan briefed Farzana animatedly about the plan to lease a place and run a food stall.

"Us on our own! Independent!"

Farzana did not react at once. She had a hundred questions in her head.

"I don't know if Javed will let me," Farzana said slowly after a good five minutes.

"Just inform him. Don't ask him," Nootan said in a hard voice.

"It's not easy," Farzana said.

"If you wish, everything is easy," Shakuntala said.

"Where will I stay if he throws me out?"

"You can stay with me," Nootan offered.

"He would murder you," Farzana replied.

"What about your aunt in Bandra? Your mother's second cousin?" Nootan asked.

"Yeah! She's the only one who knows about my situation. She's been asking me to leave Javed and stay with her," Farzana replied.

"I remember her very clearly. She would come home during the summers with nail polishes and lipsticks for Farzana. We'd hide them and listen to her tell tales about all the film stars," Nootan reminisced.

"Does she still visit *Abbajan's* home?" Nootan asked.

"Not after the HUP created problems. They burned down her ancestral home, and her husband died of the shock. And that was it."

Nootan knew that the HUP was causing turmoil back home, and there were violent incidents every day.

"Maybe you can talk to Javed. You know him too," Anusuya suggested to Nootan.

Farzana remained silent. She did not encourage Nootan to

speak to Javed, nor did she discourage her, but she looked at her carefully.

"He's changed. From what I hear, he's not the man he used to be," Nootan said softly.

"She's right. He's not the man she knew," Farzana said.

Their surroundings suddenly changed, and there were tall buildings, streets lined with food vendors, piles of waste, and people walking purposefully all around them. Shakuntala announced grandly, as if she owned the real estate, "And this is Nariman Point."

The Arabian Sea played along the coast, and Dalamal House, the last building, stood arrogantly, as if daring the sea. Shakuntala consulted the address on the paper and moved purposefully towards a shop flanked by a store that sold fresh fruit juices.

"This is it," Shakuntala said.

Anusuya looked around to see smartly dressed men and women strutting and talking incessantly to each other. Drivers stood alongside their long cars or napped or played cards. Then she saw the shop they were there to inspect. It was quite characterless. That the owner had no interest in it was evident from the fact that there was hardly anyone to drink the tea that had boiled more than a thousand times in the brass vessel or eat the flaking *khari* biscuit that had crumbled in the glass jar. Anusuya was disappointed. She had expected a swanky place like the ones she saw at Bandra. This shop was a little run down, and she said so.

"We have to create. We have to give it shape. Nobody has left anything for us to enjoy," Shakuntala snarled.

"It's so dusty," Anusuya whined.

"We have to spruce it up," Nootan explained patiently.

Anusuya had never wanted to complain, but she was frightened. This was a big step, and she didn't know whether it would work or not.

"Shakuntala is right. We'll have to slog," Nootan said with determination. "Remember the human pyramid?"

13
Stree

"Hmm..."

Shakuntala inspected the interior of the shop and mentally went over the changes they had to make. The walls had to be redone, the counter had to be cleaned, and the granite probably needed to be replaced. The electrical connections also had to be checked. Needless to say, the place required a good clean-up with soap and water.

The owner had waited for them. Nootan insisted on knowing the reason he wished to rent his shop.

"We don't want to be saddled with any legal problems," she thought.

The reason was a very common one. The owner was old, and his children were not interested in the property. He wanted to sell out and retire.

Nootan stood behind the black granite counter and watched people go by.

Farzana was quiet, not touching anything and refraining from making any comment. Her bigger problem was Javed. She had to deal with him first, and only then could she think of moving ahead.

"This is our starting point. From now on, there's no looking back. We're going to give ourselves completely to this venture," Shakuntala said emphatically.

But she knew the message had not been driven home. There was still a look of disbelief on Anusuya's face, and Nootan wore a quizzical expression. Shakuntala's larger task was to involve them completely. If she could get Nootan on her side, then Anusuya would follow. As far as Farzana was concerned, Shakuntala's opinion was that Farzana's husband had to be clobbered. Since that wasn't possible, Farzana would have to cajole or threaten him.

Nootan looked around and saw other stalls doing brisk business. She knew for a fact that every morning, thousands boarded trains from North Mumbai to reach the southern part of the city, where many government agencies offered employment.

"And they all have to eat lunch," Nootan thought.

"See! See!" Anusuya exulted, pulling Nootan closer.

Nootan and Shakuntala went over to see what Anusuya wanted them to. Farzana walked a little undecidedly and then quickened her pace as Nootan beckoned with her hand, urgently fluttering her fingers like a hummingbird's wings. They saw a man, presumably the owner of a juice shop that was half the size of the property they wanted to rent, licking his forefinger and counting a wad of notes.

"Five hundred *rupee* notes," Nootan said, squinting her eyes.

Everyone laughed, including Farzana. The thought that streaked through everyone's mind was *There is an opportunity.* There was an expression of mirth on each woman's face. This could be the key to freedom. Freedom from drudgery. Freedom for a new life. Freedom from Sakharam Alhat. Freedom from Javed Sheikh. And freedom from deprivation.

They could see that the other vendors were doing good business too, and there was no reason that they would not do well.

"Even that ghastly wagon cart seems to be making money selling plates of that red-colored stuff," Anusuya said in an attempt to convince herself more than anybody else.

The ghastly wagon cart was Hungry Stomach, and it specialized in Indianized Chinese food. The owner, an ingenious Nepali masquerading as a Chinese man, had created an entirely new form of Chinese cuisine by adding kilograms of Ajinomoto seasonings and food coloring to rice and noodles.

The women spent a few hours gazing around and witnessing the spectacle of lunch hour. The entire street was packed with people, and all of them were eating.

"There is no way this will fail," Nootan said to Anusuya confidently.

Anusuya nodded her head, for she had seen the hungry belly of the city.

Farzana too had no doubts that their business would succeed. However, her problems were, of course, entirely different. Genuflecting to Javed's wishes so often had made her spineless. Her heart was in the project, but her head warned her of the trouble ahead.

Shakuntala knew she'd scored a home run when she saw Nootan and Anusuya taking in the environs excitedly. She moved in firmly, fully aware that any delay would cause problems, especially with the fickle-minded Anusuya. She assumed the role of leader and looked around in haste.

"We can keep the hotplate here, the vessels there. And the plates… Oh, God! I didn't think of that. What do you think we should use? Disposable plates or steel ones? If we use steel plates, then one of us will have to keep washing them," Shakuntala said, as if remembering everything all of a sudden.

"Steel plates are a no-no. We should use paper plates or any kind of disposable plates," Nootan said.

"Also, for reasons of hygiene, it's better to use disposable plates," Anusuya said sensibly.

"Let's find out the price of paper plates," Shakuntala said.

"Why can't we use plates made of leaves? You know, the dried ones that we carry when we go on train journeys?" Farzana asked.

"Yes! That's a good suggestion. They'll be easy to dispose of and maybe cheaper. As for spoons, we'll have to use plastic ones,"

Shakuntala said, drawing Farzana into the conversation.

It was good that nobody daunted her with questions like *So have you made up your mind?* That would have frightened her. The truth was that Farzana had not yet decided. However, Shakuntala's excitement and Nootan's optimism had at least gotten her involved. Farzana was a woman whose life was controlled by incidents. And the person who caused the most incidents was Javed. It seemed that if he pushed her a little more, she would wholeheartedly be in this.

"We can use earthen containers for the tea, coffee, and buttermilk."

"We'll have to find out the price of the leaf plates, the plastic spoons, and the earthen containers."

"Also, we need an accounts ledger."

"I know a lady who makes plates and containers from dried leaves. At the moment, she supplies grocery stores."

"You'll have to negotiate for some credit with her. Maybe a month or so."

"She may not agree to a month's credit. But she might agree to fifteen days."

"True. Even the other suppliers might not give us credit now."

"But we must press for it."

It made them feel good to talk about the future. There was a feeling of control and, of course, a fear of failure. But their optimism strode over and surpassed everything.

"Let's give ourselves ten days to cart the utensils here. Also, I think it's the right time for us to decide what quantities of ingredients we'll need and how much we should cook," Shakuntala said.

"Yeah! And what about the money for the rent and the other stuff?" Anusuya asked.

"Now that we've seen the place, and we like it, we can discuss the brass tacks at home," Shakuntala said.

Shakuntala didn't know Nootan and Farzana well, but since they were friends of Anusuya's, she took to them. She had, in fact, immediately liked Nootan when she met her and spotted her strength. Nootan's sense of fairness appealed to Shakuntala. In Farzana, she saw a sense of desperation to break away from an oppressive marriage. And Shakuntala very rightly thought that the desperation could be valuable for their venture. Shakuntala was well aware of Anusuya's pessimism, which she knew would be a dampener. But Nootan would take care of that. After all, the two were good friends and would prefer to sink or stay afloat together. Shakuntala also knew that she had to keep the women together. Only then would their cooperative succeed.

"I swear to God, I'm going to make this big," Shakuntala said softly to herself.

*

They walked to Nootan's home, where Nootan cooked them plain *khichdi* for lunch and warmed Farzana's *bhurji.* The rice and lentil *khichdi* was Nootan's comfort food. Shakuntala pronounced that Farzana's was the best *bhurji* she'd ever tasted. Farzana was thrilled to bits. No one had appreciated her efforts in years. Javed continuously criticized everything she did and let it be known among his relatives that she was a bad wife who didn't keep his house well. At first, she had tried to gain his approval by striving harder, until she burned out. Among the women, she felt that she was accepted the way she was and, most importantly, her culinary skills were wanted. And that encouraged her to join them at all costs.

"I have to walk out of Javed's home, if I do this," Farzana said.

"Why?" Nootan asked.

"He won't let me do anything that will free me," Farzana said thoughtfully.

"You have to decide. Do you want to continue with that torture? The beatings, the taunts..." Nootan trailed off.

"Maybe I can stay with my aunt," Farzana thought aloud.

"All right. Let's decide on what our recipes will be and what we'll have to buy," Shakuntala said, firmly steering the discussion back to the business at hand.

"As we discussed the last time, let's make sandwiches, onion and potato *bhajjiyas, kaanda poha,* and *sabudaana khichdi,"* Anusuya said.

"Yes, but aren't we forgetting the *biryani* and egg *bhurji?"* Nootan said tentatively.

All of them turned to look at Farzana.

Farzana was sitting in a corner, silently staring into space. Knowing she was listening, Anusuya continued, "To start with, we needn't make *kaanda poha* and *sabudaana khichdi* every day. One of the two would be good enough."

"*Sabudaana khichdi* can be served on days people abstain from food for religious purpose. For that, we'll need bread, butter, green chutney, onions, potatoes, gram flour, oil, flaked rice, sago, and ingredients for tempering," Shakuntala said again, as if rattling it off from memory.

"Again, you forgot rice, eggs, and vegetables for the *bhurji* and *biryani*," Nootan said.

"I'm 'forgetting,' because I'm not sure whether Farzana will join us nor not," Shakuntala said.

All of them again looked at Farzana, who sat quiet in the corner. Her face showed determination.

"I am joining. If necessary, I can stay with my aunt," Farzana said.

"That's a bold decision!" Shakuntala said.

"Remember *Abbajan* and what he used to say?" Farzana looked at Nootan.

Nootan looked back, her eyes filling with tears and shame.

She had betrayed her good friend once, and the punishment was not only that her sleep had disappeared but that she had to face Farzana every day and see her sweetness.

"We should write the recipes in a notebook, and I'll keep it with me all the time. No deviation from the written word," Shakuntala said.

They also decided that they would run a trial batch, check on the taste and flavoring, and perhaps distribute it among neighbors to get their feedback.

"I'll go to the wholesale market to negotiate rates. I know a couple of merchants who might give me credit to start with," Shakuntala said.

"I'll come with you," Nootan volunteered.

"How much money would we have to chip in?" Anusuya asked nervously.

"I don't know. Maybe the picture will get clearer once we visit the market," Shakuntala said.

Farzana packed her bag and prepared to leave for home. She now believed that, with the money she would make in his venture, she'd be able to get by peacefully without depending on Javed. Still, she wished to obtain Javed's approval, largely because she wanted to stay married to him. Not for love, but to silence wagging tongues. Until this offer came up, she'd had no idea what she would do for a living. She strategized that, perhaps, if she kept her self-respect aside and sweet-talked Javed, then maybe he would acquiesce.

"I don't think he should object. After all, Nootan's involved, and it's an all-woman group. And what is it that we're doing? Cooking! Nothing that would sully Javed's name," Farzana thought optimistically.

Anusuya mentally calculated the amount of money she would have to pool in. She was concerned, not because she was a miser but because paying for Sarangi's education bothered her. She had scrimped and saved for Sarangi's college tuition and wasn't willing to spend the money on anything wasteful. Anusuya didn't even bother to tell Sakharam that she was switching trades. For one thing, he was never sober, but, moreover, she simply didn't care what he thought.

Farzana bade them all goodbye and reached the door before a thought struck her. She turned around.

"What do we call ourselves?"

"Think of names," Shakuntala said.

"The existing name is so silly — The Eating Point. Now, who would come to a place like that!" Nootan said.

"We should ask the owner to paint out that old name, so we can write our new name," Anusuya said.

"That should be no problem," Shakuntala said.

Just as they were about to part, Shakuntala said, "Wait!"

The others stopped, quizzical expressions on their faces.

"We have to promise that no matter what happens, only death can break this union among us. No deceit, no lies, no pretense, no caste, no creed, and no religion," Shakuntala said and waited for their reactions.

Surprisingly, Anusuya spoke up first. "I promise," she said, and the others too swore.

They embraced each other and felt each other's heart beating like the heart of a young sparrow fallen from its nest. Little did they know that one day they would be close to losing everything.

But at that moment, the four women were poised to take one of the biggest steps of their lives.

14

A Name

Anusuya reached home and described the day to Sarangi, who was terribly excited. This was a normal practice between mother and daughter, exchanging news of their respective days.

"Can you think of a name for us?" Anusuya asked.

"Yes! A name that everyone will like... I'll think of something," Sarangi said, closing her textbooks and putting on her shoes.

"Where are you going?" Anusuya asked.

"To Elvira's, to tell her that my mother's running her own business!"

In the meantime, Shakuntala and Nootan headed to the market to check on the cost of the recipe's ingredients. Shakuntala knew most of the traders, and she managed to get good rates for all the provisions, but no credit. Nootan did a quick calculation. Each of them would have to shell out approximately four thousand *rupees.*

"Is it too much?" Shakuntala asked with concern.

"I don't know about Farzana, but Anusuya and I can contribute that much," Nootan said.

"But Anusuya is very reluctant when she has to dole out money. She always seems disgruntled when it comes to her finances."

"You haven't met Sarangi. Her daughter, Sarangi, is in class ten, and she's a very good student. Anusuya wants Sarangi to pursue her education and opt for a good career," Nootan explained.

Shakuntala nodded her head, understanding Anusuya's concern for her daughter, but it didn't appeal to her to stay back in life for such a reason.

Sarangi had rushed off to Elvira's house to break the news. She hoped that Joachim would be there.

"So, Beverly, now you're a restaurant owner's daughter," Elvira said, a shade enviously.

Joachim overheard. He winked at Sarangi and gave her a thumbs-up sign. Sarangi blushed. It was the first time he had given her any attention. That night, Sarangi dreamed of Joachim winking and giving her the thumbs-up sign… while running in slow motion like in the movies.

*

When Farzana reached home, for once, she waited for Javed to return, feeling a little nervous. She cooked some of his favorite dishes and dressed well.

"If I can please him and get his sanction, it will be much better than walking out," Farzana thought. "My brothers will be angry if they learn I've walked out on him. But I need to be on my own. What will happen to me if I'm thrown out of Javed's home someday?"

She went to great lengths to get Javed's nod of approval for anything, which was strange, considering he behaved like a brute. She never dreamed that she could just talk to him person-to-person and convince him to let her proceed with her plans.

Javed returned later than usual. Farzana rubbed off the smudge of the impatient kohl. She served him his dinner and hovered around his chair.

"What is it you want?" Javed barked

Farzana began a little hesitantly, "My friends have formed a business venture, and they've invited me to join them. I wish to do so," she said slowly, barely able to hear her own voice.

"And who are these friends of yours? May I know?" Javed asked sarcastically.

"You remember Nootan? Well, I met her. She and two of her friends are doing it," Farzana said.

Farzana thought that if she mentioned Nootan, her husband might feel better. After all, he knew her old friend. But Javed's face darkened when he heard Nootan's name.

"And what are these grand friends planning to do? Prostitute?"

Farzana bit back a retort.

"Sell food," she said shortly, disgusted with the man.

"And what do you want me to do? Pimp for all of you?"

"I wish to join them."

"You barren bitch! Now, you'll go out and earn money to prove that I'm useless and can't look after you? I absolutely forbid it. You'll stay at home," Javed snarled and threw a plate at her, missing her by a few inches. He then struck her so forcefully that she slumped to the floor. He kicked her hard in the abdomen and screamed, "I don't want you to meet that Nootan or even talk to her!"

Farzana was in great pain and her stomach churned, but, strangely, she didn't cry. It seemed as if her eyes had dried up, but her resolve to escape only got stronger.

"Damn Javed," she thought, clutching her stomach.

That night, Javed flung himself over her like a beast in the darkness, oblivious of her pain. He smelled like an animal. She lay helpless below him, tears streaming from her eyes. But Javed did not see them. Farzana had never felt so defiled. Her mind was made up. She was certain of the path that she wished to choose.

The next morning, she packed her clothes and some money that she had saved, and she walked out, not even bidding Javed goodbye. She shut the door after her. The air was clear, and Farzana walked with her head held high. Her *purdah* flew slightly in the wind.

Farzana was never the same again. Her body too was never

the same. She suffered chronic pain from the kick Javed had aimed at her lower belly, injuring her uterus and causing her to have irregular menstrual cycles.

*

Sarangi had thought of a name for the women's venture: *Stree*.

Stree meant *woman* in Hindustani. It had an underlying tone of strength.

Elvira had suggested Hot Point and Lip Smacking.

"No… cheap," Sarangi pronounced.

"Goal!" Joachim forwarded.

"Now that's a name," Sarangi said, though she actually found it very silly.

Joachim walked out pompously, but not without applying more gel on his hair.

*

The next day, Farzana called Nootan on the telephone to tell her that she had walked out on her husband. She told her Javed had refused to permit her to join them, and the only alternative she'd had was to leave.

"What? How did you manage to do it? Does he know? Where will you stay? You can move in with me!" Nootan said in a rush, amazed at Farzana's stoic tone.

"I've moved in with my Bandra aunty. She always asked me to live with her. She's all alone and loves having me around. I took her offer," Farzana said calmly.

"Let's meet soon. There are things we need to talk about," Nootan said, prepared to contribute Farzana's share of the start-up capital, if her friend could not come up with the amount.

Nootan was happy with Farzana's decision but unsure about

what to expect of Javed's behavior. Javed on the loose was something she couldn't imagine.

*

The women's next meeting, two days later, was an eventful one. Farzana had settled in at her aunt's house. Her aunt was happy to receive her and lauded her for making the right, albeit late, decision. The aunt also took her to a gynecologist, for the dull pain in Farzana's abdomen had become almost constant. The doctor had prescribed anti-inflammatory medicines that provided temporary relief. The pain at times reminded her of Javed's last gift.

"You can now marry a nice boy and live happily," said the aunt, an eternal matchmaker.

Javed looked for her and, without much effort, discovered she was staying with her aunt. Javed had never liked the aunt, because she never wore the *purdah.* She simply covered her head with a *dupatta,* and she stood her ground on controversial issues.

Javed went to visit the aunt to ask her to send Farzana back. He knew that if word spread that he'd thrashed his wife, no family would give their daughter to him. The aunt, however, convinced him to give Farzana some time. Javed agreed, because he had no choice. He had injured her badly.

*

"How does the name *Stree* sound? Sarangi suggested it," Anusuya said proudly.

"How about Home Food?" Shakuntala recommended.

Many restaurant names were tossed around, but none of them sounded as good as Sarangi's suggestion. Ultimately, *Stree* was chosen. The strength of the name was commended. S-T-R-E-E was painted in bold red letters on a white board that ran across the food stall. That whole day, they stared at the board and did nothing else.

"Stree? Stree! *Stree.*" Farzana intoned the name in different styles.

"Well! Nootan and I went to the market. I must say we got the best prices. But, unfortunately, we couldn't get credit, despite the fact that we bared our plans to the traders," Shakuntala said.

"How much money do we have to pay?" Anusuya asked, now a little flustered.

"Four thousand *rupees,*" Nootan said unsurely.

There was a deathly silence.

"I'm ready to pay," Anusuya said.

Nootan nodded and volunteered to pay for Farzana, if she wished.

"I have a little money stashed away. I can afford four thousand," Farzana said, a trifle proud.

Their initial capital, sixteen thousand *rupees,* was deposited in an account with the State Bank of India.

"We'll assemble all the raw ingredients here. Like the batter, the dough, the chopped vegetables. And then transport the stuff to Nariman Point," Shakuntala said.

"How? A taxi's expensive. The train is cumbersome," Anusuya asked.

Shakuntala kept quiet. She had no clue how she would cart the raw ingredients to Nariman Point every day. A taxi was indeed expensive, and the local trains of Mumbai were crammed with people. There would hardly be any place for the women, let alone their large containers of provisions.

"Let's think about it. We still have five or six days more to iron out all the problems." Shakuntala was a born fighter.

The other women left for home, morose. Anusuya wondered whether the transportation problem would be the spanner in their grandiose plans.

"Thank God I didn't resign from the work I had. I can simply go back," Anusuya thought.

Sarangi saw her mother was glum and wondered about the reason. She'd never seen her mother so quiet. She was always nagging or cleaning or cooking or sewing.

"Ma, what's the matter?"

"Nothing! You study. It's already December. In another three months, you'll appear for your exams."

"Ma, don't worry about my exams. I'm studying hard. What's bothering you?"

Much against her decision not to burden Sarangi with her worries, Anusuya blurted out the problem of transporting ingredients and cookware to Nariman Point. A taxi would cost a good two hundred *rupees.* Sarangi had once taken the train from Andheri to St. Xavier's College. She was so tightly squeezed in the train that she had felt her life would be snuffed out. So, she understood the train wasn't a practical solution.

"Ma, things will work out. Nothing's easy."

Sarangi resumed her studies while her mother slept. As serendipity would have it, Sarangi thought of Asunción, Elvira's mother. Asunción was very well connected and would definitely know of someone who traveled all the way to town every day.

Sarangi ran to Elvira's home the very next day and explained to Elvira and her mother Anusuya's problem.

"So, in short, you want to know if somebody drives down to town every day and would be willing to take your mother and her pots and pans?"

"Yes."

"Now, who can it be?" Asunción thought aloud. "Professor Kiran Sharma," she said after a little while.

Kiran Sharma taught philosophy in the college and was in no way connected to Elvira. However, Asunción knew Professor Sharma through a common friend. Once, when it had rained heavily, the railroad tracks were filled with water, and the trains had stopped running. Elvira and her mother, after seeing some relatives off at the CST railway station, were waiting at the bus stop. The bus service was skeletal. Of course, cars and other private vehicles were stopping by and picking people up. Elvira didn't want to get into a stranger's car, as she had a fear of being kidnapped.

Sarangi knew of her friend's irrational fear and often wondered amusedly what ransom the kidnappers would ask for Elvira. But she never argued with her friend.

"A fear of being kidnapped is actually a superiority complex. Elvira thinks either she's very beautiful or rich," Sarangi thought.

There were reports of people walking on the tracks, and there was confusion everywhere. Elvira didn't want to walk on the tracks, as she had another morbid fear of falling into one of the uncovered manholes and finding her way into some municipal water tap. So, mother and daughter waited for a long time. Then, a white Fiat stopped in front of them, and the glass of the window rolled down with jerks, as if there were some problem with the handle. Kiran Sharma's face popped out.

"Are you Marlene's friend?" she asked.

Asunción nodded her head vigorously.

"Get in," Professor Sharma said, opening the front and back doors.

Professor Sharma was a spinster who lived in Bandra. She was in her early fifties and was known at the college as Bobby. She had earned the sobriquet because she wore her hair short and it bobbed in a strange fashion. She was of medium build, wore spectacles, and was very ordinary looking. Even her clothes were ordinary, and she didn't do anything that would make her stand out.

The car was twenty-five years old but seemed to purr in her hands. When the professor spoke, a most extraordinary thing happened. The content of her speech and the manner in which she delivered her lectures mesmerized all her students.

She dropped them both home, sermonizing all the way. Elvira later grumbled that her ears had swelled like a cauliflower, as she felt the professor had directed most of her words against youths like Elvira. Asunción chastened her for her ungratefulness. After all, they'd ridden home in comfort, and Professor Sharma had enjoyed some company.

"Why don't you speak with Professor Kiran Sharma? Use my reference. She'll be too glad to help you. After all, that day she gave us a ride home, she was emphasizing the importance of women being independent," Asunción said, darkening her lips to a god-knows-what color.

"I can ask the professor to keep the utensils on the back seat, and maybe one of them can travel with her. Why would she deny such a simple request? Tomorrow morning, I'll wait for her," Sarangi said resolutely.

"The professor leaves real early. She always has lectures at unearthly hours, so maybe you'll have to stand on the road as early as six in the morning," Asunción warned.

"Mom, what will Sarangi do in college that early?" Elvira asked.

"I'll talk to Dominique, the librarian. He's an old friend. I'll ask him to let Sarangi use the library," Asunción said. "At least she's interested in books. Not like you."

The next morning, Sarangi rushed off to catch Professor Sharma in time. She waited patiently till she saw the white Fiat on the main road. Sarangi flagged the car. The professor thought she was a student and stopped the car, irritated. She opened the door and bade Sarangi to sit inside. Sarangi greeted her and mentioned Marlene and Elvira's names. Professor Sharma shook her head, and Sarangi couldn't tell whether she remembered or not. But she didn't care. She narrated the story of the venture on which her mother was preparing to embark.

"That's very good! And why are you telling me all this?" Professor Sharma asked, getting to the point.

"Ma'am, I need your help. There's a practical problem. The ladies have no means to transport their cooking equipment to Nariman Point every day. If you could give them a ride, it would be helpful," Sarangi pleaded.

Professor Sharma remained silent. This was dicey. Her pristine car seats would get stained with the food the women carried. And the smell! The car would stink. As was typical of her, Professor Sharma didn't say no, but she didn't say yes either. She squirmed and muttered something unintelligible.

"What class are you in? What about your studies?"

"Ma'am, I'm in class ten. Elvira's mother knows the librarian. She'll make arrangements so I can sit in the library and study. The library has more facilities than my home," Sarangi said simply.

Professor Sharma nodded her head, still not confirming. Sarangi was disappointed. If the professor didn't agree to help, then there was a large problem at hand.

Professor Sharma dropped Sarangi off at the library with a shake of her head, disappointing Sarangi immensely. That evening, when she reached home, she avoided her mother's direct questions and resolved to petition the professor again the next morning.

For the next four days, Sarangi had a set routine. To Anusuya's questions, Sarangi responded by saying that she could study in the library better in the morning hours. She dared not say that the professor had, as yet, not committed.

Professor Sharma's heart sank when she saw the solitary figure standing on the corner, waiting for her car to pass by. She simply did not have the heart to drive by her. The professor stopped and motioned for the girl to get in. Sarangi simply sat inside and did not speak a word.

"All right, I'll take them!" The professor finally relented, and a smile broke out on Sarangi's face. She stopped herself from breaking into a jig as she stepped out of the car.

"When do we… I mean… your mother and her friends start?" Professor Sharma asked.

"In a couple of days' time," Sarangi said, still smiling.

"I have early lectures on two days of the week. Don't you ask me to leave later for them. I leave as early as this." Professor Sharma pointed to her wristwatch.

"That's no problem, ma'am. I'll come with the restaurant equipment. They can come by boat or ship or train or whatever," Sarangi said, sounding ridiculous.

Professor Sharma drove off, mentally calculating the amount of money she'd have to spend on car seat covers and air fresheners. She would never forget the forlorn figure of Sarangi waiting for her. The perseverance she displayed alone broke the professor's resolve.

"Ma! Ma! Your problem is solved!" Sarangi said as soon as she returned home.

Anusuya looked befuddled.

"Professor Sharma agreed to take you and whatever else to Nariman Point in her car, at least till you can afford your own transportation," Sarangi said excitedly.

Anusuya quickly informed Nootan, and the news was relayed to the other two women. Their first problem had been solved. Anusuya was secretly proud of Sarangi. If she could request a professor's help, then she must be keeping good company.

"Your daughter is very talented," Shakuntala complimented a pleased Anusuya.

"We must meet this lady and thank her. It would be very ungracious on our part to take advantage of her hospitality and not let her know that it means a lot to us," Farzana said.

Sarangi arranged for everyone to meet one evening at Professor Sharma's home. The professor found it all very unnecessary; nevertheless, she agreed.

"What have you named your enterprise?" she asked them, serving tea in gold-rimmed white cups.

"Stree," Anusuya replied.

"That's a very nice name."

"Thank you for helping us," Nootan said earnestly.

"It's not an out-of-the-way request," Professor Sharma said, looking sideways at Sarangi.

That evening, Professor Sharma saw four strong women. Many years later, she was to invest her life's savings in Stree and become a part of it herself.

15

The Birth of Bhurji

The December evening was pleasant and there was a nip in the air. Light sweaters were out and shops were lit, awaiting the New Year with anticipation. The four women walked down Hill Road "just for fun" like the other rich women did. They passed an Adidas shop, which very prophetically had the motto "Impossible is an Opinion" emblazoned on the window. They were too preoccupied to comprehend the full meaning of the statement. Too preoccupied to realize that they were living examples of that strong sentence.

A well-meaning neighbor suggested to them that they conduct a religious ceremony to please all the gods. Shakuntala was an atheist, and Anusuya was convinced that she would believe only after a miracle. And everyone knew that the miracle was Sarangi's future. It didn't matter to Farzana or Nootan, since they felt that the gods had forsaken them long ago and religious ceremonies were just shenanigans. There were no religious rituals and no money was spent on priests and the like on the day the women started work at Stree.

It was mutually decided that the *kaanda poha, sabudaana khichdi,* and *biryani* would be made at home and carried to Stree in the professor's car. Since egg *bhurji* tasted best while warm, it would be cooked at the stall.

The women went to the stall and cleaned up the place with soap and water. Shakuntala had kept the four-burner gas stove and toaster oven. Nootan had already very wisely paid a boy to clean the place of the dust and cobwebs, and he'd done a good job. The result was a spic-and-span food stall. They hung their license, issued by the municipal corporation, right in front for all to see that it was a legal operation and not an encroachment.

"Anusuya, no dirt, eh?" Shakuntala sneered.

Anusuya looked at Shakuntala from the corner of her eye. There was a trace of defiance and something inexplicable in the way Shakuntala returned the look. Like the beginning of an incomplete sentence.

They hired a local three-wheeled taxi, or *tempo,* and lugged the spices, sauces, and other commodities to Stree. They arranged them in containers that ran down the length of the stall. They did not wish to use the professor's service for the preliminary work. Later, when they had to carry the prepared food, they would use her car. The disposable plates for food and the earthen containers for tea were innovative ideas and were also eco-friendly. As per the laws of the municipal cooperation, a large blue garbage bin was placed beside the stall.

Nootan suggested putting a vermilion dot above the *R* in S-T-R-E-E. They looked at Farzana, who shrugged her shoulders in agreement. Nothing more. No "food stall." No "home-cooked food." Nothing else. Just Stree.

Professor Sharma was intrigued by the women. How their lives would unfold was something that she was keen to watch, like a soap opera. That evening, Professor Sharma suggested adding the words "A Women's Initiative" after the name Stree. Sarangi was caught up with the idea. The women neither objected nor agreed. They were indifferent. They were not bothered about what was written on the name board. They were tense about the venture taking off.

The painter climbed up again and painted the latter part, and the board read *STREE — A Women's Initiative.*

Shakuntala struck a deal with the baker's boy to supply fresh eggs and *pao* every morning. Farzana suggested giving customers a buttered *pao* along with the *bhurji.* That meant storing butter. However, there was no refrigerator in the stall. But since it was still an apology of a winter in Mumbai, the butter, like many decisions, stood firm but weakened from the sides.

Shakuntala took a call and then announced that every dish except the egg *bhurji* and the *biryani* would cost eight *rupees.* The egg *bhurji* would be priced at twelve and the *biryani* at fifteen. Sarangi wrote the bill of fare on a blackboard and the price of each item by its side.

There was a mixed reaction to their venture. Some said that it would take off, while some were vicious about it. There was a lot of schadenfreude among observers as Stree commenced operations on the fifteenth day of a cold January.

Sarangi and Shakuntala had been nominated to go with Professor Sharma, and the others would arrive by local train. Sarangi intended to help Shakuntala arrange everything in the stall and then go to the college library. And that is what she did.

"This will work out. I will make it happen," Shakuntala thought with determination.

Anusuya, Nootan, and Farzana could not stay at home for long. There were butterflies in their stomachs. Anusuya nervously twisted the end of her sari around her little finger. The three of them boarded a train bound for Nariman Point, and when they alighted, they walked to the stall to find that Shakuntala had already begun work.

*

The first day of anything was a day of anticipation. The first day of school, the first day at college, the first day at a new job, the first day in a new home — all were anxiety-driven. So also the women felt when they reached Stree. Their faces were white with fear as they thought about what would happen if their plans did not work. In a way, their lives and futures depended on the enterprise.

Mumbai was kind to people who started on her streets, but there were also times when she was destructive.

Mornings in Mumbai started at their own pace. The day Stree opened for business, the streets were deserted and only a few people walked around. They were janitors, housekeepers, and the caretakers of green plants. They had to reach town before anyone else to tend the picture-perfect gardens of big offices and rich people's homes.

The women took their places in the stall very naturally, without any direction, and these were to be their fixed places for many years to come. Shakuntala remained behind the counter, Nootan sat with the accounts book, Farzana stood with the ladle at the griddle, and Anusuya was always seated and frying something or assembling things or doing some odd job.

The weather was pleasant, and the sun was not too bright. It had a soft touch to it. The parking lots were still empty. Somewhere around 9:00 or 9:30, swarms of people arrived like ants. The women watched them disappear into tall buildings, leaving the streets deserted. Roll musters were signed, and any other preliminary activity to establish one's entry into an office at a designated time was completed. Pregnant women rushed to the tender coconut vendor, while the others made beelines to their familiar or favorite places for breakfast.

For Stree, the day started on a dismal note. There were only two people who came for breakfast, and they had such impassive faces that the women could not make out what they felt about the food. Shakuntala said that it would get better during lunch time. But nothing happened. Four days passed, with barely a few people coming to eat. The entire street was lined with lunch wagons and food carts that had been established years ago.

The women began to worry. If the trend continued, they would be forced to close shop. Shakuntala wondered what went wrong.

But she did not admit that there was something amiss, for that would have frightened the others. She assured Anusuya especially that people who ate at Stree would spread the word around, and then hoards would come. It was a slow process. Lots of food was wasted. But they had to be patient.

Actually, there was nothing to worry about. Everything in Mumbai was driven by time, which led to the formation of habits. A person could take the same train or eat lunch at the same place or walk on the same side of the road every single day, all his life. After lunch, he could go to the same banana peddler and eat a single banana or peanuts for exactly two *rupees* each day. To break away from routine and explore was time-consuming. Nobody in Mumbai had that kind of time to spare. Stree was a victim of people's habitual behavior.

Anusuya was so afraid that she spoke with Nootan in private about going back to her old job. All four business partners were tense and worried. They sat the whole day, their faces lighting up when one man or woman walked over to Stree. That their customer may have sauntered in only because the other places were crowded did not discourage them.

After about fifteen days of losing money and peace of mind, Shakuntala thought that she would burst into tears when she saw three young men wearing ties and full-sleeved shirts walk up to Stree. They spoke in English confidently punctuated with Hindi and had identity cards around their necks. She knew that they were the crowd that spread the word about food joints and would bring in the money. The women were tongue-tied and stared at the men. Farzana nudged Nootan and whispered, "Ask what they want."

"What is the speciality of this place?" one of the young men asked, lighting a cigarette and peering at the blackboard.

The men waited for a reply. The moment of silence seemed like an eternity. Their fear of the men walking away was the biggest one the women had ever experienced. What if they said *sabudana,* and the men hated it? Would they then ask what else there was? Or would they simply walk away? Did they eat eggs? Did their parents teach them to respect women? In that noiseless moment, Nootan was sure that the men could hear their hearts beat.

"Egg *bhurji,*" Farzana Javed Sheikh said, looking at the men straight in their eyes and, at that instant, making Stree synonymous with egg *bhurji.*

"Three plates please," one of them said politely.

"Will you have it with *pao*?"

"Yes."

Farzana could not resist a smile. With élan, she threw the onions, chili, and cilantro into the hot oil, cracked the eggs on the griddle and swished them with a flat ladle. The aroma was heady, and it meandered to the top before dissipating in the air. She made a sound — *taka-tak, taka-tak* — with the ladle on the heavy cast iron griddle. Farzana made the *taka-tak* sound again with glee, like a musical conductor waving his baton after a performance. The sound was soon to become a signal to the hungry — *Food is ready. Come get it!* — and later, practically a war cry.

She heaped the egg *bhurji* onto three plates and passed it to Shakuntala, who served it to the three men. They ate spoonfuls of it and appeared to be relishing it.

"Damn good!" said one.

"Sexy," said the other.

"Is this a new place?" asked the third. "What else do you serve?"

Shakuntala reeled off the menu items. By then, the women were thrilled to bits.

"How much?" the man with the cigarette asked, taking out his wallet.

"Thirty-six *rupees,*" Shakuntala said, worried that these men would launch into a tirade and quibble about the price.

But nothing of the sort happened. They calmly paid up and walked away, promising to return for lunch.

There was no looking back after that. The men did come back for lunch, and they brought some of their colleagues. Their colleagues brought some more friends. The friends brought relatives. The relatives brought acquaintances. The word had spread. The women of Stree became more or less familiar with the quantities to be cooked, and the profit was not bad. They managed to put a bit in the bank, and Anusuya no longer felt insecure.

But they had to negotiate better prices for the vegetables and the other raw ingredients to increase the margin of profit. They also learned how to deal with the customers better. The women patrons always preferred a smile and liked an inquiry about their homes and kids. The older women came to eat once in a while, since often they carried lunch with them, but the younger, unmarried women ate out a lot. The proprietors of Stree were making a profit of nearly five hundred to nine hundred *rupees* every day. Business was good, not excellent, but they were there. The finishing line was within sight.

They still rode to town in Professor Sharma's car, even though they could have hired a taxi. They suggested the idea to Professor Sharma, but she would hear none of it. She firmly insisted that it was a pleasure to hear about the activities and progress of Stree. And she wasn't lying. She enjoyed listening to the women. It was a refreshing diversion from the complex subject that she taught and more interesting than her morose life.

But the women's challenges were far from over. After a fortnight, something bizarre happened that tested the spirit of Stree once again.

16

The First Threat

A good four months later, at around 3:30 one afternoon, after the so-called lunch hour of Mumbai was over, Nootan was tallying figures and Farzana was cleaning the grease off the griddle while Anusuya and Shakuntala were making small talk. Just then, three men walked up and stood in front of them. The men were nondescript but looked menacing.

"Give us five hundred *rupees,*" one of them said, meanly placing his elbow on the ledge and leering at Nootan.

"What for?" Nootan asked.

"For letting you stand and sell here," one of them said, almost snarling.

"But… but… we've paid the money to the owner," said Nootan.

"And you don't own the footpath," Shakuntala added loudly.

"Everybody on this street pays us," the man said.

"For what?"

"Protection. So that nobody harms you," the man replied, stunned that these women were so naïve.

"But isn't it the duty of the police to protect us?" Farzana asked.

Anusuya cowered and stood quietly behind the other women. Fear had got her voice and she was visibly frightened.

"There are dangerous elements that the police can't handle. You're new here. You don't know what dangers lurk on this street," the man continued.

Anusuya almost shivered. Nobody had warned her about this.

"But we don't have any money. What we made was spent repaying loans," Nootan lied.

"We don't know about that. You've been here for months. We've watched you. You're making money. Tomorrow, bring the money. Otherwise…" his voice trailed away.

It was the infamous *hafta* system, whereby hawkers and vendors were forced to dole out protection money to gang lords. Shakuntala had read in the newspapers that even industrialists, film stars, and movie producers were harassed in the same manner.

The men walked away, leaving behind four bewildered women who left for home confused and frightened. They didn't know whom to seek counsel from. Anusuya suggested Professor Sharma, but the others vetoed the idea. According to them, the professor had never dealt with real life.

"That old lady will stop taking us to Nariman Point if she knows those goons threatened us," Farzana said acidly.

"What should we do?" Shakuntala asked.

"Shouldn't we pay up? I mean, that's what everyone does, right?" Nootan asked.

"Why should we? There's a law in this land. If we pay up now, then we'll be forever in their clutches. Why don't we register a complaint with the police?" Farzana asked sensibly.

"I'm not sure how much the police will be able to help us," Shakuntala replied.

"Those thugs may get more infuriated if they see the police. I have a grown-up daughter. I didn't bargain for this. What if those men do something to her? Right from the beginning, I knew this was a bad idea!" Anusuya whined.

"Shut up!" Nootan snapped.

"Anusuya, don't worry. It's all about how we handle the situation," Shakuntala said softly.

"We have to fight back," Farzana said, her teeth clenched.

"Yes, as usual, we have to fight," Nootan said wearily.

Anusuya began crying. She was frightened for her daughter. She'd heard and read about thugs who demanded protection money and killed those who didn't pay.

"Let's see what happens tomorrow," Nootan said, and they dispersed.

Anusuya didn't sleep a wink that night. She dreamed that hoodlums were chasing her and Sarangi. At the same time, a few streets away, Shakuntala's thoughts were drawn to Anusuya's pale, frightened face. Strangely, she wanted to console her.

"I hope I'm not becoming like those weepy women." Shakuntala shut her eyes firmly, waiting for sleep to take over.

The next day, the extortionists were not seen. The women spent the entire day in suspense. They looked at every strange person with suspicion. The other vendors prophesied that the women's insolence would not be tolerated and the gang would finish them. But to everyone's surprise, the gang members did not turn up. In fact, they didn't show up for seven days.

"I wish they'd just show up and ask for whatever they want. This wait is killing me," Anusuya said.

After a week, the four women were emotional wrecks. They were doing well with the business, but their hearts pounded when they saw anyone closely resembling the men of the gang. Then the suspense ended. The men turned up. This time, there were five of them.

"Where's the money?" one of them asked no one in particular.

The women didn't reply. They simply continued their work as if the voices of the extortionists were the voices of their husbands nagging in the background.

"Where is the money?" another man screamed.

The four women remained silent.

"If you were men, we'd have torn you up by now," one of them said.

They still remained silent and averted their eyes.

Then, one of the men lunged forward and flung the pans containing food to the ground. The pots fell with a clang. Anusuya had to clamp her mouth with a hand to stop from screaming. On the whole, however, the men's violent posturing didn't frighten the women. They had seen enough violence in their lifetimes.

One of the men moved threateningly towards Farzana.

Farzana cringed. For a moment, all of the men looked like Javed. The man waggled his finger at her. Farzana could feel his breath on her face.

"I'll cut you to pieces," he said.

Everyone watched the commotion, spellbound. Utensils were scattered and the contents of the pans had spilled. Mercifully, the thugs had arrived at around four in the evening, and the women had already sold almost all that they had cooked that day. The gang members didn't like to interrupt business or create chaos when people were around. They also knew that if any news reporters caught them in action, they'd hear about it from the don, their superior. The throwing of utensils and screaming was all for effect.

The four women stood still with expressions of terror; helplessness; and above all, impotent rage, but they did not say a word.

"We'll be back tomorrow," one of the goons threatened as they walked away.

The women collected their scattered possessions. They were white with fear. They left for home with a cloak of solemnity around them.

"Let's see what they do tomorrow," Shakuntala said.

The next day, at around the same time, the men returned.

"Did you bring the money?"

"No… and we won't," Shakuntala screamed, losing her patience.

One of the men raised his hand to strike her. Nootan moved forward with tremendous energy and held his hand with a force that surprised the man and her too. She had forgotten that she held a heated ladle in her other hand. Shakuntala grabbed a burning-hot iron stirring spoon and jumped in front of Nootan.

"One move and we'll burn you," Shakuntala said, no longer caring.

"The most they can do is tear everything down. And that was how we started. With nothing," Nootan thought.

The fierce demeanor displayed by the women was unplanned. Such shows of courage emanated from an inherent fear of losing. There were no plans or strategies in place. Instinct forced them to act. That they were taking on extortionists did not faze them, because they were confronting individuals who threatened to wipe them out.

The men were taken aback; nevertheless, they moved aggressively toward the women.

Farzana rushed at them, blindly waving the sizzling ladle, which immediately found its target — the arm of a young member of the gang. She heard the sound of skin sizzling and the smell of hair burning. The young man howled in pain and ran off. The other thugs saw the crowd of onlookers cheering the women. Many of them were yelling, "Attack! Attack!" A few well-dressed men who looked like honest taxpayers flinched when they saw four women being threatened. They screamed at the goons, who suddenly realized they were outnumbered.

Farzana saw a few human hairs on her ladle. She knew that she'd scalded at least one of the gang. She threw the ladle in the garbage with disgust.

"He'll see the scar all his life, and that will be a lesson for him. He'll never attack women again."

*

Prakash Bandodkar applied Burnol to the wound and, like

Farzana said, never attacked a woman again. He took to wearing long-sleeved sweatshirts to cover the scar, and they became his unique trademark.

Prakash Bandodkar, then a young boy cowed by an angry woman, was destined to rule Mumbai one day.

Crates of sun-yellow mangoes were entering the city in truckloads. The smell of the sweet mangoes and the golden hay was intoxicating. Summer was setting in. Very soon, the smells of sweat and powdery dust blown by the summer winds would invade the city.

17
Prakash Bandodkar, Alias Pakya

Prakash Bandodkar, alias Pakya, abhorred violence. Violence had been a dominant factor of his childhood. His father beat his mother. His mother beat him. Beating and hitting each other was an accepted way of expressing one's opinion in the Bandodkar household.

His father was a dominant personality and his mother, a weeping willow. Most of his childhood was spent playing cricket in Mumbai's *gullies* and hanging around with friends from the *chawl* in which he lived.

Pakya graduated with political science as his major. No jobs were available to the young man of twenty-one, short and slightly dark, with curly hair, thick lips, and an animal magnetism about him. Latent energy, an enormous amount of it, could be observed in him, and whenever he did anything — when he ran to pick up a cricket ball or even just to catch a bus — the energy could be felt. With deep-set eyes he saw the world.

His father always taunted him, saying he was a no-good and the money spent on his education would have been better spent on a cow. Pakya couldn't eat a morsel at home without his cantankerous father getting at him. Soon, matters came to a head, and one evening, his father started raving and ranting.

"Look at this fellow. At his age, he should be feeding *us.* He's like a millstone around my neck."

His mother looked on helplessly.

Something snapped in Pakya's head, and he walked out,

vowing never to return. He felt sorry for his mother, but there was nothing much he could do.

Pakya spent that night at his friend Ramdas' home. Ramdas made it abundantly clear that Pakya was not welcome to spend more than one night and should be making his own arrangements for living accommodations.

The next day was to change Pakya's entire life.

After leaving Ramdas' home, Pakya moved about aimlessly on the street, wondering what his next move should be. He spent a few days living off friends, carefully avoiding his judgmental relatives. He purchased newspapers, scanned the classified ads carefully, and appeared for many walk-in interviews, but luck was elusive. He was always overlooked. Because he'd completed his studies in Marathi, Pakya felt his grasp of English was not good, and he couldn't land a white-collar job. For this, he blamed his father, who insisted that the family speak Marathi at home.

"As if he is the custodian of the language," Pakya thought angrily.

But if he wasn't good enough for one kind of job, he was too good for another. His college degree prevented him from joining the blue-collar labor force. All in all, he felt trapped. He was increasingly frustrated and angry at the system that refused to assimilate him. His own worthlessness mocked him, and a desperate man emerged.

One day, while he was walking the streets aimlessly, he met Swapnil, a college classmate who appeared to be doing well in life. Pakya poured his woes out to Swapnil, who empathized with him and surprised him by saying, "Come with me. You'll have a job by tomorrow."

Pakya was incredulous. He thought his friend was simply bragging, but he had nothing to lose. The next day, Swapnil introduced him to a few men. It didn't take Pakya long to realize they were hoodlums and that Swapnil worked with them. Pakya threw a questioning glance at his friend, who shrugged as if to say, "What else?" Pakya soon learned that a don, who had started by committing petty thefts in the alleys of Mumbai and had since gone to live in Dubai, controlled the gang.

Pakya joined the gang, and his first assignment was extortion. The first few weeks were misery, for he was frightened of what he was getting into, yet there was no alternative. He was sure that the coils of his intestines had disintegrated from starvation. His lower-middle-class values were strong, and the battle between the opportunity for survival and those values was waged, but he realized there was no choice. Either he had to starve and die or grab this chance and live. Without much delay, the fear metamorphosed into thrill — the thrill of frightening people, the thrill of doing something wrong. Very soon, his latent energy was being unleashed on people who, strangely, resembled his father. Every man he hit or threatened was paying for his father's wrongdoing.

Pakya was a member of the four-man team that had gone to extort money from Stree. The women, however, reminded him of his mother instead of his father. And when he saw them, there was a lump in his throat. He didn't want to bully them, but there was no way out. Either he was in or he was out. He hid his face so they couldn't identify him. He didn't know that the women were too frightened to notice the faces and features of the men who threatened them.

He admired the spirit they displayed. The gang had to return to Stree at least three times to demand money, and then the lady in the black *purdah* attacked him with her ladle and scalded him. From nowhere, those meddling businessmen had arrived, and they'd had to flee.

Nobody had ever stood up to them like those women. If everyone displayed the same amount of courage, the gang would be out of business. Pakya couldn't get them out of his mind. Strangely, he didn't feel like taking revenge. All his friends in the gang taunted him because a woman had burned him, but he refused to be provoked.

Normally, the don's operations were carried out meticulously and with extreme professionalism. Rules were laid, hierarchy was respected, and a certain amount of red-tapism also existed.

Pakya knew that he had to catch the don's attention and bag an assignment that was worthy of praise. Extortion bored him. He'd seen Mucchad Saleem, so called because he boasted a handlebar moustache, with a gun in his pocket. The "moustached" Saleem was a man of few words who grunted or merely waved his hand when he had to convey something. The gesture was enough to incite people to run to execute his instructions. It was rumored that, in the sixties, he'd killed no less than a hundred men and that the police were also frightened of the wiry, ruthless man who knew no emotions.

Saleem was the don's favorite man, and all the prized assignments were given to him. Pakya thought of ways to usurp Saleem's position. At first, he thought of calling the police and giving them information on Saleem, a wanted criminal. But the police force had a lot of informants who were on the don's payroll, and Pakya would get caught. The only way left was to befriend Saleem and, through him, become a part of the don's coterie. But Saleem was an extremely suspicious man and never let anyone get close to him. It was rumored that he had killed his own brother in cold blood. Pakya had to bid for time.

He ingratiated himself slowly by sitting near Saleem whenever possible but not saying anything. One day, without Saleem's permission, Pakya accompanied him for the landing of some smuggled goods at a port. When the customs officials arrived, Pakya very dramatically dragged Saleem away, as if shielding him from the officials. He drove the getaway vehicle at breakneck speed.

After the successful smuggling operation, Saleem called for Pakya. The ambitious young gangster stood in front of his role model and, to Saleem's questioning grunt, said he was no longer happy with the extortion crowd. Saleem's approving grunt indicated that Pakya would join him for bigger operations. Pakya was moving up the ladder.

All the members of Saleem's gang had guns. But Pakya would have to wait for a little longer. Like an understudy in a theater company, his time to play the lead role was yet to come.

*

A little while after his brush with Stree, when his wound had healed, Pakya began stopping by the eatery to have his breakfast. The *kaanda poha* tasted just the way it was made at his home. Once or twice, he caught Farzana staring at him intently. He didn't panic but continued eating calmly and turned away from her gaze.

"I've seen this boy before," Farzana thought. But having no vivid recollection, she put it behind her.

Pakya arrived every morning at around 11:30, ate brunch, and then went about his business, whatever it was. The long-sleeved-sweatshirt-wearer was a regular customer, until he got lost in the dark streets of Mumbai.

The women had, by that time, settled down to their work and frozen their schedules. They started their day at nine and wound up by four. The last lunch was served to a harried executive who had to stay back at the office for some meeting or a salesman whose sales call extended beyond the stipulated time or a clerk who went to the bank and was delayed inordinately.

But behind the surface normalcy, danger brewed.

The Hindu United Party, or HUP, as it was popularly known, had in its cadre young Hindu men who were unemployed and angry. Some, like Pakya, chose their destiny, while others chose another course. The political manifesto of the HUP failed to address the country's innumerable problems. The party leaders attributed the country's malaise to the Muslim citizens and exhorted that they were evil. Nootan and Farzana, whose families had lived together for many years, saw no difference between them. However, Nootan's brothers and the rest of her family, who were active members of the HUP, constantly chided Nootan for hanging out with Farzana. They had hated *Abbajan* because of his secular political views.

Dilip Vakharia was an HUP recruiter. He had attempted to use his wife to recruit women for the HUP's women's auxiliary. However, Nootan's approach to life was largely influenced by *Abbajan.* The HUP had caused considerable damage with their extremist views. Yet, in a city like Mumbai, the HUP never got a foothold. The city was a place where people were more bothered about their own survival. To a man or a woman standing in Mumbai's overcrowded local train, the religion of the person standing an inch away didn't matter. They were both people eking out a living in a glorious yet unforgiving city.

Shakuntala simply didn't care for religion-driven political parties. She, like many others, only wanted a decent life. And her view was shared by the other members of Stree.

18

A Rung Up

Time flew by like the blink of an eye. Mumbai witnessed no major changes, except that skirts grew shorter and more inane Bollywood movies were released.

In a short time, Stree became well known for its home-cooked food. At eleven in the morning, the *taka-tak, taka-tak, taka-tak* sound was like the Pied Piper's flute. Farzana making the gentle noise with her ladle on a cast iron griddle, her *purdah* flying lightly in the air, was a reassuring sight for hungry Mumbaikars.

The women understood the dynamics of the crowd very well and improved their public relations. Known customers were always acknowledged and indulged with an extra dollop of butter or a slice of lemon. They improvised on the menu and introduced customized recipes like *upma* without onions for Jains, who avoided root vegetables, and different kinds of *biryanis* for vegetarians and non-vegetarians. But the egg *bhurji* ruled.

That year, Sarangi appeared for her class ten state board examinations. The marks that she would score would determine the college she would get into. Sarangi preferred St. Xavier's College, because she had used its library and Professor Sharma was a member of the faculty. The Indo-Gothic structure of the college was very comforting and, moreover, Elvira would be there. Her mother had already decided.

Unlike the parents of most of the other students, Anusuya could not afford to send Sarangi to any of the high-profile tutorials that promised to make their children doctors or engineers. Parents starved in order to send their children to the tutorials, claiming that public schoolteachers didn't do their jobs. Sarangi borrowed old notes from her upperclassmen and studied hard. Whenever she had a problem with any subject, she stayed back after class and sorted it out with her teachers, who were only too glad to help her.

Sarangi was still very much besotted with Joachim and gawked at him whenever she saw him. He continued to largely ignore her, save for an occasional greeting. Those were the days her feet never touched the ground.

As far as Joachim was concerned, Sarangi was still a gauche girl. She had nothing to command his attention, and he was riding high on his ambitions and dreams of "perfect ten" girls. He didn't spend much time in class, but he was always on the soccer ground, dreaming of playing alongside Pele, Maradona, and Baggio. Joachim concentrated on soccer, hoping that some company would select and employ him. He was aware that corporations sponsored sports and, if luck had it, he'd be playing for a multinational corporation. His mother was not too keen that he play for an Indian company. Every Wednesday, Asunción visited St. Michael's Church in Mahim and lit candles in the shape of legs, so he could kick the soccer ball harder, and in the shape of brains, so he could think better.

*

Javed, with his battered ego, was not through with Farzana. He was fuming with rage. He wanted to get even. Many times through the year, he walked toward Stree, thinking he would drag Farzana out. After all, he was the husband. But even from afar, he could sense a change in her, an aura of strength. He'd heard stories of how the women had driven away a bunch of goons. Could Farzana have been one of them, or did she sit back? He often wondered.

Javed didn't want to take a chance. What if Farzana attacked *him?* So, he resorted to maligning her among friends and relatives and fabricating stories so that he came out clean. He learned from his relatives that Stree was doing well and Farzana was financially independent.

The aunt with whom Farzana stayed couldn't help but brag about Farzana's independence at a *majlis,* a gathering of women. Word about her success reached Javed, taking him to new heights of anger.

"How can she defy me and continue to live?" he thought viciously.

Out of curiosity, Javed visited Farzana at Stree one day and was surprised to see the transformation of the place and the women. He was so angry at Farzana's effrontery that he lost the compulsion to pretend. He walked over and started calling Farzana names.

"You whore! I know why you want to be away from home. This is nothing but a brothel. How much is your rate? And where is your pimp!" he screamed.

The few customers around looked amused. Farzana's ears burned red with embarrassment. She sat down in the corner and began crying. The sudden physical and emotional pain reminded her of the past. Yet she was the same woman who had scalded a man who threatened to destroy Stree.

Like a woman possessed, Anusuya walked out of the stall with a kitchen knife in her hand. The steel of the knife gleamed. Javed, by that time, was stuttering. The sight of the frail woman with a knife striding purposefully towards him intimidated him.

"If you ever come here again..." Anusuya hissed and left the sentence unfinished. The threat was enough for Javed.

Shakuntala walked to Anusuya and gently ran her hand over her head in a show of affection. Anusuya was surprised at the gesture coming from the otherwise coarse Shakuntala.

Javed beat a hasty retreat, surprising all. They had expected him to fight back. They didn't understand their own power.

Seeing her husband retreating, Farzana, for the first time, contemplated getting a divorce.

"If I don't get rid of him legally, he'll keep harassing me," she thought.

After the episode, Javed went around bad-mouthing Farzana, telling everyone who'd listen that his barren wife was really a whore. Javed made it known to all and sundry that Farzana left him because she chose, against his wishes, to work at Nariman Point, and Mumbra was too far for her to travel every day. He was actually building a platform that would allow him to take his second wife. Rukhsana, the oldest of six children, was the proverbial sacrificial goat at the altar of marriage. Nearly twenty years younger than Javed and a distant relative, she had no choice but to give in.

Farzana's aunt had mentioned Rukhsana to her.

"Let him do whatever he wishes to, as long as he doesn't trouble me," Farzana said very calmly.

A couple of times, Javed showed up at the aunt's home and asked to talk to Farzana. When he did, his worst suspicions were confirmed — he could see no trace of the fear-stricken Farzana he once knew. Instead, he saw a bold, confident woman whose eyes, even behind the *purdah,* were smoldering. He could no longer use his normal intimidation tactics to subdue her. So, naturally, he resorted to amorous tactics.

On one such visit, he was extremely nice to Farzana and carried her favorite *mawa* cakes from Kayani. Farzana accepted them graciously, but when Javed edged closer to her and tried to hold her hand, she pushed it away with force. For a moment, Javed was frightened of her. He saw fire in her eyes.

"You barren bitch! I'm divorcing you. My sister has already found a bride for me," Javed screamed and went away.

Oddly, Farzana did not feel anything. In fact, while Javed shouted, she just looked at him coldly. Now she knew that he would take another wife. There were many poor girls whose fathers would arrange for them to marry Javed without a second thought.

"Who needs him?" Farzana thought contemptuously.

In the past, she'd had nothing much to look forward to. Her only function in life had been to serve Javed. Stree changed all that.

*

One day, Sakharam Alhat did not return home. Anusuya waited up half the night and later asked a neighbor to look for him. The neighbor went to the police station and made a report. Someone callously suggested that maybe he was drunk and sleeping on a railway platform. A boy from the neighborhood checked all the country bars in the vicinity. Anusuya made no further inquiries.

The next morning, the police called Anusuya to the morgue to view the unclaimed corpses that had arrived in the night. Anusuya did not go. Sakharam Alhat at last was given an official status — missing.

Surprisingly, Sarangi did not ask where her father was. Nobody took Sakharam's disappearance very seriously.

*

The juice bar adjoining Stree was folding. It had been run by a young man who got a job in Dubai. He suggested to the women who operated the food stall next door that they meet the owner, who was interested in leasing the place. Shakuntala thought it would be a good idea to rent the adjacent space and expand their area of operation.

The owner was Niranjan Shetty. Apart from the juice bar, he

owned a few hotels in the city that were doing well. The property next door to Stree was the smallest among his shops, and he wanted to rent it out. Shakuntala and Nootan met with him to negotiate a lease, but he was asking for an exorbitant rent and a deposit that was unreasonable. Niranjan Shetty was a greedy man.

"That man just threw a random figure out of his head," Nootan said.

"There will be some way." Anusuya was optimistic.

"Yeah, he'll just wake up one day and have a change of heart," Farzana said sarcastically.

"There is no heart in business," Shakuntala philosophized.

Over the next few days, the women calculated and scribbled on bits of paper ways to raise money for the rent and deposit. Taking a bank loan was one option, but they weren't confident of borrowing a huge sum, and no respectable loan officer would meet with them. They spoke incessantly about ways and means to raise the money. Then, one day, Niranjan Shetty's man came to them.

"We're willing to rent the place at your price," the man said.

"What do we have to do in return?" Nootan asked suspiciously.

The man walked away without replying.

"What the hell must have happened?" Nootan wondered aloud.

Farzana held her head in her hands and bowed it in disbelief.

"Is there a god looking after us?" Shakuntala exulted.

The women dipped into the money they had saved and rented the juice bar. No one had a clue why Niranjan Shetty changed his mind.

In fact, Niranjan Shetty was a frightened man — frightened for his life.

*

Pakya was by then an important figure in his gang. As he'd

desired, he had caught the don's attention. One day, Saleem, Pakya, and half a dozen others were supervising the unloading of some smuggled consignment at a deserted beach. Two hundred kilometers away from Mumbai, it was where the don normally smuggled his contraband. The don had also greased the palms of certain officials who would not harass the don's men. It was dark, still night. The members of the gang held torches, and the light was yellow. Saleem gave Pakya a gun and instructed him to shoot at any custom officials he saw. Pakya concluded that the incoming shipment was an important one. Saleem normally took part only in special operations that the don, his immediate superior, had an interest in.

Everything was going according to the plan. The crates were unloaded from the boat, and Saleem was watching with a hawk's eyes. Without any warning, the men downloading the crates suddenly dropped them and began running. Pakya could see fog lights and knew that the authorities had spotted them.

"Run! Officials!" Pakya screamed, hearing a fog horn.

"Shoot!" Saleem shouted.

Pakya fired one shot, catching his rival on the temple. Saleem died on the spot. The other men ran into the darkness of the jungle near the beach. Pakya was sweating with fear, unsure of the outcome. He stayed for a moment, until he heard the gunshots of the authorities. He knew that the other men had continued running, not to avoid arrest, but because they thought Pakya would shoot them next.

When the don heard of the incident, he summoned Pakya. He'd already learned of the ambitious and restless boy. The don knew that no port official would have shot to kill Saleem; they all knew Saleem was the don's blue-eyed boy. Moreover, it had been dark. The killing was definitely the work of an insider. The don, with his native intelligence, realized at once that Pakya must have been responsible.

The don did not wish to know whether Pakya had informed the authorities about the operation. He was indulgent. He knew his organization needed young blood like Pakya to carry on the riskiest operations. If the upstart had engineered Saleem's death, then Pakya was a man to watch. The don assigned him to assist Abdul Lakda, whose main responsibility was land deals. This meant big business in sea-locked Mumbai.

"And don't betray me," the don warned, looking straight at Pakya, his eyes unwavering.

Pakya felt a shudder down his spine. If the don wished, he could have killed him there and then.

Pakya thought about how he'd felt nothing after shooting Saleem. He'd hung around with Saleem since the time he'd joined the gang. They had shared many cuttings of chai, chuckling between gulps of the sweet and milky tea. The blood that gushed out of Saleem's head and soaked into the sand made him a little queasy, but he got over it effortlessly. It was the only way he could rise in the organization. He was now only loyal to himself, and any feeling of remorse was erased when he thought of his father's taunts. If only his father could see him kill. The emotional detachment served its purpose. He enjoyed the fear he evoked in people. Pakya was on his way up.

Pakya regularly sent money to his mother without disclosing who the sender was. Another fallout of his rise in the don's organization was that he could no longer visit Stree as frequently. He sent his flunky when, more than often, he couldn't get away to collect his breakfast.

One day, when Pakya happened to find time to eat lunch at 'Stree', Anusuya asked him the reason for his infrequent visits.

"Have you found another place to eat?" Farzana joked.

"Work," he mumbled.

"Don't you feel warm in that long-sleeved sweatshirt?" Anusuya persisted.

He shrugged his shoulders and almost smiled.

One day at Stree, he overheard the women talking about Niranjan Shetty's juice bar.

"Let's look for some other place," Anusuya said, pounding *masala*.

"Yeah! As if that Shetty's place is the last one on Earth," Farzana said, chopping onions and sniffing.

"But it is so convenient," Shakuntala persisted.

"We don't have that much money; besides, if we spend everything on that place, we'll have nothing in our reserves," Nootan said.

And so it went on. Pakya knew Niranjan Shetty. It was clear from their conversation that the proprietors of Stree wanted to lease his property, but Shetty was acting tough. They chattered about their problem, unaware that anyone might be listening.

Pakya sent a boy to eavesdrop, and in three days he knew the price they had offered and Niranjan Shetty's counteroffer.

"That bastard's fleecing them," Pakya thought.

Pakya became determined to get them Shetty's place. He sent a man to Shetty with his message. "The women are under my protection. Give them the place at their price."

Niranjan Shetty knew that Pakya was a gangster on the rise. He regularly sent gifts and, at times, money to the don. But the bigger picture was that Pakya was more closely connected with the don than Shetty was. If Pakya wished, he could create havoc at Shetty's other establishments.

Shetty did not take long to deliberate. He immediately let the women know that he was willing to rent the juice bar at their price, and he also made it known to Pakya that he'd paid heed to his word.

His power over other men reassured Pakya. He felt supreme. The spell of fear and insecurity that his father had cast over him was broken at last.

19

Maurya

The women extended Stree's existing floor plan to encompass the new place. It could now accommodate a refrigerator, to store chutneys and butter, and larger vessels. The next few days were full of feverish trips to Crawford Market to buy larger vessels and gas stoves. Farzana was happy, as she got a larger flat griddle and a new ladle to make egg *bhurji.*

When the newly expanded Stree was inaugurated, Shakuntala made semolina and gram flour ladoos and distributed them to all her friends and neighbors and their regular patrons.

The partners' places in the stall were well defined, and there was no trespassing. Shakuntala interacted with the customers, collected the money, and kept it in the drawer that was always securely locked. Farzana stood near the griddle and tapped the ladle on the coagulated mass of egg with her trademark rhythmic *taka-tak, taka-tak*. If there were many customers, then Anusuya and Nootan helped Shakuntala. If not, Anusuya fried the cutlets or the potato *vadas* while Nootan took care of the accounts.

Shakuntala was still the driving force, but her attitude towards Anusuya had changed considerably. She was less snappy at her grumblings and tried to understand her insecurity where her daughter was concerned. She attempted to alleviate Anusuya's fears and assure her that they were in the endeavor together.

Nootan and Farzana were happy to see the friendship developing between Anusuya and Shakuntala. Nootan knew Anusuya well and thought that the new friendship would do her good. It would give her the sense of security she needed.

Nootan and Farzana, at their end, were always reminiscing and laughing like young girls with no cares. Farzana was becoming her former self, now that Nootan was around.

Whenever any opinion or decision was sought, Anusuya echoed what Shakuntala said, while Farzana and Nootan were always unanimous in their opinions. But it must be said that the four never let their personal likings cloud their judgment where Stree was concerned.

*

Maurya was a sit-down restaurant at Nariman Point but, understanding that time is a luxury in Mumbai, the proprietors had a little takeaway section in the front. It had a canopy below which food was served. The place offered a decent fare at an affordable price in an air-conditioned environment with its own share of clientele — the office-goers. Most of their business luncheons, farewells, and celebrations were held at Maurya.

Mridul Pujari and Sudhir Shetty — friends and entrepreneurs — ran Maurya. They had built the restaurant from scratch, and now that its popularity had reached dizzying heights, they let professionals run it. Yet, both of them were involved in the restaurant and kept a close watch on the operations.

The two men had started their careers as waiters at Hotel Sri Vijay, a small restaurant in Bhandup, a suburb in Mumbai, after they had run away from their village in Udipi. Laxman Pujari owned Sri Vijay, and he belonged to the same village as the boys. Hotel Sri Vijay was perhaps so named either because Pujari didn't know the difference between *hotel* and *restaurant* or because he had dreams of transforming Sri Vijay into a swanky hotel. For the record, it must be mentioned that Sri Vijay forever remained a seedy restaurant.

Pujari was very clannish and preferred to employ boys from his village. He exploited them by overworking them and not paying on schedule, but he made sure that they learned everything. The *idli,* which were steamed rice cakes, and the *dosa,* or rice pancakes, at Hotel Sri Vijay tasted better because the batter was pulverized on an old-fashioned grinding stone by young boys whose sweat fell into the thick white rice and lentil batter as they bent over it, grinding it to a fine, perfect paste.

As Stree's popularity grew, it appeared on Mridul and Sudhir's radar. They were indulgent at first. But then they became worried. Their manager informed them that many of their regular clients were eating at Stree. The co-owners coaxed some friends and their chef to visit Stree as customers. The verdict was that the fare was simply excellent. It tasted like home-cooked food, and the atmosphere was friendly. It fed not only the stomach but also a starved soul. People who lived far away from their loved ones and had truncated lives enjoyed coming to Stree.

Mridul Pujari and Sudhir Shetty had never taken competition lying down and were not indulgent when their market share was attacked. They always fought back, sometimes with unfair means. This time, they felt that since four women restauranteurs were involved, it would be easy. Pujari did not want to use violence or threats, which would create a bad image. A man threatening four helpless women was a sign of weakness.

"There's no need for that," Pujari thought with a grimace.

He discussed the matter thoroughly with Shetty, who was equally worried.

"At first, let's offer a flat ten percent discount on all our dishes. That'll steer the crowd away from their stall," Pujari suggested.

The next day, a blackboard propped outside Maurya proclaimed a discount on the food. But to Pujari and Shetty's surprise, there was not much of a turnaround. It seemed to them that the crowd at Stree was only on the rise. The ladies were turning out food that made everyone want more. Pujari and Shetty became very worried. If the ladies were not checked, they would prove to be a risk.

They also knew another significant reason behind Stree's popularity. The items on Stree's menu included no additives or preservatives, unlike at Maurya, where each recipe was loaded with unwanted *masalas* to make it taste better and preservatives so food could be reused.

"We have to stop them. Do they have the licenses? Or are they operating without the knowledge of the BMC?" Pujari asked, referring to the Mumbai Municipal Corporation's business regulations.

"Yes, they have the necessary licenses," Shetty said morosely.

"Buy them out?" Pujari asked.

"*Arre bhai!* It's their independent venture, and they're making money. You know what that means? You think they'll sell out? They've started with gusto and pride, and nothing can stop them," Shetty said rightly.

Stree stood there, small, dignified, and upright. The *taka-tak, taka-tak, taka-tak* taunted Maurya's two frantic owners.

*

Anusuya was tense. Sarangi's board examinations were around the corner. Sarangi was feverishly studying, so much so that she had lost weight. Her face was gaunt and her eyes were bleary as a result of sleeping less.

Sarangi seldom went to Elvira's house anymore. Elvira's arched eyebrows and waxed legs distracted her. Sarangi, for one thing, did not have the money to pursue such fancies and, at the moment, she was focused entirely on her exams. Her day was long. It started at seven and ended only by five. Three days of the week she spent studying with a group of students supervised by a schoolteacher who conducted practice exams consisting of questions that had been included in the past years' exams. Sarangi had a goal, and at the moment, Elvira seemed a major diversion. But not Joachim, for her feeling for him was love that sprang from her heart and inspired her.

On the rare occasions that she took a break from her studies, Sarangi went over to Elvira's merely to see Joachim and remained deaf to all of her girlfriend's chatter. Elvira was nonplussed about the upcoming exams and a bit cross that Sarangi was neglecting her. Sarangi's eyes searched all over for Joachim. And Joachim, with his unmistakable swagger, sauntered in, winked at her, and said, "Hi, scholar." It was more derogatory than complimentary, but it was enough for Sarangi. One such sighting, and a fortnight would pass peacefully.

Joachim dropped out of college, because he felt that his studies were hindering his game. His mother lit more candles at the church, but Joachim's hazy future plans didn't deter Sarangi. She dreamed of marrying him, and he was her idol. The endearing aspects of youth were dreams and the ability to see everything through rose-tinted glasses.

Joachim, though, was frustrated. He had no money to spend and was dependent on his mother's income. New shoes, new clothes, all cost money. Many of his friends worked for courier companies, but Joachim did not care much for the job. Every day, when his mother gave him fifty *rupees,* he cringed. He had to find a way out. The college general secretary had forged documents indicating Joachim was still a student, so that he could continue to play on the team, but that could not be stretched further. Any day, he would be caught.

The board exams started on a sweltering March day. Sarangi appeared for her exams and was confident of high enough marks to get into St. Xavier's College. On the other hand, Elvira had no worry. She planned to take advantage of the Catholic quota, which would enable her to be admitted to the Arts stream in St. Xavier's College.

That year would be Professor Kiran Sharma's last before she retired as a member of the faculty.

*

Stree was marching towards new benchmarks with confidence. But the same could not be said about the owners' personal lives. The women were fighting their own secret battles, and the worst affected was Nootan. She wept in the loneliness of the night, longing for the companionship of a man. At times she ached with despair as thoughts of her daughter invaded her insomnia. If only there were a man around to take care of them.

At last, Nootan met someone who brought the zest back to her life.

It was Nootan's responsibility to buy the potatoes and onions from the wholesale market, largely because she haggled very well and managed to get the best quality at the right price. She maintained a notebook in which she wrote down the prices of the produce items she purchased, noting the changes in the prices and the impact on the profits. She traveled far to wholesale markets to purchase condiments.

Naturals was a renowned shop that sold garlic, onions, potatoes, organic products, and fresh produce at wholesale prices. Parimal Mehta, a partner in Naturals, often saw her on Sundays, inspecting each potato and onion and discarding those with even the slightest defects. She bought twenty-five kilograms of each and waited for the change patiently. If there was even five *paisa* due, she never let go of it.

Parimal appreciated her selectivity. In fact, the boys at his shop looked for change when they saw Nootan Vakharia approaching.

Parimal took to handling Nootan's purchases himself, mainly because he was curious about her.

"Such large quantities can't be for her home. Does she run a catering business?" Parimal often wondered, though he never asked. There was something formidable about the cotton-sari-clad figure. He had attended to many customers, but nobody had interested him. Until he saw Nootan.

20

Parimal Mehta

Parimal, who had never had a successful relationship in his life, devoted his entire energy to growing vegetables — making the soil work. He had graduated from Indian Institute of Technology Delhi in the seventies. He tried working with the government on projects, but the bureaucracy got to him. He was not very good at watching his back. Slowly, he began picking quarrels with his superiors in an effort to wake them from the inertia of bureaucracy. Nearly every day, he got into a scrap with his supervisor, who was, in Parimal's estimation, "just a bloody conformist."

One of Parimal's favorite battles was the suspension of the muster roll for scientists. The institute that employed him insisted that scientists log their arrival and departure times, while Parimal maintained that the practice killed the scientists' creativity and made them into mere clerks. He refused to accept the system and worked all night long in the laboratory and slept till noon. The institute sent him memos that he refused to read. Inevitably, he was shifted to another facility where things were the same. He moved from one state-run institute to another. En route, he collected a French wife, Catherine.

Catherine had visited the northern hills in India as a tourist. She was introduced to Parimal by a friend and became enamored by his anti-establishment views and his crusade against science labs that were set up to crush the innovative temperament of the scientific community. She liked him and his outrageous views, dated him, and proposed marriage — more so because she wanted an

Indian visa in order to remain in the country. Otherwise, she would have simply lived with him. Parimal married Catherine because he loved her.

Catherine spent most of her time in the hills, helping the women preserve fruits as jams, marmalades, and spreads. Parimal didn't mind her absence, as he needed the space. He never felt that space diminished feelings. They were together for ten years. Then, the unavoidable happened.

Catherine began to find Parimal's anti-government tirades boring, and a few friends called her back home, saying she might as well protest against her own government. Catherine was enticed by the cooler climate of France after baking in the Indian heat. She lost interest in sex and rebuffed Parimal whenever he came close to her. Disillusionment crept in. She couldn't see anything exciting happening, and she became bored. Her work with the hill women was at a standstill; their preserves were not selling, so she had no worthy cause. The novelty of India and Parimal had worn out, and her husband's laid-back attitude was disturbing. And Parimal, with his natural pessimism, reinforced her state of mind. She began finding fault, and one day, she said she wanted to go back home.

"But this is home," Parimal said shakily.

Catherine shook her head. She left for France, shrugging off her *salwar kameezes* that had helped her blend with the hill women. She also left behind old photographs of herself that seemed absurd in the Indian context — photographs of a young girl standing next to a Shetland pony, a young prom queen, and a few gangly girls holding bottles of beer. Parimal surmised that Catherine didn't identify with them anymore.

As for the jars and jars of jams that she'd purchased from the hill women, Parimal calculated that he need never buy jam for breakfast till the time he died. He and Catherine parted as good friends and promised to keep in touch, but Parimal believed that she was determined to forget him once she left India.

After Catherine left, Parimal was surprised that he didn't miss her. He didn't need her for anything, but he still hoped that she would return.

Two years later, he was transferred to another institute, where he followed the same pattern. He questioned his superiors and was even more rigid. He was getting older. His mop of white hair, *khadi kurtas,* and *chudidars* — the traditional tight cotton pants tied with a drawstring — became his trademarks. Women colleagues at the institute found him exotic. A recalcitrant scientist, a divorcé, and a nonconformist... all made for an exciting combination. It was at his new place of work that Parimal met Sushma.

Sushma was involved in research into new forms of organic farming. She was an attractive woman of forty-two. Her hands and limbs were well shaped and toned because of the hard work. She farmed an acre of the institute's land and also taught tissue culture at the institute. She was dark, with black hair and black eyes, the antithesis of Catherine. Parimal loved the energy that she exuded and was fascinated by her passion for organic farming. He loved watching her eyes light up when she saw tiny plants grow in the soil. He spent a lot of time in her company and discovered that she was feisty in bed. Very soon, they were in a comfortable relationship.

Sushma steered his creative energy towards farming and taught him all about sowing, reaping, and understanding the earth. Parimal was fascinated, and he spent most of the time on the farm or in the library, reading about organic farming. It was not unusual to find Parimal and Sushma walking in the orchards, touching and caressing every leaf and fruit they saw.

Parimal believed, and often said, that he was a great one for spoiling things. The head of the institute took note that he spent more time out in the fields and lecturing students about organic farming than talking about USB ports. After he led a demonstration against a large fertilizer manufacturer, protesting against the company's programs for farmers, he was served with a notice. Parimal was perversely proud that the institute had refused to tolerate his dissention, and he told all and sundry that the scientific establishment did not take kindly to people expressing their views. He was prepared to sever his relationship with the scientific community.

An old friend from his days at IIT, who had chosen farming as a profession, contacted Parimal by e-mail and invited him to Nashik to grow grapes, potatoes, and onions. Parimal saw the offer as a relief. He immediately e-mailed back saying he was ready for it. He knew that if he asked Sushma, she would accompany him.

When he found her, she was, as usual, admiring some cherry tomato.

"I'm leaving for Nashik. A friend of mine owns land there, and he wants me to grow grapes, potatoes, and onions," Parimal said, his mouth very dry.

Sushma kept quiet.

"I'd like it if you joined me," Parimal said.

After a long time, Sushma said no and walked away, leaving him alone, surrounded by avocados, cherry tomatoes, and broccoli. Parimal was heartbroken. At forty-five, he felt like a jilted twenty-three-year-old.

He boarded a train to Nashik and started on his work. His vineyards produced the right grape for wine. His friend made him a partner in the business. Sommeliers raved about the organic wine made from the grapes that grew on Parimal's farm. He extended the concept of organic farming and moved from village to village, educating farmers. In a short time, he had employed a hundred farmers growing onions, potatoes, and other produce.

He began traveling to Mumbai — the main market, where

most of the vegetables were sold — to ensure that the middleman wasn't shortchanging the farmers that worked for him. It wasn't long before Parimal and his friend set up a shop in Mumbai and began selling their produce — Naturals.

Parimal had become more relaxed with his life. He began treating the families of the farmers as his own. He sent e-mail messages to Sushma, but they were strictly academic. They discussed new methods of farming and ways to rejuvenate land. Often, in moments of solitude, he saw Sushma standing in the field and shedding a tear for a bitter gourd that had turned yellow. He concluded that only the things she grew could evoke emotions in her.

Parimal became a popular figure, a crusader for the farmers. A TV channel interviewed him and dubbed him The Farmer from IIT. He used the analytical skills he'd gained from IIT to understand the weather's impact on crops, and he compiled data forecasting losses. He'd already begun preparing a report on how producers could save their crops from the uncertainties of the weather. Parimal intended to present his report to the government.

And then, a plump little lady in a well-worn sari, who valued every *anna* of her money and purchased huge quantities of produce, charmed him. But her mind-your-own-business attitude intimidated him, and he dared not approach her.

One day, though, he saw his opportunity. The rains had arrived a tad early. Their wrath destroyed most of the onion crops, and prices were going to rocket. Parimal had access to the information, since he was in touch with the farmers and studied weather with scientific morbidity. The newspaper covered the excess rainfall, but the average reader didn't understand the implications.

That Sunday, when Nootan began her exercise of picking the onions, she heard a soft voice by her side unlike the voices of the men in her life thus far.

"Excuse me," Parimal dared.

Nootan turned to see a tall, fair, older man wearing a white *kurta* and *chudidar*. Nootan turned towards him, wondering whether the payment she'd tendered was not right.

"I suggest you buy more onions," Parimal said affably.

Nootan raised her eyebrows.

"The rains have begun to destroy the onion crops. The price may go up," he explained.

Nootan muttered her thanks and doubled the quantity of onions she purchased. She didn't bother to check the veracity of the news. There was something trustworthy about the man. On her way back to the eatery, she pondered why she had believed him.

The others shrieked and howled when they saw the quantity of onions she'd purchased. Although Stree was earning well, the women were accustomed to being frugal, which helped them stay grounded.

"Why have you purchased so much? Where are we going to store all this? What if they begin to get rotten?" Shakuntala screamed.

"I got a tip that the prices will increase," Nootan said knowingly.

"And who told you that?" Anusuya asked, a little suspicious that somebody could actually give them a helpful suggestion.

"The man who sits at Naturals. Looks like he's the owner. Anyway, he asked me to buy more," Nootan said.

Parimal's forecast was accurate. Onion prices did increase. But the shortage didn't affect Stree, since the owners had been forewarned. Thereafter, Nootan's visits to the market on Sundays were a pleasure. Parimal waited on her with infinite patience.

"You could charge more from your customers if Stree used organically grown vegetables in their recipes," Parimal would say.

"But why would people pay more?"

They would spend a few minutes discussing the causes of the smote on the potatoes or a blight that destroyed the onions. It would be months before Parimal spoke to Nootan about her life.

The rains that had pushed Parimal to talk to Nootan traveled over the Sahayadri mountains and reached Mumbai. Simultaneously, the results of the college board exams were announced. Elvira and Sarangi walked to school together, Sarangi a nervous wreck and Elvira confident that she hadn't failed the exams. Sarangi stood third in the school and missed making it onto the merit list by a percent. Elvira scored fifty percent.

Anusuya wanted Sarangi to apply for admission to a college nearby, but Sarangi was adamant. It had to be St. Xavier's. She couldn't forget the grandeur of the college or the library where she sat and studied. Anusuya gave in.

Asunción accompanied Elvira and Sarangi to the required interviews, and both of them were admitted into the Arts and Sciences faculty, respectively. Sarangi returned home elated that the first hurdle was crossed, and Elvira rushed to a tailor to see some new designs.

21
Farzana's Change

Pujari and Shetty continued to ponder ways and means to decimate Stree. It was a tricky prospect. To frighten the women into closing their business would mean incurring the wrath of many. Social activists, the general public — all would turn against Pujari and Shetty's restaurant.

"I've seen that hoodlum who belongs to Lakda's gang eat there," Pujari said.

"Who?" Shetty asked.

"That guy who wears a long-sleeved sweatshirt," Pujari said.

"Yeah? Maybe the women are under Lakda's protection," Shetty said, assuming wrongly.

*

Farzana had shed her judgmental role and begun looking at the anomalies of the city rather objectively. Nootan and Anusuya spoke indulgently about Farzana's change of heart. Anusuya could not get out of her mind what she'd witnessed a couple of weeks earlier.

A flashily dressed hooker, screaming for attention with her crass speech and loud clothes, had come to eat at Stree. She was usually dressed in bright pink and yellow saris and garish costume jewelry. She wore flowers in her hair, and everyone called her Phoolmati. Nobody knew whether it was her real name or simply a moniker. She arrived regularly, at around eleven in the morning, disheveled and starving. The night always ravaged Phoolmati.

The women of Stree found her not so different from the other office-going women who stopped by for a quick snack. Farzana initially was surprised when she learned of her profession, but then she warmed up to Phoolmati, who always ordered her egg *bhurji*. She ate ravenously but with hints of delicacy. She lowered her head and ate quietly, not initiating conversation with anyone.

But one day, Anusuya almost fell off her chair when she saw Farzana standing in the street, exchanging words with a policeman while shielding a frightened, indignant Phoolmati behind her. Anusuya ran towards them to see what had occurred. Apparently, ι few days earlier, when Phoolmati was at work, another girl had picked Phoolmati's client's wallet and scampered away. The client reported the theft to the police and said he suspected Phoolmati.

Police officers that patrolled the street where Phoolmati and her ilk solicited were accustomed to accepting bribes in cash or kind. The police constable arguing with Farzana grabbed for Phoolmati and, in the process, tore her *salwar*. Phoolmati howled, not because her modesty was outraged, but because she instinctively knew it was the only time she could create a scene and elicit some sympathy. But people weren't interested in gathering around an enraged hooker and a constable.

"*Namasté, Didi!*" Phoolmati greeted Farzana loudly.

Farzana, who had rushed to the scene, returned the greeting and opened her mouth to admonish the policeman.

"Please do not interfere in this," the policeman told Farzana.

Farzana saw the torn *salwar* and was incensed. All said and done, no man had the right to abuse the modesty of a woman, even if she happened to be a hooker. Farzana knew that Phoolmati was always desperate for cash. She made up her mind.

"Please pay her five hundred *rupees;* otherwise, I'm going to report that you ripped her dress," Farzana said in her sternest tone.

To avoid any adverse publicity, the police constable paid up without the slightest hesitation. Phoolmati was happy with the money, and Farzana was delighted with the irony. Anusuya was taken aback because, among all of them, Farzana had led the most protected life.

Still, Farzana, in spite of the self-confidence she'd gained, was not free of Javed. Her husband resented her freedom and, in some black corner of his brain, he wanted to possess her again. Women, according to his dictum, were meant to be treated like slaves. His father had treated his mother in such a manner, and so had his grandfather. In his family, religion had been conveniently used as an excuse to justify the otherwise inexplicable behavior.

"If you let them loose, they will cause us shame," his grandfather intoned, his father repeated, and Javed reiterated.

He continued to kept track of all of Farzana's movements and never missed an opportunity to run her down.

Pakya had seen Javed create a commotion at Stree, but he didn't intervene. After all, the madman was Farzana's husband. The first time he'd seen Javed abuse Farzana, he'd glanced at his own arm in amusement.

Farzana's total liberation from Javed came unexpectedly. One evening, she was walking down the street with Pooja, Nootan's daughter. Pooja seemed to be enjoying her company and was speaking to Farzana in baby talk. Javed appeared, it seemed from nowhere, and stood near Farzana and looked at Pooja.

"Who is this mongrel?" he snarled.

Farzana fumed and was about to retaliate when she realized it was of no use.

"Nootan's daughter," she said softly.

Javed looked at Pooja intently. Saliva was dribbling from her mouth, and she made some incoherent sounds. Javed screamed, laughed, and cried. He pulled his hair and beat his chest. Farzana was stunned. She had no idea what had come over him. He ran off like a man possessed, never to return again.

Farzana's aunt helped her obtain a divorce. It was not difficult, and Javed didn't contest the proceeding. Then, she was freed of him legally too.

At first, Farzana felt almost strange being without a man, albeit one that tormented her, but reality sank in, and she moved on with immense grace.

22

Faiz Syed

At one o' clock, Mumbai felt hungry. If viewed from above, the crowd looked like an ectoplasm swaying from side to side. Executives in full-sleeved shirts moved with haste that was largely pretentious. Custodians, clerks, and office boys ambled as if to waste time.

The first day he lunched at Stree, he had to wade through the people. Yet, Faiz was comfortable eating at the women's restaurant and quickly learned the trick of avoiding the crowds. He either arrived at twelve o'clock or at two. Stree was relatively empty at those times, because they were respectively before and past the conventional lunchtime of the other offices.

Faiz Syed had studied law at the Aligarh Muslim University. He was convinced that his vocation was to dispense justice. He came to believe that justice was not entirely a fair business, a belief that emerged from the lesson he learned first when he was a young boy. The lesson had been reinforced when he grew older.

Faiz and his family lived in Lucknow, a city in North India known for its *Nawab* dignitaries, mouth-watering *kababs,* and formal etiquette. His family included his father, mother, an elder brother, and two elder sisters. Faiz's family had chosen to remain in India rather than leave for Pakistan after the Partition in 1947. Many of their relatives chided them for staying, but the elders of the family firmly insisted. Faiz remembered a house bustling with uncles, aunts, and cousins. The adults were always discussing politics and matchmaking. The polarization of the Hindus and Muslims in various states was a much-discussed matter in their household.

His childhood was a big country with many people. Faiz's father had never worked all his life. His oldest uncle managed the family's property and distributed the proceeds among the siblings. His father spent most of the day smoking the hookah and playing chess. In the evenings, he listened to music and ate blithely. Then, suddenly, there was a turn in the tide when the oldest uncle became greedy.

The family's patriarch had made a will naming the older brother as his successor, assuming that he would take care of the family. Instead he defrauded the others. Very soon, Faiz's family was on the streets. They didn't have the money to hire a good lawyer to contest their case. They lost everything. *If only we'd had a good lawyer* was the constant refrain Faiz grew up hearing. He avowed that he would become one.

And then another blow struck.

Faiz's older brother, Aftab, had moved to Delhi and was working with a software company. He and three other young men lived in a rented apartment. Aftab, a religious and god-fearing man, was the sole earning member of his family. One night in Delhi, a bomb exploded on a crowded public bus. The police investigated and arrested Aftab. One of Aftab's roommates had spoken to Aftab on his phone forty minutes before the blast, and the roommate was a suspect in the case. Aftab pleaded his innocence, but no one listened to him. Despite numerous trips that the family and Faiz made to Delhi, he could not be saved. Aftab died in police custody. The post mortem said heart attack, but the word was that it was police torture.

Faiz was embittered. He knew that Aftab was innocent, but the damned lawyer couldn't prove it. Faiz resolved to become a lawyer. He majored in economics and later studied law. He practiced in Lucknow and took up cases whose fees were not assured. He fought because he had the compulsion and the passion. Each case was fought for his father, for Aftab, to avenge the injustice meted out to them.

Soon, the urge to handle bigger cases made Faiz consider relocating. Lucknow was like a small pond, and the matters that were brought to him largely pertained to land. It pained him to see that the only achievement he could boast of was securing adjournments.

Both Pakya and Faiz were avengers. The only difference was that they chose to be on opposite sides of the law. Faiz moved to Mumbai and lived with Rahmatbibi, an aunt at Andheri. Rahmatbibi, a widow, was a distant relative who had met Faiz only a couple of times when she was visiting Lucknow. She was a genial lady who chose to escape the rigors of widowhood by staying in Mumbai. Her husband had left her a little nest egg. She spent her time performing social work in the slums, urging women to seek help if they were oppressed. She gladly accommodated Faiz, because she knew that most of her cases could be referred to him, and he would not charge a fee.

"After all, I'm his aunt," she thought grandly.

Faiz stayed with her for a while and then moved to a place of his own in Andheri. He worked at a law firm called Lex Charter and took on *pro bono* cases for the needy in his spare time. Faiz fell in love with Mumbai, and he felt he belonged there.

*

Architecturally, the Mumbai High Court was a grand structure. Its dazzling Gothic design was flanked by the equally imposing Mumbai University. Faiz simply loved the feeling he had when he walked into the premises of the high court. He knew he was meant to be there.

The gates of the high court were always guarded. Vendors selling fruit juice, biscuits, and hot beverages occupied the footpath outside.

Interestingly, a fortune-teller sat there with a plastic palm as his signboard. Freelance lawyers flapping their black gowns like bats hovered around in the hope of getting a client. Faiz handled a few good cases, and in the evenings, he let it be known through his aunt that he was available for free consultation.

Faiz was a good-looking man standing at five feet and eight inches. His mane was largely black, but there was white hair at his temple. He was of slim build and moved with ease. The court clerks liked to hear his soft, warm voice, which had a distinct Lucknow refinement.

Lex Charter was near the court in the busy area of Fort. Normally, Faiz ate his lunch at Maurya. However, he hated the steel and chrome look of the restaurant and the food that seemed aseptic. He had experimented with eating at many places and had finally settled on Maurya. He hardly paid attention to the food as he read the newspaper while he ate.

Then, one day, he accidentally discovered Stree.

He was walking to his office when he heard the sound of something sizzling and *taka-tak, taka-tak...* The aroma was familiar. The egg *bhurji* was the trigger for nostalgia. He remembered his mother, his sisters, and the leisurely breakfasts at which, along with egg *bhurji,* he ate piping hot, butter-laden *paranthas,* and the discussions of poetry and politics whetted the appetites...

Faiz began eating regularly at Stree. He noticed Farzana pound the egg *bhurji,* and the sound of the ladle against the cast iron griddle — *taka-tak, taka-tak, taka-tak* — was music from the past. He could never find a chance to speak with her. Nootan always took his order, and Farzana silently passed the plate of egg *bhurji* with onions, *pao,* and a slice of lemon on the side.

Faiz silently admired the women for holding up. He could make out from their faces that it must have not been easy. Having lived in Mumbai for a while, he wondered how the women kept the unwanted elements at bay.

Nootan saw Faiz and, judging from his apparel, knew that he was a lawyer. She was happy that respectable businesspeople were coming to eat at Stree.

At times, sophisticated, well-dressed women arrived in long cars, stepped out regally, and ordered their egg *bhurji* and *kanda poha*.

"They must be experimenting with new tastes," Anusuya said.

But the women at Stree were disgusted to see the la-di-dah women eat and then discard the disposable plates and spoons on the street.

"Please use the waste bin," Shakuntala would say extremely politely, pointing to the container kept outside.

The double chin had merged with the neck, and whether the lady scowled or grimaced was difficult to reckon.

College and university students came like gaggles of geese and drowned the surrounding noise with their chatter. Pujari and Shetty watched with dismay as they saw larger and larger crowds gathering around Stree. They also noted that Stree had started offering takeaway orders. The women packed food in aluminum boxes and sent them to offices for people who didn't wish to step out for lunch.

Meherunissa, a girl Farzana knew when she was living with Javed at Mumbra, was employed to pack the food and hand it to the runners or office assistants who came to collect it. Meherunissa was a penniless orphan, and her employment at Stree gave her independence and spared her of the monthly trips to homes of relatives to beg for money or food.

Considering the large number of people that had begun eating at Stree, Nootan suggested introducing a coupon system. The customers would pay first, collect their coupons, and then receive their food orders. In the past there were instances of people taking advantage of the crowd and not paying. With the new method, there would be greater accountability.

Sarangi was put in charge of getting the coupons printed. She made a simple artwork depicting five *rupees,* and below it she wrote *Stree — A Women's Initiative.*

Elvira knew Rita D'Souza, a charming old woman of sixty, who had run a thriving press at Dhobi Talao twenty years earlier. Rita's sons had deserted her, and her husband had died long ago. Elvira and Sarangi met with her and gave her the printing job. The machinery was a little rusty, but Rita assured them that with a little oil, the press would run fine. Later, as Sarangi would remember, she saw a sixty-year-old transform into a sixteen-year-old.

Another woman, who was more agile, was employed to tear off the coupons and collect the money from the customers at Stree. The system worked fine after a few teething problems. Clients had to spend a little more time buying lunch, but as Shakuntala had theorized, there was more method and less chaos.

Stree was grossing nearly five thousand *rupees* a day, but it was not enough for Shakuntala. She constantly thought of ways to expand. Culinary skill was the root of their success, and it could be used for branching out further.

Anusuya knew that Shakuntala made the most delicious *rawa ladoos, besan ladoos, chaklis,* and other savories. Shakuntala had learned from her mother. On every festival, her mother would go to the local grocer to buy refined wheat and chick pea flour and oil. She would patiently make savories with old gadgets and hide them in aluminum tins away from her brood. Since Shakuntala was her mother's helper, she would give her a few of the freshly fried savories, and the taste still lingered on Shakuntala's tongue. The smell of the betel nuts, rice, and red earth mingled and stayed for a very long time in her mouth.

It was difficult to duplicate the recipes in Mumbai; however, Shakuntala unfailingly tried for every festival. Her arms ached after she pressed the brass molds to turn out wriggly, concentric *chaklis.*

Every *Diwali,* when Hindus, Sikhs, Buddhists, and Jains celebrated, she executed small orders for a kilogram or two of savories for neighbors and friends.

Anusuya was aware of Shakuntala's talent. She had heard from her mother that in their village, the best savories were made in Shakuntala's home. While discussing their expansion plans for Stree one day, Anusuya said, "Why can't we sell *chaklis* and other such savories? We have an expert here!" She looked at Shakuntala.

Shakuntala smiled at Anusuya, seeing in her the success of all her efforts. Anusuya and the other women had changed their entire way of thinking. Not long ago, they'd been employees at the mercy of greedy employers. Now, they thought of ways to use their skills to earn more money and employ others in need.

"Good idea! We can sell packs of four *ladoos* each as dessert," Nootan said.

"We could also pack the savories in 25- or 50-gram packs and sell them in the local trains and railway stations," Farzana said with a tremendous amount of insight.

Generally, such savories were sold in packs of one hundred or two hundred grams or even in higher denominations. It was too much for one person to finish eating on a train journey from office to home. The trip, on an average, would take an hour. Smaller packs made sense.

"Anybody who wanted to munch a snack on the way back home could do it without wasting the leftovers," Anusuya said.

Stree was normally closed on Sundays, and rightly so, because all offices were closed on Sundays. The women generally spent a few hours cleaning their houses, maintaining accounts, or making a checklist for the provisions needed for the next day. But on that Sunday, Anusuya and Shakuntala got together and spent two hours in the morning making *ladoos* and *chaklis*, savories made of rice and chick pea flour. They packed them in polyethylene bags. That Monday, there was a new fare to sell. Farzana began calling it Time Pass, and on the first day, it was sold out.

"We can't be spending time making this at home," Nootan said.

"But the *ladoos* and *chaklis* are selling like hotcakes," Farzana countered.

"Why can't we ask someone else to make them for us?" Anusuya suggested.

"But they can't make them as well as we do," Shakuntala said.

"Why don't we train them? We can pay them a few *rupees* for a kilogram and also give them an incentive against sales."

"We'll be helping out a few families too," Farzana continued.

Shakuntala knew Nurul Hassan and Lalita Dolwani, two women who stitched blouses and were looking for other work to supplement their incomes. She sent word that she would like to meet with them. Shakuntala explained the work to them. She emphasized that Stree would provide them with the raw ingredients and the recipe. All they had to do was follow it faithfully. They would be remunerated with a fixed amount every month and also a bonus against the sales. Nurul and Lalita jumped at the prospect of augmenting their incomes.

Shakuntala and Anusuya went to the women's homes with the ingredients. They wrote down the recipes and stuck them on their kitchen walls. Shakuntala supervised the cooking of the first few batches. The test was whether the unsupervised product would sell just as well. It did. Nurul Hassan and Lalita Dolwani became members of Stree. Very soon, Nisha Parikh, another young girl, joined them as well.

Sarangi designed a nice label with the words *Stree — A Women's Initiative* prominently printed on it and stuck it on the packets of Time Pass. Shakuntala's vision was on the way to becoming a reality.

"We have to crush them," Pujari told Shetty when he saw the increasing popularity of Stree.

*

A few days later, Farzana received a phone call from home. Her elder brother was dying, and he wished to see her before he breathed his last. Farzana hadn't returned home since her marriage to Javed. After *Abbajan* died, she had no reason to go back. Her brothers were chauvinists who had often confronted their father for his liberal methods of raising Farzana. When Farzana asked for their help to prevent Javed from harassing her, their standard response was, "All said and done, he is your husband. Our duty is over."

But, after all, blood was thicker than water.

Farzana boarded a train at Mumbai Central and reached her home town the next morning. Her younger brother picked her up at the railway station. Everything had changed. She didn't recognize the way to her own home, and her face showed it.

"We sold off the old place," her brother said.

The family's new home was an apartment in a colony bound by high walls.

"This is only for us," came the explanation. "*They* aren't allowed here."

Farzana hated the place; it was nothing more than a ghetto. She cried unabashedly at *Abbajan's* grave. The only dinner she had with the family was interposed with statements like *We will kill them* and *Let them touch our mosque.*

The HUP had forced the Muslims to form militant groups to combat them. The fight was now an everyday affair. Graves were being desecrated by the Hindu extremists, and the Muslims retaliated.

Farzana was sick. She returned to Mumbai the very next day.

23

A False Charge

Tuesday afternoon, the crowd at Stree had eased after lunch. There were five to ten hungry souls that had ambled in for a last-minute meal. Faiz walked in a little after two thirty. A client had kept him busy.

"One egg…"

Before he could complete his sentence, Nootan relayed the order to Farzana.

"One egg *bhurji,* extra chilies, less butter, two *paos,* and some onions, finely chopped."

Faiz smiled at Nootan who returned the gesture.

At the stall were also two men whom the women did not recognize. They were, by now, familiar with most of the people who came to eat.

Faiz ate quietly and read the *Mid-Day.* He glanced at Farzana, who was cleaning the griddle. He finished his lunch, paid, and rushed back to work. The three men were still eating when he left. Suddenly, one of them clutched his stomach and groaned loudly. The other two rushed towards him. The man was now crying out. Shakuntala and Nootan sprang up.

"Maybe he's a having a heart attack," Nootan thought.

The man wailed even louder. The other two put him in a cab and rushed him to the hospital. The little crowd that had gathered dispersed in the absence of any more *tamasha*. The drama was over.

"I hope it's nothing serious," Anusuya said.

"He was clutching his stomach, not his heart, so maybe he'll be OK," Nootan surmised.

The day passed uneventfully, and they assumed that the man was well and about. The next day, a police official was waiting for them when they arrived at the stall. His stance declared that he had not come to eat.

"Who is the owner?" the police official asked gruffly.

"We are the owners," Nootan said, wondering why he was there.

"There's a charge against you," he continued.

Farzana gasped and Anusuya went ashen.

"A man was admitted to the hospital. The hospital authorities say it's food poisoning. He filed a first information report naming this establishment," the police official said.

Farzana's mouth formed a silent *Oh.*

"But that's not possible," Nootan said.

"Please come with me to the police station," he said.

Shakuntala took charge of the situation.

"Farzana, you stay here. There's no point in all of us going to the station. Anusuya can also stay," Shakuntala said.

Anusuya was glad that she was nominated to remain behind. The prospect of going to a police station frightened her. Farzana and Anusuya watched Shakuntala and Nootan walk away bravely with the police official. They could barely keep their hands still.

"I hope it's not something that we have to worry about," Farzana said, in ignorance of the enormity of the case, as Anusuya nodded her head.

Faiz came for his lunch and saw the two pale and somber women. The other two were missing.

"There's some problem," he thought.

He ordered his lunch and paid. As Anusuya tendered the change, he asked, "Is everything all right?"

Anusuya kept quiet, not knowing what to say.

"I'm a lawyer," Faiz said, giving Anusuya his business card.

Anusuya accepted the card.

"If we need the services of a lawyer, this man can help us," Anusuya thought, handing the card to Farzana.

Farzana held the card in her hand and read the name over and over again.

*

The Food and Drug Administration building was located on the newly built roads of Bandra. The sleek buildings with glass façades, representative of India's new economy, stood tall. Banks, financial institutions, hospitals, and pharmaceutical companies — all were arranged in the stylish new complex. The FDA acted as a sentinel, watching the vagaries of the pharmaceutical industry. It was there that Ramesh Raote, an FDA inspector, received complaints of food poisoning. Raote's phone rang shrilly.

"Hello."

The person on the other end informed him that two persons had taken seriously ill after eating egg *bhurji* served at Stree.

"Can you give me the address, please?"

Raote jotted down the address. He asked two inspectors to go and investigate the complaint. In the meantime, a first information report was filed.

When the inspectors reached Stree, they saw Anusuya and Farzana managing the stall. The two nervous women fidgeted constantly and mopped their brows.

"We're here to collect samples of the egg *bhurji*," one of the inspectors said with a polite smile.

"But why?" Anusuya asked, suddenly feeling her world skid out of control.

"We'll let you know later," they said.

The inspectors scooped the *bhurji* into a plastic bag, sealed it, and left without further delay.

One of Pakya's boys happened to see the food inspectors take the sample. Pakya's network of young lookouts hung around the city, gathering information or looking for opportunity. It must be said that Pakya and his gang could smell authorities from a mile away.

"They were there," the boy said, gasping for breath.

"Who was where?" Pakya asked lazily.

"The police, at Stree," the boy replied.

Pakya got up with a start, lunged menacingly at the boy, and twisted the collar of his shirt in his fist until it nearly choked him.

"Tell me clearly. What did you see?"

"They walked up to the kitchen and took some egg *bhurji,*" the boy said, still trying to catch his breath.

Pakya let go of the boy's shirt and paced up and down. He was extremely angry.

"Go and find out what happened," he instructed another boy.

The second boy immediately rushed out to comply with Pakya's instructions. He reached Stree and hung around, waiting patiently to learn what had occurred earlier. He couldn't exactly walk up to the owners and ask them.

*

Shakuntala and Nootan reached the police station in a numbed state. The charge against them was adulteration of food. The two men had taken ill after consuming the egg *bhurji.*

"But that can't be possible. So many people ate it. Why did only this man fall ill?" Shakuntala asked.

The police officer was patient.

"Please. Don't get upset. The doctors are checking the man," the police officer said.

"Of what use is that now? Word will spread that people get sick after eating our food," Shakuntala said.

"Don't rush to conclusions," the police officer replied.

After about half an hour, the officer instructed Shakuntala and Nootan to sign a paper. They were allowed to leave after an hour, which they spent quietly twisting their fingers, not speaking a word to each other, watching nervously as police officers screamed at petty criminals. In that hour, both of them thought that if they had to lose everything they'd worked for, this was the most dishonorable way.

"If we need you, we'll call you," the police officer said.

Shakuntala and Nootan rushed back to the food stall.

What happened? Why did the police come?

"That man who clutched his stomach and was groaning..." Shakuntala stopped unable to continue.

"Yes..." Farzana said.

"We thought he was having a heart attack," Anusuya said.

"Yeah, the same one," Shakuntala said.

"Well, someone related to him filed a criminal complaint against us," Nootan explained.

"For what? What have we done?" Farzana asked.

"The charge is that he fell ill after eating what we served here. So our food must be adulterated," Nootan explained.

"All of them fell ill?"

"No. Only that man who was groaning."

"Can they arrest us?" Anusuya asked with fear.

"I don't know," Shakuntala said, her voice only slightly quivering.

The four women were afraid. The official complaint was something they hadn't expected. In all their years of life, no one had taken sick eating what they had cooked.

The sun raged, showing off cracks in the roads and blemishes on pretty faces carefully covered with foundation.

*

The boy from Pakya's gang gathered, partly from overhearing the women's conversation and partly from speaking with others, that the four women were in serious trouble. He narrated the events to Pakya.

Pakya was restless. He paced up and down. He knew that food poisoning was not possible. He had been eating at Stree. The dedication of the women who ran the eatery and their integrity had not been wasted on Pakya. He simply could not believe that there could be something wrong with the food they served. He'd seen Farzana distribute food to the poor, if any were left at closing time. There was nothing wrong with the people who ate it. Pakya smelled a rat.

Like a pit bull, Pakya was slow to come to decisions, but once he made them, he stuck to them, come what may. It was what the don liked about him.

Pakya got to work. He placed a few calls on his phone. The first things he wanted to know were the identities of the two men. According to reports, they were taken to a private hospital rather than a public hospital, which, in itself, was glaring. Pakya's men were sent to work while Pakya waited for answers.

*

Farzana knew that they had to seek wise counsel. As she thought about who would help them, suddenly she remembered Faiz Syed. She turned her purse upside down and retrieved his card.

"We have to call this man. We may need him," Farzana said with finality.

The other three saw the lawyer's business card and read Faiz's name.

"Yes, Farzana, you're right. We'll need somebody to represent us if anything goes wrong, God forbid," Nootan said, looking upwards.

Shakuntala called Faiz. After the preliminary greetings, she explained the tight spot in which they found themselves.

"There is no way those two men took ill after eating egg *bhurji*. Lots of people ate it, but there were no complaints," Shakuntala explained.

"Yes. You may be right," Faiz said guardedly.

"The FDA inspectors took samples of the egg *bhurji* for analysis," Shakuntala said.

"I'm coming over there," Faiz said and hung the phone up. He was a little worried. Should any arrests be made, the bail amount would have to be paid. Faiz wondered if the women had any money with them. *Prima facie,* Faiz felt the case against the women was weak. It wasn't possible for only one man to take ill. Faiz headed for Stree.

A pall of gloom had descended on the stall. The four women sat glumly, and a few people hovered around with curiosity ranging from mild to harsh. On seeing Faiz, all four women sprang up.

"At the moment, there's nothing to worry about. The police haven't pressed charges. They'll only proceed once they have the laboratory results," Faiz said.

"So… at the moment, there's nothing much we can do except wait?" Nootan surmised.

"Yes," Faiz replied.

"You can get back to work. We'll call you if the need arises," Farzana suggested.

"No, I'll stick around," Faiz insisted. He made several calls to the police station. After a while, he left to prepare papers for anticipatory bail, should it be needed.

*

Pakya's men went to the hospital where the two men had been admitted. It did not escape Pakya's attention that they'd been taken there in a cab that happened to be waiting conveniently. Pakya's men recognized the ill men. They called Pakya, who arrived at the hospital in a rage. He stormed off the elevator, past the nurses' station, and into the room where the men were lying in hospital beds. His fury shook the men up.

"Please! We're not responsible. We did it for the money," one of them pleaded. The other simply sniffled.

"Who paid you?"

"We were asked by Kalidas," the more vocal of the two troublemakers replied.

Pakya knew Kalidas. He was another small-time rogue, working for another don. Pakya and Kalidas never trod on each other's path. Now, that would change. He left the private hospital, his men trailing in his wake. There was a briskness in his movement and he got out of the hospital quickly, not wanting to draw attention.

Pakya dialed Kalidas' private phone number. "Tell your men to retract the charge and confess the truth."

Kalidas knew Pakya's power and didn't want to give offense. "But what about my honor?" Kalidas attempted.

"In harassing four women? Who put you up to this?"

"Pujari and Shetty."

"Who are they, and why would they want to harm those women?" Pakya asked incredulously.

"They own a restaurant, Maurya. The women were a threat to their business. So they contacted me," Kalidas said in a matter-of-fact voice.

"Kalidas, you have to pull out of this," Pakya said.

"I didn't know they were under your protection," Kalidas said.

Pakya didn't reply. The women were not under his or anyone's protection. But he was fond of them. Kalidas, misattributing the meaning of Pakya's silence, acceded to his request.

Pakya left the two men in the hospital unharmed, but not without ensuring that the same evening, they told the police the truth. Soon after, the police received a written statement that the report of food poisoning had been falsified.

The next morning, the FDA analysis also cleared Stree. There was nothing wrong with the egg *bhurji*. The women heaved sighs of relief.

"But what about the rumor that's spread?" Farzana asked.

"You can counter it by working even harder," Faiz said.

Farzana looked at Faiz with gratitude. All of them thanked him profusely. He had been a major support in a time of crisis.

Faiz wanted to know why the men confessed to falsifying the charge against Stree. He asked the inspector in charge, who looked at him and said, "Repentance," with a twinkle in his eye.

The women opened the shop and resumed business. Little did they know that the gangster named Pakya was responsible for their acquittal.

When Kalidas called Pujari and Shetty to inform them that their deal was off, they were shocked at the turn of events. As an adversary, Pakya was not only industrious, he had connections.

"Wait and see," Pujari said.

Shetty nodded his head.

The women need not have worried about their reputation. Word did spread, but only about the women's strength. There was also a whiff of gossip about a gangster being involved, but business did not wane.

There were more hungry stomachs. Two more girls were employed at the stall to serve food to customers and to serve it faster. As usual, they were girls known to one of the women — this time, Nootan — and they were looking for a livelihood.

Farzana trained one of them to make the now famous egg *bhurji*. The recipe was engraved in the cells of her brain, a part of her genetic code. Onions, chilies, a little bit of spicy *garam masala*, and fresh eggs. All on the griddle and pounded with the ladle, *taka-tak, taka-tak, taka-tak*.

24

Time Passed

The week changed Nootan's life. As usual, she went to the market to buy potatoes and onions. The brush with the police had shaken her, and it was evident from the dark circles under her eyes. The fear of losing everything that they had created had shaken Nootan the most.

Parimal saw her and in an instant knew that something was wrong. Nootan chose the potatoes and onions with the utmost care, turning each one over in her hand.

"Is something the matter?"

Nootan heard a soft voice by her side. She turned to see that it was Parimal. She smiled at him.

"Would you like to have a cup of tea?" Parimal asked.

More than the cup of tea, it was his kindness that moved Nootan. She nodded her heard.

Nootan wanted to meet with him in a place where they could be alone, so when he suggested a nearby restaurant, she agreed. Over a cup of tea, Nootan poured out the happenings of the previous week — the charges investigated by the police; the trip to the police station; and, at the end of it all, the realization that it was a trumped-up case. Tears flowed. She could not stop them. All the repressed emotions were given vent. Parimal heard her out and held her hand affectionately. Nootan gave in when she felt his support.

"When the time comes…" Parimal said and stopped.

Nootan nodded her head and left the restaurant a very happy

woman. She didn't understand what he meant by *When the time comes.* Did he mean marriage? Or did he mean companionship? Whatever he meant, she felt good. She could not stop smiling.

As she reached Stree, Farzana sensed her happiness.

"What's the matter?" Farzana asked.

"Met someone?" Shakuntala taunted.

Nootan brushed them off and continued with her work. If she did disclose her secret, it would be only to Farzana.

*

Sarangi studied with a feverish vigor. Her final class twelve exams were a year away. They were the exams that Sarangi had to toil for. Her mind was made up. She planned to study to become a doctor of medicine. She knew that her mother couldn't afford to pay for a seat. There were colleges mushrooming across India. For a hefty sum, one could buy admission, but the only way that she could fulfill her ambition was by studying and scoring exceptional grades.

Elvira was all set to become an air hostess with a foreign carrier. She practiced by carrying trays laden with cups, much to Asunción's annoyance. Elvira was also, of course, not very bothered about the exams. This she made clear every time Sarangi dropped in to see Joachim.

Sarangi's heart beat faster whenever she saw him, and she swore that when she was studying botany, she could see his sweaty face amidst the petals of a flower. That Joachim whiled away his time, spending most of it hanging out with his pals or on the soccer ground, did not cause her passion for him to wane.

Joachim, oblivious to all of it, was reaching the nadir of desperation where his professional life was concerned.

Joachim was an average soccer player, and he'd been

overlooked by all the companies that came to the college to select players for their teams.

"Why didn't Burmah Shell pick you?" his grandmother asked.

"God! She's demented! She doesn't know that Burmah Shell doesn't exist. It's Bharat Petroleum now," Joachim thought in despair.

Joachim wrongly blamed his plight on everyone else. He made up his mind that if he didn't get a job within six months, he would migrate to Australia or New Zealand. Glen D'Costa and Shelton Fernandez had, and they were a happier lot. But go there and do what? Joachim gave himself time, and that was the only thing he could give himself.

It was good that Sarangi didn't learn of Joachim's plan to migrate, for she would have been heartbroken.

Whenever Sarangi took time from her arduous studying, which was rare, she met with Elvira, whose chatter had begun to sound plain silly. But silly Elvira was an ace at smelling out romances, and she sensed her friend's longing for her brother. She wasn't sure how her brother would respond to Sarangi, for Elvira knew that her brother had a thing for girls who wore their hair and skirts short. Nevertheless, Elvira decided to be a conduit for Sarangi's romance. Whenever Sarangi called to meet her, she successfully steered Joachim to join them for coffee.

As for Joachim, he needed someone to hear his tall talks and share his pipe-dreams. Nobody else seemed to want to spend much time with him. Moreover, when he went out with the two girls, he didn't have to pay for anything. Sarangi readily paid for him. Her naked admiration encouraged Joachim to speak more on his favorite subjects, soccer and himself.

Other times when she took breaks, Sarangi would help out at Stree. Afterwards, she, Elvira, and Joachim would walk through Fashion Street, cross over to the footpaths of Fountain, and turn from the Institute of Science back again to Fort. If they were in an extravagant mood, they'd visit the Iranian café, Kayani. Kayani always hosted a motley crowd, and the quaintness of the place lent it a certain charm.

One day, after a long walk and a half-hour discussion on Pele's style, they stopped at Kayani for a cup of tea and *mawa* cakes. Joachim ordered scrambled eggs, claiming that he was an athlete and needed the nourishment.

"The girl I marry must know how to make the best scrambled eggs," Joachim said with finality.

The color on Sarangi's cheeks went unnoticed by Joachim, but Elvira saw it and wondered how dense her brother could get. As usual, Joachim rushed off without paying his share of the check. Thus passed their youthful, ephemeral evenings.

*

Javed's sudden disappearance, and their divorce, gave Farzana the freedom to pursue her life the way she wanted. She never told anyone about Javed's bizarre behavior on seeing Pooja. She wondered why he reacted in such a strange way. His weird manner towards the little child sealed her belief that he was stark raving mad.

Nootan would have been very amused if she'd heard of Javed's behavior.

Perhaps Javed's guilt played tricks with him. One of the issues that bothered him to no end was his infertility. The fear of having to hear a doctor pronounce his condition prevented him from seeking corrective medical treatment. The easier way to reaffirm his masculinity was to spread gossip about Farzana and hold her responsible for her barrenness.

Often, when Farzana closed her eyes, she thought of Faiz. The manner in which the lawyer had stood by the women during the food poisoning episode was engraved in their hearts, and he enjoyed their trust. Even Shakuntala, who was usually skeptical when it came to men, fell completely for him.

Faiz's routine was fixed. On afternoons, even blindfolded, he could reach Stree. He still read the newspaper or went through his legal briefs while he ate. He had a soft spot for Farzana, but he dared not show it. Her dignity and silent strength came through from afar.

One day, Faiz was delayed at the court. He came for lunch long after the lunch hour had passed. Farzana was clearing up. Faiz saw that she was all alone and felt good about it.

"Is there anything left for me?"

Farzana smiled and nodded. She hurriedly splattered oil on the griddle and began making fresh *bhurji* for him. From time to time, she pushed aside the flying *purdah*.

"Where are the others?" Faiz asked.

"Nootan and Shakuntala went to the city offices, and Anusuya went to purchase some writing paper for her daughter," Farzana replied.

"Where do you stay?" Faiz asked while eating.

"Bandra," Farzana replied.

"Alone!"

"No." There was an awkward silence. Farzana enjoyed Faiz's discomfiture.

"She must be married, and that too happily," Faiz thought. After a moment, Farzana spelled things out.

"I was married, but not anymore."

Faiz smiled at first and then laughed. He did not stop laughing. He suddenly noticed that the afternoon was a little cloudy. A slight wind blew, evaporating sweat on lips and foreheads. People on the street spoke about rain in the northern parts of the country as the reason for the cool winds. The Gulmohar trees were beginning to turn red and tiny *mynas*, with their brown and yellow plumage, perched on the trees.

Faiz was feeling light and thought that if he willed, he could fly in the air.

Farzana was bemused. She was happy with the interest that Faiz showed in her. Maybe…

*

Stree's reputation spread, and the tantalizing taste of the egg *bhurji* lingered on everyone's tongue. As the months passed, Nootan and Farzana often remembered their past and spoke about things back home. They could never forget their childhood — that period of innocence when the pleasures of life were simple. The flowering of the *champa* or the first rains or the smell of peanuts being roasted. At times, when Nootan closed her eyes, she could still see her brothers ploughing the field with bullocks and calling out to her to bring them buttermilk spiced with the special *masala* that her mother ground every summer. All that had become a picture in the part of her brain where all the good shots were stored.

*

There were rumors that Dilip Vakharia, Nootan's husband, had been reinstated in the HUP in their native town. On hearing about Dilip's release from jail, Nootan surmised that he'd completed his sentence. Dilip, in fact, did not return home. The party had plans for him, and envoys picked him up the moment he was released. He didn't have the time to think of his family. As far as Nootan was concerned, Dilip Vakharia was dead.

The political situation was volatile. Tridents and spears were used as weapons. Communal tension was like a rubber band stretched. It was *us* and *them*. The high walls that bound Farzana's brother's new home got higher. Areas were clearly marked — the

Hindus lived in one area, and the Muslims in the other. Arms were stocked, with each side believing that the other would attack. The call of the *azaan*, *Allah u Akbar*, that woke Nootan on time was viewed as a call to action.

Nootan was glad that *Abbajan* was not alive to see all of it. He would have been heartbroken. During *Eid,* his house had been filled with people, no matter what religion they practiced. Farzana still kept in touch with her relatives back home; however, Nootan did not maintain contact with her brothers. Farzana informed her that many Muslims had moved to Mumbai and other places, where they felt safer.

"But that is their home," Nootan said.

Farzana had no answer. The commercial areas where Muslim businesses were prominent were targeted by the HUP. Abdul Miyan's lumberyard was frequently attacked. Rasoolan's bakery was stoned. Pamphlets were distributed by the members of the HUP, exhorting Hindus to keep away from Muslims.

To Nootan, it seemed that the smell of henna in her memories of her town had been replaced by the smell of blood. She remembered the times when she attended the meetings of the HUP, and everyone was asked to stand up and swear to abide by the edicts of the party, which declared that all people who respected other religions were mere slaves. The atrocities during the Partition of the country into India and Pakistan — and extending centuries back in history to emperors like Mahmud of Ghazni, whose rule extended from Afghanistan into Iran and Pakistan, and Aurangazeb, whose religious fervor resulted in perpetual war during his reign — were all recounted. Nootan had come to agree with Farzana that history and historians should be banned.

"And whatever happened to the handsome Mr. Patnaik, the history professor," Nootan wondered.

25

Realization

The good reputation of Stree was strengthened in another strange manner. Anusuya almost started believing in miracles. And, in a manner of speaking, Nimmi Rastogi was responsible.

Nimmi wrote for a leading newspaper. She had no fixed topic; the editor indulged her and let her pen be. She wrote about the city. Nuances, eccentricities, vagaries, and everything that would have escaped a casual onlooker were captured by her words. Nothing escaped her eye and her pen.

She was an innovative person, born and raised in Mumbai, and she loved the city in spite of its traffic congestion, pollution, and other flaws. She was thirty-four and quite attractive. Nimmi lived alone. Her parents had retired and moved to Delhi with her brother, but she simply could not leave Mumbai. She had completed her master's degree in journalism, and it didn't take her very long to get an entry-level job as a reporter with one of the leading newspapers.

Nimmi lived with Abhimanyu Patel, a fashion designer. She didn't feel the need to marry, and neither did he. They enjoyed an easy relationship, and since both of them were fiercely independent, the arrangement suited them. Nimmi loved Mumbai's liberal attitude. Nobody raised an eyebrow at Abhimanyu and her relationship.

Her typical day was spent searching the streets of the city, especially South Mumbai, looking for stories. One afternoon, while walking, she discovered Stree tucked confidently along the street. The name board, with its vermillion dot on top of the letter *R*, fascinated her. And there were four women staffing the stall, serving quite a varied crowd!

Nimmi had never taken ill after eating any type of food from a stall. She was immunized, and friends often joked that she had an iron stomach. She regularly ate *bhel* and *vada pao* from various street vendors, but her stomach managed to churn it all. That particular day, she saw the little stall with the powerful name— Stree—that appealed to the independent woman in her. She walked towards it, and the aroma made her salivate. It was noon, and she was hungry.

Like a zombie, she ordered a plate of egg *bhurji,* a plate of *kande pohe,* and a *rawa ladoo* as dessert. Nimmi watched Farzana throw the finely cut onions, cilantro, and fiery green chili into the oil. The smell that emanated was heavenly. When the eggs joined the medley, the aroma wafted past, and she was sure that it reached CST station. She'd never had that kind of food before. The taste was very cooked-at-home, and yet there was a zing of some special masala. Above all, in the food was a lot of warmth. The women who ran the stall had a smile for everyone, and they seemed to be familiar with most of their clients, as they asked about their health and their families' well-being.

Nimmi wrote a review of Stree for the newspaper. She used evocative words to convey the taste and the smell of the food she'd relished. She mentioned the warmth and love that was an accompaniment to it. She rhapsodized on the tantalizing egg *bhurji* that stimulated one's senses. And the *taka-tak* sound of the ladle that stirred one's soul. Stree roused people from the depths of their escape. Her piece ended with, "Four women dare. The egg *bhurji* is to die for. Do not miss this delight."

Suddenly, eating egg *bhurji* at Stree became very fashionable. Fancy cars with well-dressed women passengers stopped by, or drivers from long cars took parcels of the *bhurji* home.

Nimmi Rastogi's writing always set trends, be it in eating

or shopping. She had forced restaurants to close down with her criticism and enhanced sales of embroidered kurtas at an unknown shop in a nondescript area as the result of her praise. She had an eye for excellence and was seldom wrong.

The women did not see the write-up; however, Sarangi, who scanned the newspaper from beginning to end, saw the article and was elated. To be reviewed by Nimmi Rastogi was a great feat, and it was rumored that one had to pay the newspaper to be featured by her.

Sarangi showed the newspaper article to Anusuya, who was not too thrilled. Parimal decried the writing as cheap. However, Shakuntala was excited, because she knew the crowds would throng. Faiz rued that the article didn't carry photographs, while Farzana and Nootan were simply indifferent. Elvira went around telling everyone that her friend's mother ran the exquisite shop.

Predictably, Mumbai's glamorous set arrived in long cars and parked in front of Stree to eat the home-cooking Rastogi had written about. These people were a novelty to Sarangi. She stared unabashedly at the baubles of diamonds sparkling on their fingers and streaks of L'Oreal color shining in their hair. Sarangi realized that theirs was a life totally different, with a different set of rules.

"Now, look at that hemline. If I were to wear a skirt as short as that, I'd be termed a 'loose girl'," Sarangi thought.

The seasons had changed. Stree had stabilized and was showing steady profits. Six girls were employed to sell Time Pass — three of them at CST and three at Churchgate. Shakuntala was a little sated. Her dreams seemed to be coming true.

Sarangi was preparing to appear for the mother of all exams. She was very confident of being admitted to medical school. By the time she finished the tests, she was a pale, thin girl, but she'd done well and hoped for the best.

During her vacation, Sarangi helped her mother at Stree. Anusuya felt it was much better than sitting at home and corrupting her brains watching useless serials on television. Sarangi assisted with the sales of Time Pass, which had been a roaring success. Passengers purchased the small pouches of roasted peanuts, gram, or the occasional *jaggery* sweets for as little as three *rupees.* Their long journeys home became a little easier.

*

Another reason Sarangi chose to work with her mother during her vacations was because of Joachim, who came to play soccer at the Cross Maidan, one of the last open green spaces left in Mumbai. Lying between Fountain and Churchgate, it was a period of green between two long sentences. Normally, youngsters played Mumbai's favorite sport — cricket — in the *maidan*, and office-goers who worked in the Fort area cut across it to get to Churchgate and vice versa. Inside the Cross, dogs were walked, children played, and Joachim dreamed.

Elvira had begun working evenings at the retail counter of a watch shop at Fort. In a sense, she was a practical girl. She knew that she wasn't brainy enough to score good grades and pursue higher education, so she began taking part-time jobs and earned enough money to buy her stock of Lakmé lipsticks and depilatory wax.

Normally, when Sarangi caught up with her, Elvira would thoughtfully suggest going to the Oval, where Joachim played. The trio would then walk to Kayani for their customary tea, each lost in thought. If they'd had a crystal ball, they would have known that the moment was no more than a second in time, there and then gone.

One day, Elvira excused herself, saying that she had to meet someone Sarangi and Joachim didn't know. Refusing to accompany them, she left a disgusted Joachim and excited Sarangi alone.

"At least she doesn't speak much," Joachim thought as he walked along with the flushed, palpitating Sarangi.

Sarangi wasn't sure of what was happening to her. She felt like a balloon wanting to fly yet grounded by strings.

At Kayani, she sipped her tea in silence and listened to Joachim weave his web of fantasy in which he played for India and become as famous as Pele. Normally, when Elvira was around, she also staked a claim in the talk time. Today, Joachim was unbridled. He found a perfect sounding board in Sarangi. She neither agreed nor refuted. She simply listened. Joachim had always wished for an audience like her. His family and his friends really didn't care to listen to him. They were involved with their own plans, and Joachim was not moving forward in life.

Joachim was too selfish to see Sarangi's burning passion for him. Their tête-à-têtes continued for a good month of Sarangi's vacation. Elvira stayed away but was acutely disappointed that Joachim still hadn't gotten the message.

Then, one day, Elvira spilled the beans.

Brother and sister were returning from church on a Sunday morning and making plans for the evening. As usual, Joachim grumbled that he had no money to do anything, hinting that Elvira should lend him some.

"You don't need any money. That poor girl pays for everything."

"Which poor girl?"

"As if you have a harem of women dying to pay for your extravagances."

"And why does she pay for what I eat?" Joachim asked, running his hands in his hair in an attempt to push it back. He kept arranging his hair so often that it threatened to leave his head.

Elvira looked at him disgustedly and shook her head at his impenetrability. "Because she's in love with you."

"No way."

"Why is that impossible to believe?"

"She's a bookworm!"

"Humph…"

There was a silence in which Joachim's brains churned. He knew it but didn't want to know it. Sarangi was different from the girls Ryan and Rob hung around with. She wore only *salwar kameezes* and never applied makeup. The most important thing going against her was that she looked intelligent. At the rate she was studying, she'd soon start wearing spectacles.

"Ugh! Kissing a spectacled girl is like the end of life," Joachim thought, pompously forgetting that, let alone kiss, he'd never even held a girl's hand.

That night, he couldn't sleep a wink. He recollected all the evenings he'd spent with Sarangi and her patient ear to his tirades. She would quietly pay for whatever he ate. Suddenly, he realized that she had only sipped a cup of tea. She probably ordered tea because she had no money. Joachim felt strange. Suddenly, he missed her and felt something indescribable towards her. He couldn't wait to see her, and her simple figure was a solace to him.

The next evening, Joachim pulled out of his game and waited for her, unlike most days, when he made her stand by for a good thirty minutes because it made him look good in front of his friends to have a girl wait for him. As usual, they walked to Kayani. Joachim ordered a pudding and tea for Sarangi. She could feel a difference in Joachim. There was an air of passion around him. He stared at her long enough to make her feel shy.

Joachim asked the waiter for a napkin. Kayani did not have any extra trappings on the table. If you needed anything, then you had to ask for it and, worse still, pay. The napkin, however, was free. He took out a ballpoint pen and wrote *I LUV YOU* and pushed it across to Sarangi with a great amount of courage.

The Iranian eatery, with its long-necked fans, round tables and chairs, showcases of fat cakes waiting to be gobbled, and rope hanging at the entrance to help the elderly enter, seemed to stand still in time. The old Parsi owner looked knowingly at the waiter. They'd seen a lot of notes passed in their lifetimes.

Crazily, birds began singing in and out of Sarangi's ears, and she felt a shiver run down her spine. She took the sacred tissue paper, tucked it in her physics textbook, and could not meet Joachim's eyes. She blushed and was tongue-tied. Her body seemed to be behaving in a manner that was alien to her.

They walked towards the Marine Lines railway station amid the crowds of people rushing to reach home. Sarangi was oblivious to the whole world and was only aware of Joachim's presence by her side. Joachim came close to Sarangi and brushed his shoulder against hers. His little finger, like a hook, trapped her finger, and he very naturally held her hand. Sarangi enjoyed the experience. She was in love.

Joachim told his mother, his sister, and all his friends that he was "friendly" with Sarangi. Elvira gave Sarangi a small crucifix that Sarangi hung round her neck when she went out of the house. Asunción didn't mind Sarangi coming over; after all, she was her son's first girlfriend.

Farzana noticed the crucifix on Sarangi's neck and shrugged it off as being some new fashion statement.

Sarangi didn't utter a word of it at home. Anusuya would have wrung the life out of her.

Joachim couldn't understand why Sarangi spent so much time with her books. Now that he'd claimed her time as his own, he was enraged when she refused to go out with him. He didn't recognize her ambition and often threatened, "If you don't meet me tonight, then I'll never see you again."

At first, Sarangi put her books away and went to meet Joachim, for she was afraid of losing him. All the time she was with him, however, she was in a hurry to get back to her studies, and she barely heard what he said. One day, she mustered the courage and declined to go out with him.

"After my exams," she promised.

Joachim didn't throw a fit, as she'd feared, but turned meeker and hung around her like a puppy. Sarangi's preoccupation with her exams left him with a lot of time on his hands.

*

Stree was progressively making profits. Shakuntala's conviction that no one in Mumbai minded spending money to eat was justified. Nootan spent more time settling accounts, and sometimes she had to accept Parimal's help. The tax laws confused her, and the income tax returns baffled her.

By now, they had stopped traveling in Kiran Sharma's car. The former professor had retired and was at a loss for how to kill time at home. The broken-down white Fiat stood in her garage. She contacted Shakuntala and expressed her desire to sell the car. Anusuya insisted that they buy it, since she felt that the car was a good omen for them. Thus, they became the proud owners of a four-wheeler — a big achievement for them.

*

Jagvinder Singh was a sixty-five-year-old Sikh taxi driver. Long ago, he'd zipped through the streets of Mumbai in his taxi and was nicknamed Speed Master by the other taxi drivers. Age caught up with him, and he couldn't drive as he once had, but he treated his taxi as a demigod or, rather, venerated it like a farmer revered his bullocks. He raised two good-for-nothing sons and married off his daughter to a wastrel, all on the income accrued from the taxi. He blamed the misfortune on karma. His health was not too good, and arthritis was claiming his bones. Passengers grumbled that they were uncomfortable, because the car wobbled and, at times, he didn't see approaching vehicles. Retiring was not an option, since his finances were still in a mess. He sold off his taxi, and his sons promptly grabbed the money.

Faiz's aunt knew Jagvinder and recommended him to Faiz, who, in turn, suggested him to Farzana when he heard the women were looking for a driver.

"I hope he doesn't crash us," Farzana said laughingly.

"He's lucky that he gets to spend more time with you than miserable me," Faiz thought.

Jagvinder lived at Koliwada, and every morning he had to present himself at Shakuntala's home at 7:30. It was a funny sight to see all of them traveling together. The battered old white Fiat, Jagvinder with his blue turban and flowing beard, and the four women with pots and pans and fresh vegetables. After Jagvinder dropped them off, he hung around doing odd tasks and brought them back home late in the afternoon.

Jagvinder genuinely liked the women and enjoyed listening to their chatter. He nodded whenever asked for an opinion. He had a special fondness for Nootan. On being asked why, he replied that she resembled his dead wife.

Mumbai remained insulated from the polarization of the Hindus and Muslims that was happening everywhere else. The proprietors of Stree purchased their bread and eggs from Latifbhai, who was not only their vendor but also their friend. On his delivery rounds, Latifbhai stopped at Stree for a plate of egg *bhurji*, and Shakuntala never charged him.

Back in Farzana's home town, however, the situation was getting worse. There was mistrust all around. Farzana's brothers were storing weapons and ammunition, fearing an attack from the Hindus, while Nootan's kin were doing the same.

The Babri masjid, a mosque without minarets, was making news. The Hindus asserted that the mosque had been built to replace a temple commemorating the birthplace of their god Rama. There was news that right-wing parties were planning a destructive act. Rumors were sweeping the country.

26

Farzana Goes Back to School

Pakya was no longer the boy who, earlier, could amble into Stree unnoticed. He'd become a man one could not ignore, a man who spoke few words and walked around with a loaded pistol. The don trusted him implicitly and called him over twice to Dubai. A hardened criminal with at least fifteen prior arrests, he'd spent some time in prison. In fact, being in and out of prison was no longer a big deal for Pakya. He knew his game was treacherous and he could be killed anytime, but he couldn't get out. He was caught like a spider in a web. No relatives, no friends outside the business. For that matter, his own mother had disowned him.

The underworld machinery of Mumbai is eulogized, but Pakya knew the truth. There were no long-gowned, cigarette-smoking molls hanging on his shoulders. There was grime and dirt. Pakya began to worry about encounters with the police. He lost three of his trusted men to police gunfire. And the media hounded him. He was more afraid of the camera than the gun. The dark streets of Mumbai had trapped Pakya.

It was yet another journalist who was responsible for giving Pakya the fame he did not deserve.

A cricket match pitted India against a neighboring country. There was heavy betting. Pakya and his troupe were in favor of the Indian club. Suddenly, one of India's bowlers pleaded a hand injury and was taken out. It meant losses in millions for Pakya, who was suspicious.

"He was fine, and suddenly this morning his hand is sprained?" Pakya thought with a degree of amusement.

Obviously, someone had paid off the player. Pakya made discreet inquiries and found out that the cricketer's game at the nets was uneventful. Pakya's flunkies learned that the bowler owned two Labradors that he loved more than his life. The player was obsessed with the Labradors and took them wherever he went. Page three of the daily newspaper featured the dogs, and an article mentioned that the cricketer had severed relations with two women because they didn't like his dogs. The cricketer's pidgin English, his dogs, and his starlet girlfriend-of-the-month always made more news than his game. He was in good form and was expected to perform well that season. And it was because of him that Pakya had put money on the team.

"And now this," he thought disgustedly.

Pakya made up his mind and issued instructions. He knew that the cricketer wouldn't care if a knife were driven into his starlet girlfriend's gut, so one of the two flunkies stabbed one of the Labradors and killed it. The bowler returned home and was devastated when he discovered his dead dog. Tears ran down his face, and he was on the verge of suffering a breakdown, but he got the message. He didn't want to lose the other dog. He immediately sent word that he was willing to play. Pakya became an unseen hero.

As he sat next to the don and watched the next match, he felt sorry for the bowler, but such was life. A journalist spotted the don and clicked pictures. The newspapers splashed photographs of Pakya and the don watching the match. Farzana saw the pictures and recognized the man who never met her eye but always looked down, as if with humility. And in the blistering Mumbai heat, he wore a long-sleeved sweatshirt.

She showed the picture to Shakuntala who circulated it to the other women.

"As far as we're concerned, he's a customer. We don't have anything else to do with him," Anusuya said sensibly.

But deep down in their hearts, they were shocked at Pakya's occupation. Shakuntala could clearly recall the days when Pakya came to the stall at the stroke of eleven and ate his breakfast. He had seemed to be a shy boy, and he never failed to pay. These days, whenever Pakya was in Mumbai, he sent a boy to collect his breakfast from Stree.

Pakya always wondered whether the women at Stree saw his picture in the papers. Strangely, he felt sad when he thought of them. His only consolation was that his father could no longer say he was worthless.

*

In the murky city, with all of its dirt and grime, there was also passion. Or something close to it, anyway.

Nootan had been very discerning when it came to relationships with men. Even though she missed the companionship of a man the most, the mistrust she had for men overrode all other emotions.

Parimal, on his end, had developed feelings for Nootan. Men like Parimal didn't love or like women, they "had feelings" for them. These feelings were then analyzed and classified as emotions, definitely not love. Parimal was attracted to Nootan's sheer grit. Catherine and Sushma had been lotus-eaters, but Nootan was a fighter, and the quality attracted him to her. However, she seemed aloof. Parimal often made attempts to hold her hand or, at times, even to hug her. But she edged away. Parimal didn't understand why she behaved so prudishly. He gave her time to come to terms with what she felt for him. Parimal was a man who enjoyed a physical relationship with a woman, but he respected the liaison and never treated any woman with contempt.

Nootan also wondered why she shirked away from a physical relationship when she wanted one with Parimal. Whenever she closed her eyes, the image of that strange tiger in pursuit still haunted her. She felt inadequate and believed she couldn't satisfy Parimal. Dilip Vakharia had been a fundamentalist even in bed. He enforced his dogma and was unmindful of the other person's sensitivity. The past had left Nootan incomplete, but she held herself responsible for her failed relationships. Assuming rejection from Parimal, she never got close to him. His body ached for hers, and she knew it but made no move. There were times when she wished to cast everything away and run to Parimal. But there were fetters on her feet.

Despite their physical distance, the relationship between Parimal and Nootan was a strong and mature one. Strong because they respected each other, and mature because they understood the limits of their friendship. Parimal liked spending his time with Nootan and talking about his grand plans for organic farming. For Nootan, Parimal's interest in Stree and in her was novel. Over cups of tea, he would enthrall her with stories of his life and set her thinking. Whenever she returned from meeting with Parimal, she was infused with energy and felt like running barefoot through the streets of Mumbai.

Friends have a knack of sensing new emotions, and Farzana perceived the change in Nootan. The excitement to go to the market and the last-minute preening didn't go unnoticed. But she never pried and made Nootan uncomfortable. She knew that her friend would speak with her when she was ready. And that was what happened. When the exhilaration made Nootan buoyant, she told Farzana about Parimal.

"Is he married?"

"No, divorced," Nootan replied, trying to tally two reconciliatory figures.

"Has he proposed marriage?"

Nootan shook her head and smiled thinking, "When the time comes…"

"Has he touched you?" Farzana asked with a naughty look in her eyes.

"Hmmm!"

"Where?"

"We just held hands, silly."

"That's all?"

"He's not riffraff. From IIT," Nootan justified.

"What? Men from IIT don't do it?" Farzana let out peals of laughter.

Nootan could not hold back either and was in splits.

"Just let go," Farzana said, thinking of her friend's bad marriage. "Does he know about Pooja?"

Nootan nodded. "I want you to meet him."

There was a crashing sound of a car's bumper hitting another car. The drivers stepped out and began yelling at each other, and at the far end of the street, a traffic constable was whistling as he raced to the spot.

"Come with me to the market tomorrow."

Farzana laughed and nodded her head. It wasn't clear what caused her so much mirth. A flashback?

History and historians should be banned.

The next Sunday, Farzana accompanied Nootan to the market; she looked beautiful. Nootan introduced her to Parimal as her "best and childhood" friend. Farzana took him in at a glance, and an expression of naked admiration crossed her face. Farzana had absolute esteem for erudite men. *Abbajan* had always surrounded himself with learned men. Farzana used to tag along behind *Abbajan* and listen to every word they said. That day at the market, she listened to every word Parimal was saying in his soft voice. He inquired after her health. She wanted to tell him about all her troubles — the nagging pain in her stomach and Javed, the worse pain. Parimal asked about Farzana's home town and began postulating his theory on Fascism, applying it to various places in the country.

"You are a very lucky woman to have such a man besotted," Farzana said, a shade enviously, as they returned home that evening.

Nootan was happy that her friend liked Parimal, but she was also confused. She had no clue what the logical conclusion of her relationship with Parimal would be.

*

As Stree was gaining ground in the city, religious sentiments were flaring in the country. Every second day, the Mumbai police pursued an extremist group or locked horns with underworld gang members. A group of Islamic extremists, *Aman-e-Watan,* which translated as *a peaceful nation,* a misnomer, approached Faiz and asked him to help them counter the HUP. Faiz declined and was reminded of the true teachings of Muhammad, "The strong one is not he who knocks out his adversary; the strong one is he who keeps control over his temper."

The *Aman-e-Watan* recruited young boys and was rumored to send them to foreign lands for training in warfare and weaponry. The Indian government had banned the group, though in certain quarters, people criticized the politicians that enacted the policy.

Pakya's don didn't care which religious party approached him to orchestrate acts of vandalism and violence. He was always getting requests to desecrate a Hindu idol or a Muslim mosque. All he cared about was money. It was rumored that he had a champagne fountain in his home in the deserts of Saudi Arabia. Pakya had never seen it, but he was sure one day he'd have something just like it. Pakya was of the opinion that, in the underworld and

Bollywood, religion, caste, and creed didn't matter. Prove your worth and stay at the top.

While the city, with its seven million people, was rumbling along, the four women were as secure in Stree as a fetus in the womb. It was their own world. Them against the others. In their world, they put down their reserves and lived. Crowds teemed to eat, and they saw self-educated young women living life on their own terms.

If they had one lament, it was that none of them had completed a formal education. Shakuntala consoled herself by saying that they had reached far in life without having studied, and Farzana answered that, if they had, they would have reached their destiny much earlier. Despite Farzana's misgivings, the uneducated women were grossing a profit of nearly four *lakh rupees* a month.

Farzana began to accompany Nootan regularly to the market. Nootan didn't mind having Farzana with her. She was happy to see that she'd taken to Parimal. Whenever Nootan was alone with Parimal, he grumbled that it was impossible to meet and share a word of affection with Nootan, since Farzana was always with her.

"But you're the one who's always chatting with her," Nootan laughed.

"I can hardly be impolite," Parimal retorted.

Strangely enough, Nootan always lied to Farzana when she went to meet Parimal by herself. At times, she wondered whether Parimal was paying a little too much attention to her friend. She felt guilty for being jealous, so she justified her behavior to herself. She thought of herself as the right companion for Parimal.

Farzana started dressing to the hilt and was always a little eager and nervous before meeting Parimal. His views exhilarated and freed her, and when he said that anarchy would save the country, Farzana believed it.

One such Sunday, the two women were with Parimal, drinking a cup of tea and talking about everything under the sun. Nootan was quiet. Farzana and Parimal showed no signs of winding up. Jagvinder waited for them, wiping the windscreen of the car till it was so clean that it seemed like there was no glass. Jagvinder was obsessed with cleaning the car until it shone. No amount of pleas to rest a while dissuaded him.

"Why don't you resume your studies and graduate?" Parimal asked Farzana out of the blue.

"Are you joking? I've only finished the second year of college. Too much time has passed. I don't think I can start again. And now, working at the restaurant all day, I don't have time," Farzana said.

Despite her apparent negativity, when Parimal made the suggestion, Farzana almost felt that she could hear her *Abbajan.* He would have been the only one to goad her into completing her studies.

"Well, the university has long-distance programs. It all depends on whether you wish to," Parimal said, looking at her seriously.

"I can't," Farzana said matter-of-factly.

"You can. You comprehend well, and I've noticed you're a fast learner," Parimal insisted.

Farzana kept quiet. She was thinking. It sounded almost like flattery, but coming from Parimal, it could not be. She looked at Nootan. Surprisingly, Nootan was expressionless. The fair, rational Nootan sat there, deadpan.

"What do you think?" Parimal asked Nootan

"About what?"

"Farzana studying," Parimal said.

"If she wishes to, then she can," Nootan said and got up.

Nootan was not at all happy with the interest Parimal was showing in Farzana. She didn't understand why he goaded her to complete her education. Did he see a spark in Farzana that she, Nootan, didn't possess? She was jealous. It was true that she loved Farzana the most, but she'd seen Faiz look at Farzana longingly, and their relationship was growing. She couldn't bear to see Parimal's interest in her friend, but she was too polite to say so. Expressing her feelings to Parimal would be pointless, since he wouldn't understand. On the contrary, he'd accuse her of being petty.

Farzana was just as confused. She respected Parimal and his views. It especially pleased her when he said that she was a fast learner. She wanted to read poetry and understand metaphors. Yet, she was intimidated by the University of Mumbai, its tall, Gothic structure standing formally upright. She could see it from almost anywhere. She tossed and turned the matter in her head and decided to take counsel in Anusuya's daughter, Sarangi. After all, Sarangi was an expert in matters of education. She did not consult Nootan.

Sarangi unhesitatingly told her to go ahead and fill out an admission form at the university. Sarangi debunked her apprehensions about her age and very rightly said that one could study at any age. And so, in her thirty-third year, Farzana decided to graduate, much to the elation of everyone, including Nootan, who chided herself for being so trivial.

Somewhere in the city, a yellow and black auto rickshaw had a sticker on its black Rexene back that read *Educate a woman; progress is assured.*

*

The four women's quality of life had vastly improved. Anusuya and Nootan had moved into bigger apartments near each other, but Anusuya retained her one-room tenement for sentimental reasons. Shakuntala moved to a better place just a furlong away from the other two, while Farzana still lived with her aunt.

"Why buy a house? A rich man will marry you, and you'll live in Malabar Hill," Sarangi teased Farzana.

No such dreams for Shakuntala. Driven purely by her desire

to make money and succeed, she was blinded to everything else. She only saw the strength of the team and thought about how she could harness their energy. She was determined to make Stree strong, like the human pyramid she had created for *Janmashtami*.

The *Bombay Times,* a popular tabloid, rated the egg *bhurji* at Stree among the best in their annual food review's takeaway category.

As time passed, and Faiz had devoured hundreds of plates of egg *bhurji,* he became acutely aware of the attraction he felt towards Farzana. Every day, it was the same pattern. He ordered his egg *bhurji* and ate it in silence.

He caught Farzana's eye when she passed him a side dish of onions. At first, she merely looked away; later, she looked at him pointedly. Yet, he knew no way of starting a conversation with her. Of late, he'd seen her poring intently over a college prospectus. If only he could muster enough courage…

Still, he waited.

27
The Furtive Kiss

The furtive kiss had its own charm. The brushing of lips hurriedly behind a bus stop or near a water cooler at a railway station or behind a deserted office in a high-rise building sent tingles down the spine. Sarangi experienced the sensation too. When she didn't have to attend college classes, she came to Stree a little late in the morning and helped Nootan with the accounts or simply pottered around. She liked being around and helping, but mostly she enjoyed watching the people who came to eat. Anusuya noticed her watching young girls her age eating their egg *bhurji* with manicured fingers, and she said to herself, "That poor girl never had it easy." Little did she know, the dreamy look on Sarangi's face was for entirely different reasons.

For Sarangi, the days never seemed to end. Summer saw a stubborn and winters saw a lazy sun. After she finished at Stree, Sarangi went to the Oval to watch Joachim play soccer. Of course, Sarangi didn't tell her mother the truth. She lied, saying she was going to meet Elvira, which Anusuya did not discourage — she was thankful to Elvira and her mother for bailing them out a couple of times. Even though her maternal instincts warned her that there was something undesirable about Joachim, she gave Sarangi a free hand, in gratitude for all the work she'd been doing.

Sarangi walked from Nariman Point to the Oval, a good ten-minutes away, but she didn't mind the distance, because she was meeting Joachim, who was all clammy and laden with dust after playing. The sight of Sarangi brought new vigor, and he kicked the ball with greater energy. Still, it was short of the goal. He'd always been an average player, but being ignored made him lose his zest for the game.

Joachim had already proclaimed loudly to everyone on his team that Sarangi was his "girly," and he would marry her. He was besotted, and his face flushed whenever he thought of or saw her. Like the young always did, he made grandiose plans for a future with her. He was a little skeptical about two aspects, though: her mother, who he thought would dislike him, and the fact that they followed different religions.

"I can convince her mother, and religion… Well, if necessary, I can become a Hindu. Most importantly, I need a job. Hindus will never respect a career in hospitality management or music. Doctors and engineers…" He looked at the ball forlornly. "Maybe I should joint TNT Express as a courier boy. They pay well and, who knows, they might send me abroad to Australia," Joachim thought hopefully.

Joachim's obsession with Australia started when many of his friends migrated there and sent him glowing reports of the beer and food Down Under. And so his thoughts raced while he ran all over the ground, chasing the ball.

Joachim finished his practice, wiped his face hastily, ran his fingers through his curly black hair, and strode indifferently to meet Sarangi, who'd been waiting for a long time. Joachim would have been happy if life just went on as it was. Practice, meet Sarangi, talk about Pele and soccer, and return home. His mother and Elvira provided for his daily needs, and he didn't have to worry about the nitty-gritties of life.

Elvira applied to various foreign airlines for a position as an air hostess. She was rejected on various grounds, like inadequate height, or for being a little flabby. So, she planned to join a gym to tone her body. She needed money for the gym membership and her cosmetics. Unlike her brother, she hated asking her mother for money. She, being more realistic, found a summer job at a call center where they trained her to speak like a Yankee. She attended to irate customers as far away as Texas without them realizing that she was Elvira Pinto from India. She spoke like a Yank even at home. The drawl irritated Sarangi to no end.

"But I have to speak like this," Elvira insisted when Sarangi protested.

Sarangi and Joachim walked towards their usual haunt, the Iranian tea shop, Kayani. Elvira was busy at work.

"I am sosos00000 bored with Kayani," Joachim whined.

Sarangi remained silent. Just walking with Joachim was good enough for her. It didn't matter where they went.

"Some other place?"

"Where?" Sarangi asked.

Joachim led Sarangi to another Iranian restaurant, New Era, which stood bang opposite the New Excelsior Theatre. In the past, people went there for a cup of tea or coffee before they went to watch a movie. But all of that had changed. A couple of hurried office-goers, a few college students, and sometimes hookers came for a cup of tea or an omelet. When it got dark, the hookers, garishly dressed to attract clients, walked the street outside. It was not a strange sight to see a balding, potbellied accountant haggling with a hooker or exchanging a few dirty words for instant titillation. New Era's most popular clients, though, were courting couples.

The reason Joachim preferred New Era was because the mezzanine floor had a board announcing *Family Only.* It was actually for couples who went upstairs, smooched, necked, and petted. The waiters didn't rush them out, unlike the other places and, most importantly, they didn't pronounce judgments with their glances. The waiters were an older lot and were so desensitized by what they saw come in and out that they always had poker-faced expressions. Joachim knew of the place through Sheldon, a friend who had taken his girlfriend, Daphne, to New Era many a time.

"No… Not here," Sarangi said, knowing the reputation of the place. She was sure of Joachim's intent.

"But you love me, no?" Joachim asked.

Sarangi nodded.

They walked up the stairs. To their dismay, only one table was left. The entire place was occupied by office-goers who had come in with their companions. Sarangi was aghast to see a man unbutton his companion's blouse and dip his hands inside, oblivious to all who were looking. Sarangi sat down with trepidation.

"I'm not comfortable. Let's get out," she pleaded.

"But I'm here with you," Joachim said as he moved from his place and sat next to her.

He held her hand. They ordered a cup of tea. Joachim took Sarangi's chin in his hand and turned her face towards him. He brought his face forward and was about to kiss her on the lips when the waiter thumped the cup of tea on the table with all his might.

"Stupid man!" Joachim thought.

Sarangi felt like everyone was staring at them. She became very self-conscious. Then, suddenly, Joachim pulled her closer and kissed her on the lips. Sarangi felt Joachim's force, and her body surprised her. The feeling was heady, as if someone had banged her head with a ton of bricks. Sarangi was tongue-tied. They went home in silence, holding hands.

"If only it would stay like this forever," Sarangi thought wistfully.

*

Faiz had none of Joachim's youthful enthusiasm. His youth was spent in such bitterness that there was no time for him to learn about love, let alone express it. And there was no one to counsel him. He contemplated asking Farzana out, but he was afraid of rejection. Days passed in indecision, and if love could be sensed in the words *Onions, please,* then there alone it was.

However, one afternoon, Farzana had a pleasant surprise. After lunch, Faiz diffidently handed her something wrapped in newspaper. He waited for a long time till everyone else was busy with chores and then gave her the packet. Farzana was delighted.

"What is it? And what for?" she asked, excitedly tearing the package open. It was a book of couplets by Faiz Ahmed Faiz.

"I enjoyed reading it," Faiz said.

Farzana was touched.

"Nobody has ever given me anything," she said plaintively.

"If only I could hold your hand," Faiz thought. But he could not come around to telling her of his affection for her. He preferred that she sense and acknowledge it herself.

Farzana devoured the book and memorized some of the couplets. Very soon, Faiz and Farzana could be seen over lunch, talking animatedly and holding long discussions about everything except what Faiz felt for her, of course. It hung in the air heavily, almost suffocating him at times.

Faiz walked her to the railway station every evening. The others sensed that something was going on between them and left Farzana alone. The two walked past the magnificent buildings of the high court and the university. Sometimes, they were so engrossed in their conversation that they walked right up to the traffic on Colaba Causeway and still did not want to stop, but the Arabian Sea was the limit.

With Faiz, Farzana was rooted to the ground. He spoke of his life, his law practice, his parents, his sisters, and his future. He spoke of real problems and workable solutions and, most importantly, he had no illusions. Faiz wished to fight the system by staying inside it. His views on the communal problems were practical, and he was wise to admit that, at the moment, an answer to the problem of religious extremism eluded him.

On the other hand, Parimal, Nootan's friend, made Farzana want to undo her hair and ride on the crest of the wave he created. It was a euphoric feeling. Parimal whisked Farzana away to a place where she could see no fences.

Nootan was the happiest to see the relationship developing between Faiz and Farzana. She encouraged Farzana to spend more time with Faiz.

"If she settles down with Faiz, life will be easier on her. Faiz will take care of her," Nootan thought. Also, she hoped it would mean that Farzana would get over her childish admiration of Parimal.

Nootan liked Faiz and was comfortable with him. He was rational and pragmatic. There was no trace of servility in him, but he had no grandiose dreams like Parimal. He was an ordinary man who lived a real life.

Peculiarly, Farzana had shown the college catalogue to Parimal and not to Faiz, and Parimal had helped her select a course of study. He'd suggested a bachelor of arts course with a language as a major. Farzana hadn't questioned his judgment; she'd calmly accepted his advice. Sarangi and Farzana had gone to the university and paid the fees. In the column for *Guardian,* Farzana had written "Parimal Mehta."

It was a good thing that Nootan didn't know of it, but Farzana had an explanation. Nootan's friend Parimal was the most learned man she knew, and she believed he was the one best suited to be her guardian.

Faiz was proud when Farzana informed him of her decision to graduate. He lauded her for it. On one of their walks, Faiz was unusually quiet. Normally, he was the one who chatted, and Farzana quietly listened, nodding her head. Faiz's head was spinning. He had to confess his feelings. At times, he feared that maybe Farzana wasn't the right woman for him, since she didn't feel the pain he experienced. Other times, he could think of no other. And so finally, that day, Faiz proposed marriage right outside the University of Mumbai. The question just came out like marbles tumbling from a bag.

They had, as usual, proceeded on their walk. There was a slight wind in the air. A yellow flower from a large *sonmohar* tree sailed down and fell on the *dupatta* that covered Farzana's head. With a delicate flick of the wrist, she brushed the flower down, and that was the moment in which he asked.

"Will you marry me?" Faiz looked at her intently.

A *vada pao* vendor gently slipped the large fritters into the oil. They slid gracefully along the walls of the wok and bobbed in the liquid. The bell of the sugarcane juice machine jingled loudly, and a newspaper boy screamed *Mid-Day* even more loudly.

Faiz himself was surprised. He'd never acted in haste, but he couldn't contain himself anymore. He wished to spend his entire life with Farzana and have children with her. He also wished to have a huge house, like the one he had in Lucknow, with vast courtyards. Farzana did not accept or decline. She continued walking, but he could see that she was flustered.

The wind blew a little, and the evening was pleasant. In a little while, the streets would be filled with people.

Faiz was very sure that her answer was not *no*. The color had rushed into Farzana's cheeks, and very soon the same color would tinge the Mumbai skies.

*

"Faiz proposed. What do I do?" Farzana asked the other women nervously.

"I think you should accept. He's a sensible man. I quite like him. That is, only if you're comfortable with the idea," Nootan advised sensibly.

"You hardly know him," said Anusuya. "You've barely gotten

out of the clutches of one husband, and now you want to trust another?"

"God! You women will never learn. If we hadn't mustered the guts to start this business, these men would have raped us like dogs," Shakuntala ranted.

Nootan observed the hatred that Anusuya and Shakuntala felt for men, and she thought it was unhealthy. Shakuntala, in particular, launched a diatribe against men at any opportunity. Anusuya and Shakuntala had been disappointed by their husbands and extended the opinions they had of their husbands to all men. They kept away from men completely and preferred the company of women.

Nootan also noticed that Anusuya had started spending most of her time with Shakuntala. They were always giggling and whispering and, to Nootan, they looked like schoolgirls or lovers, she couldn't tell which. Anusuya seemed to worship Shakuntala, and she was extremely grateful to her for rousing her from her inertia. Shakuntala made Anusuya feel secure and often came to her rescue when there was a disagreement. Evidently, Anusuya did not miss her still-missing husband at all.

Much to Nootan's consternation, Farzana decided to seek Parimal's counsel regarding Faiz's proposal. But she did not object. Shakuntala, an astute observer, noticed Nootan's discomfiture whenever Farzana accompanied her to the market, and she saw the look that crossed her face whenever Farzana mentioned Parimal. Shakuntala hoped and wished that the man would not become a cause of contention between Farzana and Nootan. But she stayed out of it. After all, they had promised each other: *No caste, no creed, no religion will come between us.* They had forgotten to add *no men.*

*

About two hundred kilometers away from Farzana and Nootan's

home town, a skirmish took place. A mosque was desecrated. It was never established who was responsible for the act. The Muslims thought that the Hindus were guilty, and the HUP, in turn, neither denied nor accepted the blame for the crime.

"If they want to react, we're ready," said Bhavan Singh, one of the prominent members of the HUP.

The Muslims did react. They led a *morcha,* or procession, asking the local politician to intercede and help. The Hindus, in an unprecedented move, attacked several Muslims in the *morcha.* There was a free-for-all. Each wanted to kill the *other.*

The riots spread, and two villages were affected. Khairunnisa, a young pregnant woman, was chased by the mob. She'd already seen her father murdered and her mother and sister raped till they were dead. Khairunnisa managed to run, in a bid to save her life and the life of her unborn child. Into the night, the mob, with their torches and their cries of "*Mian ko maar dalo,*" "Kill the Muslim," and "*Bintok Pakistan vapas jao,*" "The circumcised go back to Pakistan," pursued Khairunnisa, who couldn't manage another step and fell under their feet. Mercifully, she died instantly.

The mob was not sated for, like a pack of wolves, it had not yet tasted blood. A twenty-three year old man cut open Khairunnisa's womb with a sword, lifted the dead fetus on the tip, and cried, "*Jai Bhawani!*" "Hail, Goddess!"

Shabana, a middle-aged woman belonging to the same village as Khairunnisa, filed a first incident report with the police, since she had seen the mob chase the girl. She managed to get an old man, Trilok Patel, to agree to testify that he'd seen Kishore Shah with the fetus.

Kishore Shah was Nootan's younger brother. The stage was being set for the ultimate act against the Muslims of the country.

Yet, Mumbai remained insulated.

28

Two Relationships

After work one evening, Nootan was bored, so she went to Shakuntala's home. The door was ajar. Shakuntala was not in the habit of closing it. She lived with the supreme faith that nobody would mess with her. Anybody could walk in and out. Nootan pushed the door open with her hand. The television was switched on, but she could see no one around.

"Maybe she's gone out somewhere," Nootan thought.

Nootan walked into the bedroom. There was absolutely no natural light in the bedroom, because a building right in front hogged the sun. Nootan saw Anusuya inside, reclining with her head on a man's lap. Seeing Anusuya there did not surprise Nootan, since all of the women who worked at Stree had unrestricted access to Shakuntala's home. Nootan could not recognize the man with Anusuya, but there was something vaguely familiar about his profile, which was all she could see. The man was caressing Anusuya's hair and staring out of the window. The orange sun brushed every object with a burnt earth color.

"Surprising that Anusuya never mentioned this man to me. And why are they here, in Shakuntala's home?" Nootan thought contritely. She was hurt. After all, they were neighbors and had been confidants till not long in the past.

Nootan turned to walk away, but she felt the compulsive need to look back at the man. She'd seen him somewhere. Instead of leaving, she turned towards them, shamelessly peering through the darkness. On closer inspection, she recognized the man was Shakuntala.

Anusuya looked up instinctively, met Nootan's eyes, and recoiled as if caught doing something wrong. The darkness made it impossible for Nootan to see Shakuntala's expression. The orange light danced in the room, making grotesque shadows. She couldn't decipher what was going on, but something told her that what she'd seen was a travesty. What business did Anusuya have in Shakuntala's lap? Was it a game? Shakuntala pretending to be a man? Nootan sensed the passion in the air and a humid, animal smell. She walked away without saying anything.

"We've never interfered in each other's lifestyle. I must keep a free outlook," Nootan thought, shaking off the need to be judgmental. But she was taken aback and shook her head several times. She thought she'd vomit when she replayed the scene in her head as she walked back home. Was it possible? Between two women? Nootan was all muddled when she went to bed that night.

Shakuntala couldn't say when the change had come over her. She was married once, and she often tried to recall what had gone wrong. Did her husband leave with another woman because he sensed something in her response, or lack of response, to him? Shakuntala being Shakuntala, she gave in to her impulses, because that was the way she operated — purely on instinct. She behaved like a man, wore clothes like men, and used the look to scare off others. She was also a little surprised by the way her body behaved when she saw women and by the intense hatred she felt for men. She tried to ignore it at first. Later on, it became difficult. She realized how awkward it was for a woman to confess her love to another woman. At night, she wailed like a baby, and in the mornings, only Anusuya saw her red eyes and sympathized.

Anusuya's dependence on her made her feel good. The whiny nature that she'd found irritating once had become endearing to her. She felt the need to shield Anusuya — a feeling that changed to warmth and grew into physical love. When she touched her, Anusuya offered no reproach. On the contrary, she quietly reciprocated, encouraging Shakuntala.

Anusuya ached for an intimate relationship, and she was confused by what she felt for Shakuntala. Her experience with Sakharam, her husband, had been disappointing and shattering. Shakuntala was kind to her, not harsh like Sakharam. The paramount point in Shakuntala's favor, though, was the gratitude Anusuya felt towards her for changing her life. Anusuya needed a protective figure to guide her through the maze of life. It did not necessarily need to be a husband. After Sakharam's disappearance, Sarangi donned the role. With Sarangi busy studying, the burden had shifted to Shakuntala.

They had a special look for each other while they were working at the stall. In the evening, they often visited each other's homes. At first, they felt happy just holding hands when they were alone. One evening, Shakuntala kissed Anusuya. Anusuya readily gave in, and that was the beginning.

"What will Sarangi think?" Anusuya wondered.

"She won't find out," Shakuntala assured her.

However, the fear of being caught by her daughter troubled her. "Do you think Nootan will say anything?"

"No. She's the most sensitive," Shakuntala said.

Anusuya smiled, thinking how true it was. Nootan was indeed the most sensitive of them all.

Shakuntala suspected Farzana already knew of their relationship, but she couldn't be sure. "Why would Farzana leave the room quietly when we're together?" Shakuntala thought. She remembered Farzana telling them how her mother thrashed her when she caught her reading Ismat Chughtai's "The Quilt."

The next day, Nootan called Parimal on the phone and with great difficulty managed to tell him what she'd seen.

Parimal said nothing. "It's their life," he thought.

Nootan couldn't get around to telling Farzana. Parimal's nonjudgmental silence made Nootan realize that such matters were personal and should be left alone.

At Stree, there was no mention of the incident, and the women got to work just like every other day. Anusuya glanced at Nootan with guilt, and sometimes her eyes pleaded with her, whereas Shakuntala wore a defiant look. Whenever Sarangi chatted with Nootan, Anusuya's heart almost missed a beat.

"You don't have to worry. Sarangi won't know anything," Nootan said to her later.

But Farzana's shrewd eyes observed that when Anusuya accidentally touched Nootan, Nootan shrank from her as if she'd been scalded. Farzana saw that the other women were on edge. "They're hiding something," she thought.

They were high-strung, like the country. Shakuntala was always belligerent, Anusuya her old weepy self. And Nootan moved about like a high priestess. Whenever Farzana was around, they pretended to be like their old selves. The thought that their tension was because she was a Muslim crossed her mind occasionally. Had the propaganda changed them? She chided herself for thinking so, but at times, the thought walked softly back into her mind.

The state of her studies was bothering Farzana. She wanted to pursue the college course and fulfill *Abbajan's* dream for her, but it wasn't as easy as it had seemed. She knew she could speak with Faiz if she had any problem, but she chose not to. She had a preconceived notion that Parimal was wiser in matters of academia, and she also wished to speak to him of Faiz's marriage proposal.

Farzana called Parimal one day, and they decided to meet on a Sunday evening. The plan was to discuss the effect marriage would have on her studies. After all, she'd made a mistake once.

Of course, she mentioned the meeting to Nootan.

To Nootan's surprise, she was not invited to join them. Parimal did not even tell her about the meeting. But then, he would have brushed off the whole thing by saying, "Look, I don't tell you about everything that goes on in my life."

Nootan very thoughtfully sent Jagvinder along with Farzana. "It's not safe for you to travel alone in taxis. Who knows? That mad Javed might still be stalking you," Nootan explained.

"Parimal can't do anything wrong if Jagvinder's there," Nootan thought and was immediately ashamed.

Farzana and Parimal met at the David Sassoon Library, where Parimal was a member. They sat on a bench that overlooked the Jehangir Art Gallery of Rampart Row. Farzana's *purdah* blew in the wind. It was a pleasant May evening. The old buildings on Rampart Row looked grand in the evening sun. Young artists lazed around on the steps of Jehangir.

Farzana listened to Parimal speak about Kafka, Hitler, Bertolt Brecht, Chopin, the singer Begum Akhtar, the filmmakers Akiro Kurosawa and Satyajit Ray, and on and on. Farzana didn't understand everything, but the enormity of the world and his knowledge of it stunned her. She sat unashamed and just soaked it in. They never spoke of Faiz.

The birds twittered, and suddenly it was dark. Night fell and caressed her. It appeared as if the harshness of the night succumbed to her softness. The gibbous moon looked down, and its light explored her face. Jagvinder Singh waited, cleaning the windscreen of the car and gazing upwards.

Farzana had serenity around her and a beauty enhanced by her inner tranquility. She felt like a woman.

Later, Nootan, like a jealous wife, asked Jagvinder for a blow-by-blow account of what happened between Farzana and Parimal. He shook his head, and Nootan didn't have the courage to ask him whether he was ignorant or something untoward had occurred. She could never get around to asking Farzana or Parimal for fear that her questions would make her look petty.

Nootan laughed in irony. Many years ago, she'd lived in mortal fear of Farzana finding out about the smudged henna on her hands.

*

Farzana always looked forward to her regular walk with Faiz, but those walks were very different from the time she spent with Parimal. Parimal was a heady, intoxicating brew, while Faiz was a comforting cup of tea.

Two days later, Faiz reminded Farzana of his proposal. He was painfully shy, but he hemmed and hawed and finally brought it up. Farzana seemed very quiet and even more beautiful. It was a pleasant afternoon. People hurried about doing their business, and Farzana walked quietly by his side.

"I guess her answer is no," Faiz thought dismally.

They walked to the Sassoon Docks, taking in the smells of the city. The sky was clear and there were the beginnings of a few clouds that would eventually take over the sky. Farzana still did not say anything — neither yes nor no. He walked her back to Stree in silence.

Later that evening, Farzana asked Jagvinder to take her again to the Sassoon Library. She wanted to vanish in Parimal's magic. But Parimal never joined her there again. She returned that night, disappointed. She didn't call Parimal to ask why; she construed his absence as a rebuff. She became more withdrawn, and Nootan watched her closely.

Faiz persisted and asked her once again for her hand.

"I don't know what to do," confessed Farzana.

"It's better that you accept Faiz's proposal. It will be good for you and all of us," Nootan said tearfully, sizing up her childhood friend's reaction.

Farzana nodded absently.

Nootan knew. She went to a corner and cried her heart out.

They'd come full circle.

Shakuntala saw her and placed a hand on her shoulder, but Nootan did not react.

"Do you think she'll leave us?" Shakuntala asked.

"No," Nootan replied confidently.

Farzana accepted Faiz's proposal the next day in front of the high court. Faiz felt that the location was a good sign. They were married in the court without any fanfare. The official witnesses were Nootan and Shakuntala. Anusuya looked on and, for some strange reason, started crying. Parimal was conspicuously absent. Nootan phoned him a hundred times but he didn't answer.

"Humph! Men!" Shakuntala said contemptuously.

Sarangi was also present for the wedding. She made up her mind that it was the way Joachim and she would get married. No one would be offended. Her mother would not be disappointed and neither would Joachim's mother.

"But I've always wanted to wear a white bridal gown," thought Sarangi, imagining herself in one of the elaborate dresses she'd seen on display at Castellino's in Crawford Market.

Farzana went home with Faiz, to his apartment in Andheri. He had insisted that she remain economically independent and that she continue with her work at Stree. In any case, Farzana had no plans to give up her work.

On their wedding night, Farzana gave herself to Faiz readily, and he took her with love. However, Faiz felt aloofness in her, as if she held back something. There was a gibbous moon that night.

"Give her some time," Faiz thought.

Nootan, realizing why Parimal hadn't come to the court for Farzana's wedding, met with him a day later. Surprisingly unlike himself, he held her tightly. He caressed her hair, and slowly she gave in. He hailed a cab and took her home. That night, Nootan slept for the first time untroubled by bad dreams.

Farzana attended to work as usual while Faiz continued his

practice as a lawyer. He'd become widely known for taking on cases for people who could not afford legal advice. He represented a young student, Riyaz Shaikh, who had gone with a few friends to Gujarat on a tour. Unfortunately, there was a bomb blast in a railway station, and the phone records of one of the suspects showed that he'd spoken to Riyaz two hours before the blast. The police picked Riyaz up and questioned him until he was reduced to a wreck. The media labeled him a young terrorist. All the while, he maintained he was innocent. One of Riyaz's distant relatives knew Faiz and asked him to take the case. Faiz studied the case intently. On speaking with Riyaz, he learned that the bombing suspect was Riyaz's cousin and their phone conversation had been a casual one. Faiz took up the case in memory of Aftab, his older brother. He sought vindication.

A TV news channel covered the case, and some groups branded him as being on the *other side,* which hurt him to no end. The thrill he got when he saw the tricolor fly could not be explained to anyone.

"Truth and terror have no religion," he said to all.

*

The big event — the twelfth class examinations — was a week away. As usual, Sarangi came down with a fever, and Elvira couldn't be bothered. She'd given up on her dreams of becoming an air hostess. The rigors of staying slim were too much, and call centers paid equally well.

"Who wants to live in terror of being hijacked?" Elvira thought, her old fear of being kidnapped resurfacing as a consolation.

She decided to continue working at the call center and make it her career.

"Our English is good," she told Sarangi as her reason.

"If she'd known of this call center business earlier, then the poor thing wouldn't have had to live with steel wires in her mouth for a year," Sarangi thought.

Elvira, it was expected, would join the bachelor of arts program at St. Xavier's College, while Sarangi would be admitted to the medical school if she scored good marks.

"I'll pray for you, Elvira" said Sarangi, a lump coming to her throat.

She was fond of Elvira, who never grumbled when Sarangi was too busy studying to meet her. Elvira had the same warmth towards Sarangi.

Surprisingly, Anusuya was less tense, knowing there was an option for Sarangi.

"If Sarangi doesn't make it into medical school, she can join Stree," Anusuya thought.

"If I don't score good marks, then I'm ruined," Sarangi told Joachim.

Sarangi was a witness to the growth of Stree, and she was proud of her mother; however, she wanted to become a doctor and had no intentions of joining Stree. Realizing her ambition was a way to escape from her life.

In the past, Anusuya had often said, "My daughter will become a doctor or engineer and save me." The statement stuck. It didn't matter that Anusuya already had been saved.

Joachim didn't understand Sarangi's fervor or her obsession to get good scores. He'd never worked hard for marks. Nor did he comprehend how she would be ruined if she didn't score well. All he wanted was an opportunity to kiss her, but there was always somebody hovering around. Anusuya was like a tigress when it came to Sarangi. She gave those Siberian looks to Joachim, who responded with watery smiles, infuriating her even further. Joachim decided that he hated his future mother–in-law.

*

Sarangi appeared for her exams confidently.

It was June, and Mumbai had experienced the first showers of rain, as usual proving the India Meteorological Department wrong. Trains were late and certain areas were waterlogged. The bright side was that the roads were clean, the BEST buses looked redder, and the trees were green.

The results of Sarangi's exams were available on a website. But Sarangi preferred to go to the college and see them on the notice board. She was pale and suffered from irritable bowel syndrome, fully convinced that she had failed. To add to her misery, Shakuntala, Farzana, Faiz, Nootan, and Parimal came over to her house. It seemed to her like a wake after a funeral.

"It doesn't matter if you don't score high marks," Anusuya consoled, knowing that young students unable to handle the pressure were taking their own lives.

"Of course, if you wish to study at IIT, you should score ninety-nine percent in pre-college mathematics," Parimal said.

"Even if you fail, you can appear again," Faiz said, invoking a sharp nudge on his side from Farzana. The remark sent Sarangi back to the loo.

She went with Elvira to see the results. Sarangi didn't have the courage to look at the notice board herself.

"You go and see." Sarangi gave Elvira her roll number.

She saw Elvira merge with all the others. For an instant, Sarangi was brain dead. She leaned against the bumper of a car and stood still. Some of the students were calling their parents to inform them of their marks. Sarangi closed her eyes. When she opened her eyes, she saw Elvira walking towards her with a deadpan expression.

"I'm doomed," Sarangi thought.

29

A Death

One day, Nootan invited Parimal to visit Stree and have lunch with her. Parimal accepted wholeheartedly. Contrary to what Nootan expected, he appeared to have no qualms about meeting Farzana. He was happy to see the crowd thronging.

"I've never had such excellent food," he said, eating the *poha*.

Nootan blushed.

"Why don't you marry him?" Anusuya suggested after he left.

"I'm comfortable like this. I don't need a man to constantly be in my life."

Anusuya nodded.

"Parimal is there as my support system. I don't want to mess with that," Nootan said sensibly.

"Not very long ago, Nootan wished a man would stay in her life forever. And now..." Anusuya thought.

To Shakuntala, who said nothing, Parimal was a harmless, ineffectual man who wished good but was incapable of any action.

*

After a month of marriage, Farzana missed a period. At first, she ignored it, assuming the delay was due to emotional stress or her old injury. But later, she began feeling sick and nauseous.

The other three knew immediately that she was pregnant. Nootan was the happiest. They were pleased because they knew that Farzana had longed for a child. When she was married to

Javed, he had almost convinced her she was sterile.

Faiz was overjoyed, and his mother sent Farzana a talisman to wear. It was a sliver cylinder, like a bullet, and it contained verses from the *Quran.*

*

Nootan's daughter, Pooja, at nine, was not showing any progress. Nootan left her in the care of the same woman who had been looking after Pooja for many years. The *ayah* was becoming exhausted. It was tough at her age to keep up with Pooja, who was nearly the same size as the old woman. She continued looking after the child only because of the affection she felt for Nootan.

Once Nootan had enough money, she showed her daughter to most of the good doctors in Mumbai. Parimal surfed the Internet, spoke with many people, and explored various methods of developmental rehabilitation to no avail. All the doctors said there was nothing they could do. Pooja was simply a case of a brilliant mind trapped in a disobedient body.

Pooja seemed the happiest when she saw Shakuntala and always shouted with excitement when she was around. Shakuntala found spending time with Pooja relaxing. She would throw her up in the air or play handball with her or tell her about games like *kabaddi*. Pooja developed a fascination for Shakuntala, who let her take part in the difficult games. Shakuntala, unlike the others, never treated her as an invalid; her serene side was awakened by the little girl. At times, she would not even hold the child's hand when they walked the streets, not because she was uncaring, but because she felt it was the best way to bring out self-reliance. The little taste of independence that Pooja got brought her closer to Shakuntala.

Pooja had attained puberty, and the times of her menstrual cycle were the worst for Nootan and the *ayah*.

"Why don't you consider a hysterectomy for Pooja? I remember reading about it. If you wish, I can inquire," Parimal said in his clinical, scientific manner.

Nootan didn't reply. She looked at him like a well-heeled person looked at a man with open sores. She wondered about Parimal's true character and questioned her attraction to him.

"How could he even make such a suggestion?" she thought.

Parimal hadn't meant the comment to sound cut-and-dried, but he knew his tone had upset and hurt Nootan. He meant well and empathized with her. He had never apologized to anyone. However, he was sure that he didn't want to lose her.

"I'm sorry," he said, and Nootan could see that he meant it. Parimal wasn't the sort who apologized on a whim.

They patched things up, and Parimal was glad that Nootan understood there was nothing malicious about his statements. He was simply objective and realistic.

One day, the *ayah* went out to the pharmacy to have a prescription refilled. She took longer than necessary, because she met someone who made small talk. Before leaving, she'd given Pooja a toffee to suck on.

"She won't scream and bring the roof down," the *ayah* thought.

When she returned, Pooja lay slumped on a chair. The *ayah* called for an ambulance that rushed the unconscious child to the hospital.

A police officer responded to take a first incident report from the *ayah,* and he called Nootan on the phone. Pooja had been declared dead on arrival. She had choked on the toffee.

Nootan was benumbed. Farzana and Faiz never left her side.

Parimal rushed to be with her, embraced her, and consoled her. She cried in his arms, and her nails dug his shoulders. He stayed with her, fed her, and ensured that she was looked after.

After a time, Nootan lost all her senses and could not even cry.

Shakuntala and Sarangi wept with grief. Sarangi remembered the times she played with Pooja and read her stories.

Parimal wanted to light the pyre, but Nootan asked Shakuntala to do it. According to Hindu custom, Pooja's body was to be consigned to a bed of logs and lit with a fire by a male member of the family. In Nootan's mind, Shakuntala was Pooja's surrogate father.

The day of Pooja's funeral was the only day the four women did not go to work; yet, Stree did business.

30

Joachim is Employed

When Sarangi, leaning against the car, opened her eyes, Elvira was in front of her. She suddenly thought Elvira's face resembled a pig's — those thick lips and beady eyes. Elvira thrust towards her a paper with something written on it. Sarangi glanced at the print and did a quick mathematical calculation. Her combined score for chemistry, physics, and biology was ninety-eight percent. That meant she could get into any of the premier medical schools in the city. She couldn't contain her happiness. She ran all the way to Stree with the chit of paper in her hand and hugged Farzana, the first person she saw.

"Ninety-eight percent!" Sarangi screamed.

Amid the noisy cheers and yelps of happiness, Shakuntala lifted Sarangi and screamed, "*Jai,* Sarangi!"

"My daughter's going to be a doctor. I can't believe it!" Anusuya said, crying softly.

Sarangi soon left to collect the admission forms for the Grant Medical College at Sir J.J. Hospital.

That day, Stree gave away one *rawa ladoo* to all of its patrons, among whom was a group of well-dressed women smelling of Kenzo, who'd forgotten their diet and were slumming it. Anusuya offered them *rawa ladoos.*

"My daughter has been admitted to a medical college."

"Must belong to some reserved category," Anusuya heard one of them say.

"General category! She's plain intelligent," Anusuya sneered.

The *rawa ladoos* crumbled in some of the hands.

Sarangi was admitted to the Grant Medical College, where, after four years of rigorous studying, she would receive her degree.

Joachim was not exactly happy when Sarangi informed him of the news. He tried to frighten her by suggesting that all doctors died of AIDS. Sarangi was not shaken. Joachim couldn't understand what it was to realize a dream.

Everything changed when she stepped onto the grounds of the medical college. The belief that nothing would ever change was typical of young people untouched by disillusion. That love would erase discrimination and iron out creases of trouble was what Sarangi had believed. She did not wish to see the distance between her and Joachim or realize that she was on the threshold of a new life. Her values were such that she was conditioned to love one man, come what may. But time would change all that.

Every day, Joachim very patiently waited at the gates of the Grant Medical College. At first, Sarangi was glad to see him and rushed to tell him of the day's events. Once, a few of her classmates asked Sarangi who he was. Joachim was within earshot, and he expected her to say *my boyfriend.*

"My friend's brother," Sarangi replied.

Joachim brought the roof down. He accused her of refusing to acknowledge their relationship. Sarangi had no explanation. She definitely wasn't too shy to admit that she was dating. But most of the young women who were her classmates were dating young men who were studying to become doctors.

Joachim threatened to leave her, but he could see the cold look in her eye, and he didn't pursue the strategy. Sarangi felt a little guilty about her shoddy behavior. She called and asked him to meet her for coffee at the college cafeteria.

"Why that stupid cafeteria?" Joachim raved.

"Because there are no coffeehouses in that area," Sarangi replied sensibly.

Joachim finally gave in and dressed in his best Sunday church clothes, styled his hair à la Elvis Presley, and soaked himself in cologne. He was a little early, so he waited at the Byculla bus stop and reached the cafeteria well after the agreed-upon time. Sarangi waited patiently for him. Joachim was pleased that she'd invited him there, since all her friends could see him.

Nobody noticed him.

"Why don't you invite your friends to join us?" he suggested.

"They're in the library," Sarangi replied without any interest, ordering two cups of tea.

He saw young men and women wearing white coats with stethoscopes dangling around their necks.

"When are we going to New Era?" Joachim asked.

Before she could reply, a group of fourth-year medical students came by and greeted Sarangi with a loud "Hi!" Sarangi got up and went to chat with them, leaving Joachim with two cups of tea that threatened to go cold. He was angry but controlled his rage.

"When are we going to New Era?" he persisted when she returned.

Sarangi began getting irritated. She couldn't fathom why Joachim was dressed like a dandy. She felt guilty going to that shady restaurant with him and even worse letting him kiss her.

"I have no time," she replied brusquely.

Joachim became sullen. He grumbled that he was going to make more money than her, and she'd end up dying of AIDS.

"I have to leave," she said and began to walk away.

"When are you meeting me next?" he whined

There was no reply.

"Please..."

"I'll call you," she said shortly.

Sarangi could no longer identify with Joachim. She found his appearance disgusting and his obsession with soccer childish. She had begun to see her future in a larger perspective. She was sensible or shrewd enough to realize that she couldn't jeopardize her future career for a silly crush. The dedication her chosen profession demanded would be inconceivable to Joachim, who had lots of time to spare. His lack of ambition reminded her of her father, who had been the cause of her mother's endless struggles. She didn't want to end up like her mother.

Soon, she began avoiding Joachim and outgrowing her infatuation with him. She hid behind the stone walls and slipped out through the college's numerous exits whenever she saw him.

Joachim was heartbroken. He pined for Sarangi at the gates of the college. He felt useless, and slowly it dawned on him that Sarangi was gone forever. There was no way he could woo her back. He thought about asking for his sister's help but changed his mind. Elvira had started bringing home a large paycheck, and it made his mother and sister brand him as a failure. If he confided that he was unsuccessful in love too, he'd be reduced to a laughingstock.

"Why would Sarangi want to be with me? What have I achieved? Nothing," he despaired.

The air in the soccer ball whooshed out.

Joachim played with the idea of finding a job or, rather, making a lot of money. The courier companies were not paying enough, just five or six thousand *rupees* to start. It wasn't enough for Joachim.

"Even Elvira earns more," he thought.

He spread the word around among his soccer teammates that he was looking for a job. Frustration was setting in, and a rage against the unknown was beginning to take over.

Joachim still loved Sarangi and wanted to win her back.

"I'll earn money, buy a car, and wait outside that two-bit medical college and show her what I can do," he thought with a vengeance.

Joachim quit soccer practice when he finally saw it for what it really was. It was going nowhere. He often went to the Bandra

Bandstand and gazed at Mannat, the opulent bungalow of Shah Rukh Khan, the popular Hindi actor.

"After all, he came to Mumbai empty-handed," Joachim thought hopefully.

One day, Joachim received a call from his old pal Bandya.

"I heard you stopped your soccer practice," Bandya said.

"Yeah, I wasn't getting selected, and I need to make a living," Joachim said morosely.

"Girlfriend?"

"She's studying to become a doctor," Joachim said, not able to hide the desperation in his voice.

"If you're interested, I can get you a job." Bandya said.

"What do you mean 'if I'm interested'? Of course! Where can I meet you?"

"Meet me tomorrow at Kayani."

When they met the next day, the first thing Joachim noticed was that Bandya was standing against his new motorbike.

"He must be doing well," Joachim surmised.

Bandya was a member of Pakya's gang. He was a rung above the lowest. His work involved collecting mobs for political rallies, inciting riots, and stirring up unrest. For every rally he started, Bandya was paid a thousand *rupees.* But more than that the money, Bandya enjoyed the power. He could simply grab a *vada pao* from a food vendor, and there would be no protest.

He also had the responsibility of recruiting new gang members. Joachim seemed like a good target. Frustration and desperation, along with a need for money, were the ideal combination for the right candidate.

Joachim walked into Kayani with a lump in his throat. He remembered days with Sarangi when they visited Kayani and dreamed of their future.

"I wonder why I agreed to come here," he thought.

Bandya greeted Joachim with a nod.

"What's the work?" Joachim asked eagerly, without any preamble.

"Tomorrow, you'll have to join me at Lower Parel," Bandya said, referring to central Mumbai, where old textile mills had been transformed into thriving new businesses. Mumbai had once been referred to as Manchester of the East, known in particular for its cotton mills. Slowly trade unionism and the advent of synthetic textiles like polyester doomed the industry. All the old mill land had since been converted to malls.

"And do what?" Joachim asked.

Bandya gestured to a motorbike without saying anything.

"Is this for me?" Joachim asked, disbelieving.

Bandya nodded his head.

Joachim did not even ask what his job would be. He was in. The deal was that, in Lower Parel, Bandya was going to extort money from an industrialist. For the operation, he needed Joachim.

That evening, Joachim went looking for Sarangi at Stree but only met Anusuya.

"How are you?" she asked warmly, now confident that Sarangi was out of his reach.

"I'm fine," Joachim said, brandishing his new bike and hoping that Anusuya would see it and tell Sarangi.

Anusuya was past all that. All she saw was a young boy, a hungry young boy.

"Did you get a job?" she asked.

"Yes. They gave me this bike. Important job. I have to be always in touch with the bosses."

"I'm proud of you," Anusuya said with a smile.

Joachim's chest swelled with pride. "I'm going to give you more reasons to be proud of me," he thought.

How wrong he was going to be.

That evening, Anusuya mentioned to Sarangi that she'd seen

Joachim. Sarangi's heart sank. But when she heard that Joachim had found a job, she felt better.

Sarangi's world had changed almost overnight. She rued the day she'd started dating Joachim. She was on her way to becoming a doctor of medicine, and Joachim was still an aspiring Pele.

All her girlfriends in college dated older students or young men studying to get their degrees. When they teased her and asked about her boyfriend, she said she had none. Joachim's pipe dreams, his mediocre athletic skills, and his failure to grow up were now clear to her. She wondered why she hadn't seen it all earlier. At times, she felt that she should tell him to stop waiting for her outside the college gates, but she didn't.

"If I ignore him, maybe one day he'll give up," she thought.

As for Joachim, he never walked into the college looking for Sarangi. He waited outside, chewing his nails till he tasted blood.

After his meeting with Bandya, Joachim walked to Sarangi's college to give her the good news. He stood outside the gate, riding the bike up and down and racing the engine, hoping Sarangi would see him. Suddenly, he saw her walking out with a group of classmates, and a sense of inadequacy stopped him from calling out to her. Tears stung in his eyes.

Sarangi had seen him from the corner of her eye. She laughed a little louder and merged with the crowd.

Joachim made up his mind never to wait outside the gate for her again. One day, she'd come groveling to him. He went for his first job with Bandya, who treated him well, which made Joachim feel good. He understood the deal. He knew that they were playing a dangerous game. But the thousand *rupees,* the impressive motorbike, and the rush of young blood made him oblivious to the risks involved. Joachim officially became a member of Pakya's gang.

Ironically, it fell to Joachim to pick up Pakya's breakfast from Stree every morning. He didn't tell anyone about his job; he knew that it was a shame. In response to Farzana's questioning, he said that the food was for a senior colleague.

Joachim had once liked going to Stree, because Anusuya fed him information on Sarangi's life, but he began to find her chatter irritating. Joachim's new life was dangerous and exciting. Sarangi was a figment of his past — a forgotten past.

*

Farzana was five months pregnant when the proprietors of Stree finalized a deal for a new location at Cuffe Parade, an upscale neighborhood in the southern part of the city. It was a tiny shop at the World Trade Centre Mumbai. Unlike in the past, a real estate agent negotiated the entire deal for them.

Shakuntala and Anusuya would manage the Cuffe Parade branch, while Nootan and Farzana would remain at the flagship store. They dipped into their funds and found a ready investor in Parimal. An unexpected investor also appeared in the form of Kiran Sharma. Their rides in her rickety Fiat had started off the business at Stree. The women never forgot the favor. They often sent sweets to her house, and one day they learned that she had a heart condition that was incurable. Anusuya swung into action and arranged for a girl to stay with the retired professor, who still lived alone. She goaded Sarangi to visit her, but Sarangi never found the time.

Kiran Sharma heard from her bank manager that the women were looking for money to buy a new place and that they were approaching banks and financial institutions. The old professor had told the bank manager how she had carted the younger women to Stree in the early days. She could still clearly see, in her death-ridden eyes, four women huddled in the back of her car. She sent word through her maid to Anusuya that she wished to meet with her.

Anusuya rushed to Kiran Sharma's home in the evening after work. She was taken aback when she saw the old professor. Age and sickness had taken their toll on her. The elderly woman had collected her life's savings, and the relevant papers were in an envelope.

"Invest this in Stree," she said in a raspy voice.

Anusuya was stunned. The ill woman thrust the envelope into Anusuya's hand. They needed the money, but she didn't want the professor's life savings.

"Give me the returns as per the industry rates. The investment is not for free," the wizened old woman said with a shrewd look.

"But you don't have to..." Anusuya said.

"I believe," the old professor replied.

There was a silence that hung heavily in the air like a wet raincoat on a hook.

"I don't have much time. You can use the money wisely to empower women."

Both of them stared out the window vacantly. They were thinking about the trips in the old car, Sarangi going to college early, and the futility of it all.

When Anusuya narrated the events to the rest of the women, they were overwhelmed. The money solved the immediate cash crunch.

They employed an accountant to take care of Stree's finances and taxes. The chartered accountant was Betty D'Lima, a hard-working young woman and the sole breadwinner in her family. She prepared the financial report for each month, and copies were sent to Kiran Sharma and Parimal.

The new place at Cuffe Parade was also christened Stree. Its sign declared it to be a branch of the original. And, sure enough, there was success at the new location too.

Nootan took the lead in organizing a group of four women to make pickles and conserves from fruits and vegetables that were on the threshold of rot but still firm. Parimal had suggested the idea after observing post-harvest waste and considering ways to make good use of it. The bottled items were retailed at shops under the brand name Stree, with the label that Sarangi had designed years ago for Time Pass. Women identified with the brand and felt that it belonged to them. Rita D'Souza still printed their labels and had two orphans from a local parish help her deliver them.

*

Nootan had never mentioned to anyone other than Parimal what she'd seen between Shakuntala and Anusuya. She wasn't sure the relationship between them still existed. Perhaps she'd imagined it all. The four women surged ahead, comfortable with their lives and focused on their pursuits. They hadn't bargained for so much, but their hard work had paid off.

"What if something happens to us?" Anusuya's perennial fear at times resurfaced.

*

Between the temple and the mosque, the country remained tense. Mumbai had never before distinguished between the two. And then, as planned one day, another mosque was demolished. This time, the HUP claimed that the mosque was actually a former temple and the Hindus wanted it back.

Shakuntala was contemptuous of the hatred that sprang up after the desecration. Young men climbed atop the mosque and with tridents and spears began hitting at the façade.

Nootan's breath caught in her chest when she saw Dilip Vakharia among the rabid multitudes. The women watched the news carefully. There was speculation that the extremist sentiments would reach other parts of the country. Conspiracy theories were thrown around. The HUP surged ahead with its plan to assert its religion on everyone.

*

Joachim had become ingrained in Pakya's gang. Asunción was happy that her son was employed. He bragged to her about his job and insisted that he could kill if necessary. Asunción laughed out loud, not really believing him. Her son hadn't really changed. Power, recognition were perks of the job.

Pakya began to spend more time in Dubai, and for Joachim, it was a relief. If Pakya were in Mumbai, then Joachim would be compelled to go and collect his breakfast and listen to Anusuya's second-hand medical knowledge. It had all started to sound very trivial. The students that walked out of Grant Medical College seemed insignificant compared to Joachim, who thought that one day, maybe, he would rule the streets of Mumbai.

Elvira, in turn, was contented with her job at the call center. She'd always thought that Bandra was all there was to Mumbai. Having lived all her life at Bandra, she never really had to go anywhere beyond her neighborhood. To get to the call center, however, she had to travel to Malad. There, she worked nights, handling complaints for a computer firm based in the U.S.

Elvira enjoyed speaking like a Yank. She was also developing a crush on Rajuvelan Santhanam, a colleague and another Yank-sounding guy who couldn't make it to the U.S. but settled for the second best thing. He was the guy who always knew to which coast a particular U.S. city belonged and who America's twelfth president was and where Wal-Mart was located.

The company's bus dropped Elvira at and picked her up from the nearest railway station. She didn't have much time to spend with Sarangi. She knew that Sarangi was busy studying, and

Joachim's anger whenever Elvira spoke about his former girlfriend assured her that Sarangi was no longer interested in her brother.

"She's going to be a doctor, and her mother's business is doing well. Why would she dance with my brother?" Elvira thought.

Yet, Elvira sent Sarangi cards for her birthday and Christmas, still addressing them *Dear Beverly.* The cards always had a creamy pink cake and lots of hearts with arrows, in her effort to capture a lost time.

31

Elvira Looks for Beverly

One Wednesday night, Elvira, as usual, left for work. She waited by the curb for the bus to pick her up. She was a little early, and she hugged herself because there was a nip in the air. There was no one around. Unexpectedly, two men crept up behind her and held her tight. Elvira thought they must be friends of hers.

"Come on… Let go," she said.

One of the men hooked his arm around her neck and placed his gloved hand on her mouth. They dragged her into a shanty and raped her till she was unconscious. Then they threw her back where they had grabbed her, leaving her for dead.

Mercifully, Elvira slipped in and out of consciousness, not fully aware of the attack. Pain tore through her and tears ran down her cheeks. Blood trickled down her legs. She could feel it like ants crawling. She couldn't find the strength to sob out loud. Her larynx seemed to have stopped functioning.

She thought of her mother and brother and wanted to be safe again with them. Vivid images of her childhood flashed: Beverly's visits to her home, Joachim playing soccer, the church, Kayani, Beverly's joy when she handed her the exam results. Images of it all ran at top speed in her head, yet her surroundings were hazy.

A group of young people who were pub-hopping saw her lying at the bus stop. One of them noticed that she was still alive. They pulled her into their car and took her to the emergency room at Sir J.J. Hospital, where she was admitted.

Elvira kept asking for a Dr. Beverly. The head nurse, who knew the names of all the doctors on call, was sure that a Dr. Beverly did not exist. The nurse had no way of knowing that Elvira was asking for a young girl studying to be a doctor who once liked the name Beverly and had been Elvira's friend for many years.

Elvira's attackers had beaten her severely. Deprived of oxygen and losing blood, she'd gone into shock. After arriving at the hospital, she remained comatose for a couple of hours before she died.

When Joachim learned what had happened to his sister, he fumed with anger. He clenched his fist and hit a pillar in the hospital's waiting room so hard that his knuckles bled. His mother and he lodged a complaint with the police, but Joachim knew there were higher powers. He called Bandya. As soon as Bandya picked up the phone, Joachim began crying.

"What happened?"

"The motherfuckers killed her."

"Who? Killed who?"

"My sister. They not only killed her, they…" Joachim broke down.

"Don't worry. We'll handle it," Bandya said. It was all he needed to know.

Joachim kept quiet.

"They must be outsiders. No one in this city would've dared touch your sister," Bandya said.

Bandya sent his boys out, and they learned that the police had made some progress in the case. The police had apprehended Raja Singh and Raghu Sharma, two laborers who were suspected of committing the crime.

Joachim was shattered, but after taking his mother home, he called Anusuya and informed her of Elvira's death. Anusuya immediately located Sarangi and told her before she saw the news reports. Sarangi choked on her emotions. It was as if a fragment of her past had vanished. Elvira, once her closest friend, was gone, and the reason was difficult for Sarangi to digest. Even though their paths had diverged, Sarangi had nothing but warm feelings towards Elvira. When she heard the shocking news, she unknowingly caressed her waxed arms.

The funeral service at a Catholic cemetery was well-attended. Elvira had been popular and made friends easily. Joachim and Asunción were wearing black, and the son held his mother tightly. Anusuya went, for she could not forget that it was Elvira's mother who had introduced them to Professor Sharma.

Joachim, standing next to the grave, turned behind to see Sarangi standing quietly. She was always dignified and mature, but that day she looked aloof and distant. If tears hadn't been flowing down Sarangi's cheeks, then Joachim wouldn't have believed that she felt sad at the loss of her friend.

Sarangi saw Asunción and Joachim dressed in black, but she wasn't inclined to make conversation with her old boyfriend. Everything went to dust. Elvira's mother and grandmother were devastated. Elvira had been their only hope after Joachim turned out to be a wastrel.

Sarangi placed the crucifix that Elvira had given her on her friend's grave. Beverly died along with Elvira.

*

Five years had passed since the inception of Stree. The business employed one hundred and fifty women and grossed nine hundred thousand *rupees* every month. The egg *bhurji* was mentioned as a must-eat in many magazines, and a few other delicacies had been added to the menu.

Farzana had tried various innovations with the *bhurji,* but people still preferred the original version. The recipes were neatly written in a wide-ruled notebook, and the house rule was simple: no variations. The recipe had to be followed to a T.

Stree received the Best Food Award in the takeaway category from the Indian hotel management institute that rated the quality of food provided by the Mumbai hospitality industry. Stree's owners also received accolades from the Ministry of Small Scale Industry and from the Ministry of Social Welfare for providing employment to women.

Sarangi instinctively knew that there was more to the relationship between Shakuntala and her mother, but she chose not to look at it. It was easier not to know the truth and be at ease. She never forgot that she was where she was all because of her mother. She knew she had no right to judge her.

Sarangi visited Stree rarely, but Anusuya kept her informed of the daily operations. Sarangi hoped to go to the U.S. to pursue further studies. Her ambitions had surpassed Anusuya's level of understanding.

32

Taka-tak

The newspapers were filled with reports of the disturbances between the Hindus and the Muslims. The Muslims had retaliated after their mosque was demolished. There were bloodshed and violence all over the country. Shakuntala felt that it was all irrelevant. The Hindus could build a temple anywhere. She simply could not fathom why they would want to zero in on the location where the mosque stood. She watched very carefully on television the frenzy with which rioters climbed over the dome of the old mosque and shouted slogans. The political parties took advantage of the situation as the election neared.

"What can you do if you're born into a particular religion?" she thought when she saw Hindus hunting down Muslims and killing them.

The genesis of the riots in Mumbai occurred when a Hindu family was burned to death. The Muslims had evened the score. Business in Mumbai was called to a halt for a day, but Stree remained open with its shutter partially down. If there was any further trouble, the women planned to pull the shutter completely down. A few brave hearts who had dared to venture out came to eat at Stree. They were served in a hush-hush manner.

"The Muslims deserve it," said one.

"We'll teach them a lesson."

"*Arre bhai!* Why kill the innocents?"

And so it went on.

Farzana cloaked herself with the *burkha* and looked around nervously.

There was mayhem everywhere. The situation worsened as both communities lost any semblance of sanity. In some cases, the police aided the terror. The riots were the worst ever to hit the city. The Hindus were baying for the blood of Muslims, who, in turn, attacked to avenge the destruction of their mosque. Municipal hospitals could not accommodate the injured, and the blood banks were short of blood.

The local trains were the lifeline of Mumbai. If the trains stopped running, then there was a serious problem. It was a portent of danger. For the yellow and brown caterpillars to halt, there either had to be a natural calamity like heavy rains or a manmade disaster like a riot. The first question people asked when they heard of any catastrophe in Mumbai was "Are the trains running?" Public transportation was the barometer of the city's normalcy.

The day the riots reached the old mosque, the trains stopped plying.

The repercussions of the mosque's demolition affected the entire country. There was tension between both religious communities across India. Faiz kept a close watch on the unrest. He was appalled that members of both factions were hacking each other to death.

Faiz met with leading Muslims in the city, and they distributed pamphlets exhorting peace and calm. He formed a peacekeeping group, and they traveled to areas like Pydhonie, Dongri, Behrampada, and Bainganwadi. These suburban areas of Mumbai were largely populated by Muslims, and they were communally sensitive. They were the areas that burned whenever Mumbai witnessed religious terrorism.

Faiz also visited Mahim, where he knew some people. He spent time with them discussing the situation. He sat outside the *dargah* of Makhtum Fakir Ali Paru, a Sufi Muslim saint, and returned home late, often stressed and sometimes terribly tense. Faiz had never been so driven. At times, Farzana caught him brooding as if he were the keeper of a terrible secret. He strained himself by meeting with Muslim leaders all across the city, discussing the incidents of rioting being reported from all over the country. Mumbai was not spared.

The streets were naked like trees in autumn. BEST buses plied with metal meshes over the windows, anticipating incidents of stone pelting. Ghettos sprang up, and people chose to stick with their clan. The police ventured out on the streets, and everyone else stayed at home. The riots changed the landscape and rendered a fragility to the city, so that in years to come, unrest in even the remotest part of the country caused Mumbai to shiver.

Shakuntala was the most upset. The women did not have the luxury to close Stree, because they had a loan to repay. More so, they had other women working with them. These women were paid incentives against sales, and they ran their homes with the money they made.

"It's better to keep the shop closed. Some fanatic might burn it down to prove his love for his religion," Anusuya said.

Shakuntala decided to keep the shop open with the shutters half down. A compromise.

After a day, reason seemed to have returned to the city. Everything was back to normal, and Stree opened again. Everyone was talking about the loss of property and lives during the riots. But there was temporary calm, an uneasy quiet. The Arabian Sea was still. And Shakuntala knew that it would be very difficult to break the fortitude of the city. Mumbai was truly Shakuntala's city. It was there that she could build, and it was there that she could love.

Parimal, true to his Utopian nature, printed copies of Kabir's poems and gave them to Faiz. Faiz looked at him, puzzled in a sarcastic *Rome is burning and Emperor Nero is playing the fiddle* manner.

"Distribute these. Sense will emerge," Parimal said very seriously.

Faiz accepted the copies but not without sneering. He didn't bother to debate with the likes of Parimal, who would expound every theory on earth but never actually do anything to help. Parimal would never travel and distribute the printouts himself.

"His *khadi kurta* would get dirty," Faiz thought viciously. He threw the papers into a sewage drain.

"It's not over. I can feel it. There's more to come," Faiz told Farzana.

"What do you mean?" Farzana asked.

Faiz remained silent. Farzana was worried. He seemed withdrawn and was spending a great deal of time filing cases on behalf of the riot-stricken victims. He also worked with charitable organizations to provide basic amenities to families that had lost everything. Farzana couldn't help but notice that most of the people he helped were Muslims. When she questioned him about it, he claimed the *others* didn't come to him. Farzana remained silent.

A month had passed since the riots. Farzana was sure that Faiz's fear of further unrest was unjustified. If anything more were to happen, it would have already happened.

"He's probably stressed," Farzana thought.

Farzana didn't say much to Parimal, except the occasional perfunctory greeting. She knew the heartache they had caused Nootan, and she didn't wish to do any further harm. Especially after Pooja's death, she didn't want to do anything to hurt Nootan.

And then, two months later, Faiz's worst fears were confirmed. Six powerful bombs exploded at key establishments across the city in a carefully planned operation. Within a span of thirty minutes, six blasts killed thousands. Severed hands and limbs and splattered human blood marked the locations. Many innocent people, both Hindus and Muslims, lost their lives. The city shut down.

Stree also remained closed. There was no way it could open amidst the mayhem. The streets were like battlegrounds. The wails of ambulance and police sirens punctuated the silence. The smell of destruction hovered. The religious communities were openly accusing each other. It was rumored that the police had also remembered their religion. There were talks of foreign aid to the Muslims.

Rumors circulated that shops like Noor Mohammad, Akbarally's, and Suleiman Bakery had been burned. Sarangi watched the television news reports. She did not go to class, but some of her classmates organized a blood collection drive for the riot victims that had been hospitalized. Anusuya would not hear of Sarangi stepping outdoors, however noble the cause. After what had happened to Elvira, Anusuya didn't want her daughter to take any chances.

Farzana and Faiz were worried. They heard of hoodlums going into buildings, checking the name plates on doors and mailboxes, tracking down the Muslim residents, and killing them. Faiz was distressed. He once again mobilized forces and spent time helping people. Many of the police officers knew Faiz Syed as a respected lawyer, but even some of them stood back and watched the massacre take place.

Pakya was shaken by the bloodbath. His good friend Noor had died in one of the blasts. Noor had gone to collect his visa to Oman from the consulate and never returned home. There were rumors that Pakya's don had a hand in orchestrating the bombings, but Pakya knew better. The don never got involved in riots so large in scope. And the don had nothing to gain from the mêlée. On the contrary, his business was disturbed.

"This is someone else's handiwork," Pakya thought.

Pakya largely stayed indoors for fear that the police might lock him up under the Terrorist and Disruptive Activities Act. Criminals were booked by the police under the act, but, surprisingly, the police turned a blind eye to many atrocities. Pakya received information from his many informers that at certain police stations, the officers in charge did nothing to abate the crimes against Muslims. They just watched.

Pakya had never made distinctions based on caste, creed, or religion. For him, violence was simply a job executed with finesse.

"*Khallas?*" "Finished?" he would ask after a job. Religion and every other categorization be damned.

Pakya also heard rumors that Suleiman Bakery had been razed. It saddened him when he thought of all the people he knew who worked there and the delicious flaky biscuits, or *aflatoons,* they made.

Politicians began asking people to maintain calm. A few arrests were made. The police commissioner called Pakya to the station. Pakya readily went and answered his questions honestly. He was released after an hour of intense interrogation. Pakya left the station wearing dark glasses and headed straight to his car, fielding a few questions from members of the press who were waiting for a culprit. He had notified the don that the commissioner had summoned him. The don had encouraged him to go and, before hanging up, he'd said, "The commissioner knows my style. No one will touch my boys."

After three or four days, the politicians decided to make the best of the situation. Like jackals coming for a dead body, a right-wing political party, an ally of the HUP, called for a *bandh* — a cessation of all activities, commercial and otherwise — in the city. The protest was a political expression. Mumbai was groaning, but nobody wished to take chances. The right-wing party was notorious for its hard-line approach.

Pakya was paid by the political party to create chaos, and his boys, including Joachim, contributed their might to making the *bandh* a success. Pakya knew that he had to make sure no vehicles plied on the roads. If any person dared to come out, in violation of the *bandh,* the person had to be threatened with death. Terror was the name of the game.

People sat ensconced at home, watching their televisions or catching up with the news on the Internet. To enforce the *bandh,* local hoodlums walked around the city with hockey sticks and cycle chains and yelled loudly as a sign of primordial power. Young boys, they simply did what they were told in exchange for a few hundred *rupees.*

Essential services like milk vans, ambulances, and the like were allowed to ply. The city still had a heart. People were rushed to hospitals in taxis and rickshaws. But scores of middle-class citizens, who were the most easily frightened, just sat at home. The upper middle classes sat with their magazines and glasses of beer and expounded on political theories. Junior surfed television channels searching for cartoons, and the lady of the house used a Chinese butterfly massager intended to help one lose weight as a vibrator to have an orgasm.

Shakuntala, Anusuya, Nootan, and Farzana were very disturbed. They couldn't keep Stree closed any longer. Buses and trains were running only a skeletal service, and the windows of the buses were covered with wire mesh. Taxis with their meters down lined the sides of the roads. The four women had seen enough of fear in their lifetimes. They'd been battered and bruised, but every time they had emerged. They'd always been easily subjugated, but they did not submit this time. Stree was all about strength. Strength against oppression.

On the day of the *bandh*, Faiz left for the court. Farzana looked at him questioningly. She was pale and tired. The doctor had warned her that the pregnancy might be complicated, given her fragile health. Stress would only make it worse. Then, relatives called to inform her that her aunt, who had given her asylum from Javed, had been killed, her head hacked from her body. The last few days had been demanding on Farzana, but when Faiz held her hand, she understood and didn't even try to stop him from going. Faiz had a few friends who wished to venture out, and they planned to drive to work.

Shakuntala called Nootan on the telephone. She wanted her opinion.

"What do you think? Should we open today? It's a *bandh,*" she asked.

The answer was unhesitatingly and unanimously yes. Nootan spoke with Anusuya, who seconded Nootan's opinion. Nootan was surprised at Anusuya's decision to work. A few years back, she would have whined, but on the day of the *bandh* she was stoic. Perhaps her relationship with Shakuntala was not such a bad thing after all.

Farzana was well into her eighth month of pregnancy, and Shakuntala felt that she was the most vulnerable. Should anything unforeseen happen, they could run, but not Farzana. Considering the heartlessness of the rioters, they would not spare a pregnant woman.

"It's best that we don't tell her," Shakuntala said.

Nootan and Anusuya agreed. They knew that if Farzana found out they were opening Stree, she would insist on joining them. She wasn't one to stay back.

"I hope she doesn't misunderstand," Anusuya said.

"No. She won't," Nootan replied.

Jagvinder Singh drove them to Stree.

"Are we not waiting for Farzana?" he asked.

"No," Shakuntala said emphatically.

"Good," Jagvinder said in a very strange tone.

Shakuntala wondered whether he meant that it was good she stayed back because she was in a delicate condition or because he harbored ill feelings toward Muslims. She never got the answer, because it was the last time he would ever drive them to Stree.

Jagvinder was losing it. He looked upwards and kept

murmuring and shaking his head. He spoke about another partition and claimed that Farzana was a fallen woman. He had terrible memories of the riots that had claimed the lives of his brethren years earlier in Delhi after the assassination of then Prime Minister Indira Gandhi.

The roads were empty of vehicles, and urchins seemed to have made a cricket ground of the streets. They weren't frightened of anybody as long as they had a bat and a ball.

The Fiat, with Jagvinder at the wheel, reached Stree in a record span of twenty minutes. Normally, parking the car in the city was a problem, but that day, the entire stretch was available to him. Jagvinder parked the car just a furlong away from Stree.

"Are we going to Cuffe Parade?" Jagvinder asked with a silly smile on his face.

"Not today."

Shakuntala opened the lock and raised the shutter. Nootan saw that the blackboard proclaiming the bill of fare was smudged. She rubbed it clean with a wet mop and took a chalk to write. But she didn't know the day's menu.

"Look!" Anusuya screamed suddenly.

Shakuntala and Nootan turned to see two sari-clad figures walking towards them from a distance. They recognized Rima and Soha, who had walked from Victoria Terminus. Apparently, they had reached Lower Parel Station, where they lived, and had seen a train. They hopped into it and to their surprise the train moved. Surjit Kaur also managed to come to work.

"Where is Farzanadidi?" Soha asked.

"We thought it better that she stay at home. Now, get on with the work. Soha, clean the vessels, and Rima, take stock of what's in the refrigerator," Shakuntala barked.

Farzana remained at home, not knowing that the others had gone off to work. Faiz called to say that he had reached the courts safely. She decided to lie down with her feet up. Just then, the phone rang. Farzana stood, ambled across the room, and picked it up. It was Javed, after five years. She wanted to hang up but was compelled to hear what he had to say after so long. The place where he had kicked her years ago suddenly hurt.

"You bitch! You haven't gone out to whore? The other whores are there. You are an insult to our community. You join hands with the *kafirs* and shame us like you have shamed me with your fat belly," he snarled.

It was Javed's last attempt to create trouble. Farzana was enraged, not because of Javed's madness, but by the fact that — if what he said was true — she had been excluded. Shakuntala hadn't even called her and sought her opinion. They'd just gone ahead with their plans. Did they think that she had become one of the *others?* Did they harbor any resentment towards her? She didn't have any answers.

Farzana dressed and walked outside to hail a cab.

"Sister, don't travel today. Anything can happen," the taxi driver said kindly.

"I'll pay you double the fare," Farzana said and got into the cab.

She reached Stree and saw that the shop indeed was open. She was furious with rage. She waddled towards the shop.

"Farzanadidi! Farzanadidi!" Soha screamed.

Shakuntala, Nootan, and Anusuya turned simultaneously to see a black billowing figure walking towards them. The *purdah* flew angrily in the wind.

"Why? Afraid that the rioters will attack us because of me?" Farzana taunted.

"No. No," Anusuya placated her.

"You stop blabbering, you whimpering woman. I know what you must have thought. After all, this is me against you!" Farzana yelled.

Nootan went towards Farzana and held her.

"You're misunderstanding us. We were only concerned about your safety. Do you think that we've made a distinction? We've always been proud of you," Nootan said quietly.

"Yeah, so proud that when Parimal was meeting me, your heart broke," Farzana taunted.

Nootan's face fell. She let go and turned her back to Farzana.

Shakuntala knew that what was happening was what she'd feared the most. They'd begun hurting each other.

"And you! Dressing up like a man! You think I don't know. I've seen you salivate when you look at Anusuya!" Farzana screamed at Shakuntala.

Farzana had lost all sense of proportion, wrongly believing that the other women thought that she, being a Muslim, would attract the attention of the Hindu rioters.

Shakuntala took charge. She knew that if they survived that day, they would remain together forever, and if they did not, they were finished.

"Stop!" she screamed.

There was a deathly silence.

"I don't care what you think," Shakuntala said. "We didn't inform you, not because you're a Muslim, but because you're pregnant. I want you to remember the oath we swore years ago!"

The sun was shining brightly, and the only sounds were of the cricket-playing urchins who screamed, "Out!"

Tears welled up in Farzana's eyes. She hadn't wanted to make the remark, but the turn of events had taken her by surprise. People who had lived in peace were killing each other. Hindus were turning against Muslims who had been their friends for years, and Muslims were betraying their Hindu friends. She sat down and held her face in her hands. Tears were running furiously, and she couldn't stop them. Shakuntala held her, looked around, and said gruffly, "Start working! Don't waft around."

The four had indeed come a long way. They couldn't destroy

everything they had created. Nor could they let the perverts who were fighting in the name of religion take charge of their lives.

Anusuya hastily wiped her eyes with the edge of her sari and went to check the state of the vegetables.

Farzana composed herself and got on her feet. She saw that there were only a dozen eggs, as the delivery boy hadn't come. Suddenly, she remembered his name: Rashid. The bread had the beginnings of a green fungus forming on it. She cleaned the griddle, placed it on the flame, and looked out. There was a slight ache in her womb, but she ignored it.

"It'll pass," she thought.

In the past, she'd ignored many aches and pains and had trekked ahead. This was also a journey.

The sky was clear, as if it had been given a thirty-minute rejuvenating facial. The day was bright, and the steamers on the Arabian Sea passing the Gateway of India looked like a picture postcard. Pigeons perched on the promenade looking for grains, and the Hotel Taj stood imperially. Needless to say, the streets were deserted. That day, if anybody visited Stree, it would be the taxi drivers who were sitting idle in their cabs or police constables on the beat.

Suddenly, on the horizon, a mob largely comprising boys surged towards them. From afar, it looked like a swarm of locusts, shapeless but buzzing and threatening.

"Pull the shutters down, you motherfuckers! Don't you know today is a *bandh?* Ten minutes! If the shop is still open, we'll raze it," Bandya said menacingly.

"Ten minutes is all you have," another adolescent voice said. A boy-demon.

Joachim was part of the mob — an integral part. He was doing Bandya proud by playing the role of second in command. However, he'd hoped that Stree would remain closed, so that Anusuya wouldn't see him at work. When one of their gang had informed Bandya that a shop was open and there were four women in it, Joachim knew that it had to be Stree.

"Why couldn't the cows sit at home and enjoy a break?" Joachim thought viciously. He was worried that Bandya might set the shop on fire or shoot the women. He knew Bandya carried a gun.

Joachim tried to stay concealed behind the other members of the mob, but he was unsuccessful. Nootan spotted him.

"Look at that boy! You know him, right?" Nootan asked Anusuya.

Anusuya was surprised to see Joachim with the rioters.

"What is he doing? He prays to a God that speaks English," Anusuya echoed, remembering what Sarangi had told her. It then struck her that it didn't matter what language God spoke.

Anusuya tried to catch Joachim's eye, but he mingled in with the others.

Joachim was embarrassed when he saw Nootan notice him and more so when he knew Anusuya had seen him. He felt very sad, and he didn't know why. This wasn't how he wanted things to be. He'd always hoped that Anusuya would see him while he was sitting in his Mercedes. He brushed at the tears in his eyes and walked away with the mob, swinging the cycle chain in his hand a little harder.

"If *sala* Dhirubhai Ambani could, what happened to me?" he thought.

"What do we do?" Anusuya asked, looking at the mob getting smaller.

"First, we'll call for Jagvinder and send Farzana home," Nootan said.

"Why me? Why not all of us? I'm not going," Farzana said. "I'd bet my last *rupee* that those boys won't have the courage to touch us."

Nootan knew that it was foolish to argue with her.

"Farzana has a point. They won't dare touch us," Shakuntala said.

Police vans moved about smartly with cops looking out to see if everything was OK.

"Let's all stay," Shakuntala said.

"At the most, we'll have to pull down the shutter and stay inside," Nootan said.

"Those demons really meant what they said," Anusuya said, unable to shake Joachim's image from her mind.

Farzana went to the heated griddle. She poured the oil and added the chopped onions. She knew the recipe by rote. The *bhurji* was synonymous with Farzana, with Stree, and with Mumbai. They had to be there.

The onions sizzled, the cilantro and the *garam masala* merged, and then the eggs joined the browned mixture. The yolks and the whites leapt out with joy from the shells. Like a zombie, Farzana took the ladle and began tapping the griddle, completely numbed to what was happening around her. *Taka-tak, taka-tak, taka-tak,* slowly, so slowly that no one could hear. Then she increased the intensity and the frequency, feeling a strange strength overcome her.

Taka-tak, taka-tak, taka-tak. Like a possessed woman. Like an enraged woman.

The sound reverberated in the silence all around. It was amplified by the quietness. Farzana began hitting the griddle with even more force. It became easy when she thought of her aunt who had disappeared; her friends who had been killed; the egg delivery boy; the quiet chimney of Suleiman Bakery; Parimal; and Faiz, whose return wasn't certain.

Taka-tak, taka-tak, taka-tak… more loudly when she thought of why she didn't stop Faiz from going out on such a day.

Taka-tak, taka-tak, taka-tak… even more loudly when she

thought of the blood that had been spilled on the roads of Mumbai.

Taka-tak, taka-tak, taka-tak... so loud that it resonated with an intensity that conveyed her anguished *Why?*

A few taxi drivers who were sleeping in their taxis heard the sound. The noise roused them all.

"*Arre bhai!* Has everything started?" one driver asked.

"Think so."

Taka-tak, taka-tak, taka-tak...

"What's that noise?"

"Egg *bhurji.*"

The sound continued. *Taka-tak, taka-tak, taka-tak...*

"The women have started work!"

"Are we eunuchs?"

"If they can, then why can't we?"

The drivers looked around, shrugged their shoulders, ambled to Stree, and ordered three plates of egg *bhurji.* Two police constables who were tired and hungry also heard the sound and found themselves at Stree. Very soon, people began getting out and coming towards Stree to appease their hunger. Like rats from their holes.

"Everything is normal. I'm eating egg *bhurji* at Stree," someone said into a public phone.

The angry mob of boys returned in a little less than ten minutes. Bandya froze in his tracks when he heard the familiar sound, *taka-tak, taka-tak, taka-tak....* He was surprised to see people eating and behaving as though everything were normal. The sound — *taka-tak, taka-tak, taka-tak* — frightened him. Farzana had not stopped.

"Let's kill all of them," one of members the mob screamed, but nobody moved.

"Burn them down," another screamed.

Anusuya saw that some of the rioters had cans of gasoline and other inflammable substances. There was a look of terror on her face. Even Shakuntala was shaken.

Pakya had not ordered Bandya's mob to attack, and the activists for whom they were working would get unfavorable press if four women were targeted. Joachim was impressed by the women's gumption and the way they dug their heels in the ground.

"That pregnant woman is perspiring, but she's not stopping," Joachim thought.

Soha and Rima continued with their work, their faces pleasant, with no trace of terror. Bandya didn't know what to do. He tried calling Pakya. Pakya didn't take the calls; he didn't want to be incriminated. News traveled fast.

Taka-tak, taka-tak, taka-tak…

Like the drumbeats of an ancient warrior.

Nimmi Rastogi was covering the city beat. She walked to a phone kiosk and called her editor. When she mentioned that Stree had opened and people were eating as if it were a normal day, Nimmi smiled. She knew that the four women could not be cowed. She relayed the information to all her friends in the media.

They began filing their stories: "The Bandh a Flop," "Four Women and an Egg Bhurji Show the Way," "Citizens Foil the Bandh." NDTV's Mumbai correspondent Srinivasan Jain headed for Stree to cover the events.

"It was indeed brave of these ladies to take on the political party who wanted the city to remain closed for a day," he said.

Taka-tak, taka-tak, taka-tak…

Farzana was perspiring and panting. Sweat dripped in rivulets from her forehead. Her black *purdah* clung to her as if she were drenched in the fabled Mumbai monsoon rains. She felt a strange sensation, as though her insides wanted to come out. The ache that she'd been trying to forget was gnawing at her. There was something trickling down her legs. She looked down, feeling faint.

"I think my water is breaking!" Farzana cried.

"Oh! My! God!" Anusuya screamed.

"Faiz! Faiz!" Farzana moaned.

Nootan ran out and looked for Jagvinder to rush Farzana to Bombay Hospital, but Jagvinder was nowhere to be seen. The Fiat was abandoned. Nootan tried to get in touch with Faiz by phone, but a recorded message said he could not be reached at the moment. Nootan called Parimal and asked him to look for Faiz. One of the taxi drivers rushed to bring his taxi around to Stree, but by then Farzana had slumped down to the ground. The pain was excruciating. She held Nootan so tight, the half-moons of her nails bit into Nootan's wrist. Nootan wiped the sweat from Farzana's face with the end of her sari. She could not stop her tears.

Anusuya asked Shakuntala to keep some water on the flame and to try to sterilize a pair of clean scissors. There was no time to lose. Parimal went to the court and looked for Faiz, but he wasn't there. Someone said he got into a white Ambassador that sped away. Someone else said that he'd been killed. Somebody even dared to say that Faiz Syed finally became disillusioned and joined the extremist movement. The same recorded greeting played whenever callers got Faiz's voice mail, and it irritated everyone who was looking for him.

"Push. Push harder!" Anusuya told Farzana.

Shakuntala prayed for the first time in her life, and Nootan clenched her fists and wept. Farzana screamed in pain and pushed with all her strength. She remembered the first time she had met Anusuya at Nootan's home, she remembered Javed, she remembered how she broke free, she remembered Stree, she remembered her egg *bhurji* burning on the griddle, she remembered Parimal with shame, and she remembered how she had accused her friends of being disloyal. She remembered them not as friends but as blood. Somewhere, she heard someone calling her. A memory was calling her. She felt an acute pain, and there was a haze of blood and then a wail. A lusty wail.

"It's a girl!" Anusuya said.

Shakuntala and Nootan cried out. Anusuya held the baby and showed it to Farzana, who looked at her child with a smile. And then there was a serene expression on her face.

Farzana died in Nootan's arms, but not without having seen her daughter, Nushrat Syed.

The inheritor.

Epilogue

Anusuya Alhat and Shakuntala Ponkshe lived together and spent their days watching Stree grow.

Nootan Vakharia and Parimal Mehta became surrogate parents to Nushrat and took joy in rearing her.

Sarangi migrated to the Americas with her husband, also a doctor, and returned to India years later to set up a model rural health clinic.

Nushrat grew up to be an independent woman and took to handling the affairs of Stree.

Pakya escaped to Dubai, one of the United Arab Emirates, and made his home there. However, he kept eye on Stree. Someday, he planned to sell his story to a Bollywood film director.

Joachim grew frustrated with the gang system and opted out. After his mother's death, he sought refuge in alcohol and regaled everyone at Alcoholics Anonymous with his tales of bravado.

Nimmi Rastogi became the editor of a celebrity gossip magazine that covered Indian film stars. She chose to remain unmarried and at times sauntered in with film stars to eat at Stree.

Javed's whereabouts remained unknown; however, Pakya swore he saw him on television with Al Qaeda.

The HUP never came into power, but Dilip Vakharia enjoyed the status of a demigod in the party.

Sakharam Alhat remained missing.

Jagvinder Singh was killed, ironically run over by a cab. Mercifully, he was not in his senses, having become mentally unstable when the riots broke out.

Faiz Syed was lost in the crowds of Mumbai. Lost amongst the millions. Lost between the many lanes. Lost in time.

Stree and the numerous women who were part of it survived and had the honor of being reviewed as a case by the Harvard Business School. Stree expanded to seventy-five locations across India and one in America. With Sarangi's aid and under Nushrat's leadership, it employed over seven hundred women.

In the riots that ravaged Mumbai, thousands died, and property worth millions was destroyed. The ineffectiveness of the systems that were supposed to protect citizens was exposed. But the spirit of Mumbai remains unvanquished. Like a mother, despite all the wrongs committed against her, she still does not care about caste, creed, or religion.

Glossary

Abbajan/Abba
An Urdu word meaning *father*

Aflatoon
A sweetmeat, or candy

Arre Bhai
A Hindi expression meaning *Hey, brother*

Ayah
A Hindi word meaning *nanny*

Azaan
The Islamic call to prayer

Bajaj
A brand of Indian oven, toaster, and grill combination, often referred to as an OTG

Bandh
A day when everyone stops work at the direction of political activists

Besan
Chick pea flour

Bhajjiyas
Vegetables, such as potatoes, dipped in flour and deep fried

Bhel
A mixture of puffed rice, onion, and spices. Vada pao: A potato patty between an Indian bread

Bintok Pakistan Vapas Jao
An insult to Indian Muslims meaning *The circumcised go back to Pakistan*

Biryani
A rice dish from the Indian subcontinent made from a mixture of spices, basmati rice, and meat or vegetables

Bollywood
The Hindi film industry based in Mumbai

Britannia and Amul
Popular Indian brands of bread and butter, respectively

Burnol
A brand of ointment used to soothe burns

Chakli
A circular Indian savory consumed as an appetizer or snack

Chawl
A four- or five-story community housing system with ten to twenty small apartments on each floor

Chudidars
Indian pants

Dosa
Indian pancakes

Dupatta
A long scarf worn over a *salwar kameez*

Egg Bhurji
A dish popular in northern and western India, its preparation and appearance are similar to scrambled eggs. The difference lies in the addition of fried chopped onions, chilies, and optional spices such as coriander powder and chili powder.

Eid
An Islamic festival marking the end of Ramadan

Ganeshotsav
A Hindu festival celebrating the birth of Ganesha, the elephant god

Garam Masala
A mixture of five spices

Garba
An Indian form of dance that originated in Gujarat

Gullies
A Hindi word meaning *lanes*

Hafta
Hindi slang meaning *extortion*

Handi
A deep cooking utensil

Henna
A plant dye

Hindustan Times
An Indian English-language daily newspaper

Idli
Steamed rice cakes

Jai Bhawani
A Hindu greeting saluting a goddess

Janmashtami
A Hindu festival celebrating the birth of the god Krishna

Kaanda Poha
Puffed rice cooked with onion

Kabab
An Iranian or Turkish term for grilled or broiled meat

Kabbadi
An Indian game

Kafirs
A Hindi expression for non-Muslims

Kayani
A Iranian eatery in South Mumbai

Khadi Kurtas
Shirts made of Indian spun linen

Khallas
Hindi slang meaning *finished*

Khari
A flaky biscuit

Khichda
A dish of wheat and lamb popular among Indian Muslims

Khichdi
A dish of rice and lentils

Ladoos
Ball-shaped sweets often prepared to celebrate special events

Maidan
An open public park

Masala
A mixture of spices

Mawa Cakes
Cupcakes famous in Mumbai

Mian ko Maar Dalo
A Hindi expression meaning *Kill the Muslim*

Mohalla
An Urdu word meaning *local neighborhood*

Mucchad
A Hindi term for a man with a moustache

Navratri
A nine-day Hindu festival of worship and dance; a Sanskrit word literally meaning *nine nights*

Nawab
Indian prince

Pao
Indian bread

Purdah
The veiled dress of Muslim women

Rawa
Semolina flour

Sabudaana Khichdi
A dish made of sago

Salwar Kameez
Traditional dress worn by various peoples of South Asia, *salwars* are tight-fitting cotton trousers, and a *kameez* is a long tunic

Sari
An Indian woman's garment

Sherwani
A long coat-like garment

Somnath
An ancient Hindu temple located near Veraval in Saurashtra. The temple has been destroyed six times and it has been rebuilt each time.

Sorpotel
A Goan delicacy

Stree
A Hindustani word meaning *woman*

Sunni Muslims
The largest denomination of Islam

Tamasha
A Hindi expression meaning *entertainment,* taken from the word for a traditional folk drama

Toran
A garland of beads or flowers strung outside the front door of a residence

Vadas
Fried lentil roundels

Vindaloo Masala
A Goan delicacy

ACKNOWLEDGEMENT

I wish to thank T N C Nair, my father and Shamala, my mother for their unconditional support; Ketan, for everything; Usha, my aunt for holding the fort; Chetan, who heard the story first; Pragya, for being there; Shaila, my friend; Manu and Sheba, for their encouragement for anything that I do; Tanushri Shukla, for the first revision of the book; Arvind Satheesh of Grootslang for the help with the website; Chiki Sarkar, who encouraged me with her kind remarks; Robin Mizell, my literary agent, who believed in me and the book; Suman Chakraborty, my publisher; and all my family and friends who cheered me on.